What's her Secret?

THE INGREDIENTS
OF BLISS

LISABET SARAI

The Ingredients of Bliss
ISBN # 978-1-78430-196-5
©Copyright Lisabet Sarai 2014
Cover Art by Posh Gosh ©Copyright August 2014
Interior text design by Claire Siemaszkiewicz
Totally Bound Publishing

Published in 2014 by Totally Bound Publishing, Newland House, The Point, Weaver Road, Lincoln, LN6 3QN, United Kingdom.

Totally Bound Publishing is an imprint of Total-E-Ntwined Limited.

THE
INGREDIENTS
OF BLISS

Dedication

To K., who loves my cooking.

Chapter One

"What's eating you, Em?"

Harry looked up from one of his favorite positions — crouched between my spread legs — and searched my face. The usual mischief gleamed in his cinnamon-brown eyes — a bit unfocused without his glasses — but his lush mouth showed no trace of a grin.

"Shouldn't that be *who*, rather than what?" My laugh sounded forced, even to my own ears. It turned to a squeal as he swept his tongue along the length of my cleft, ending with a neat flick to my clit.

"I'm serious. Something's bothering you."

Sometimes his intuition scared me. "It's nothing, really." How did this guy know me so well, after a mere three months?

"Tell me!"

"Ow!" He'd pinched the sensitive flesh of my inner thigh.

"Do I have to beat a confession out of you — again?"

His casual reference was enough to send my mind spinning back to that wild night when he'd first revealed his kinky streak. Tied to the iron railing at the look-out atop Twin Peaks, my panties around my ankles and my dress bunched up around my waist, I'd received my first searing lesson in submission.

Unruly hair fell into his eyes, making him look younger, and rougher, too—a bit like Brando in *A Streetcar Named Desire*. I wanted to brush those black locks off his brow, to touch him, to soothe and reassure him—to feel his lovely muscles shift under the tanned skin of his broad shoulders. Bound hand and foot to the bedframe, all I could do was writhe and yelp as he burrowed his face in my pussy, while raking my thighs with his fingernails.

Pain and pleasure. Pleasure and pain. Wasn't there a time when I could tell the difference?

Whatever he was doing, I liked it. I couldn't pretend that I didn't.

He knew exactly how to play me, when to suck my quivering clit like a piece of hard candy, when to back off and trace my labia with the barest tip of his tongue.

"Oh God…Harry…" Everything felt exquisite, but I was far, far from release. I knew this and so, of course, did he.

"Damn it, Emily, I thought you trusted me." His lips looked redder than normal, maybe even a bit swollen.

The distress I read in his face felt like a physical blow. "I let you tie me up…"

"So why won't you tell me what's on your mind, love?" He settled back on his heels and regarded me gravely. "You've only had one orgasm, all morning. And it took half an hour of work to get you there. That's not like you at all, Em. You're preoccupied, or worried, or something."

"I didn't realize you consider making me come to be 'work'."

"Don't change the subject. You know what I'm talking about." With a sigh so deep it almost broke my heart, he stretched his body out on top of my bound form. The soft curls on his chest caressed my flattened breasts. His steely erection settled against my mound, reminding me that he hadn't yet come at all.

For a moment, guilt smothered any traces of arousal. Then he nuzzled my neck and breathed in my ear, striking sparks and rekindling my terrible, unsatisfied need.

"I won't mind. I won't judge you," he murmured. "You can tell me anything — anything at all."

Oh really? Even that I want another man?

Had I spoken aloud? But no, his lips were on mine now, firm and familiar, relieving me, for the moment, of the necessity for speech. The flavor of my pussy mingled with the mint of his toothpaste. Sweet comfort flowed through me like warm honey. I stopped straining against the straps looped around my ankles and wrists and simply relaxed. He could take me wherever he wanted us to go.

I did trust him. He probably didn't realize how much. I'd lowered my guard with him, letting him see both my fierce lust and my raw ambition. Neither had fazed him. And I'd allowed him to use my body in ways no previous lover had ever attempted — ways I'd never even imagined until he'd whispered his filthy suggestions in my ear and planted the seeds of new fantasies.

He broke the kiss and raised himself up on his forearms, gazing down at me. "I love you, Emily." He didn't need to say the words. The truth blazed in his face.

I love you too. I choked on the admission, unable to give back what he needed and deserved. How could I say I loved him after what had happened yesterday? Miserable, confused, drowning in self-reproach, I remained silent.

"It's about Etienne, isn't it?"

"What?" His insight shocked me into a response. "Um...no... I mean..."

"Whatever else you may or may not feel, don't lie to me. Please."

I swallowed the lump in my throat and scanned his handsome face. I saw no trace of anger. In fact, a hint of a grin played on his lips. I nodded.

"Tell me. Every detail."

"I can't..."

"Mei Lee Wong, I swear that if you don't confess this instant, I'll thrash you with that paddle we bought last week until you can barely walk!" Yet even as he voiced this threat, he levered himself off my body and thrust two fingers into my cunt, triggering a spasm of exquisite pleasure.

How could I refuse him?

"Well...the last few days—few weeks, really—he... I mean, Etienne, seems to have *changed*." I stopped, trying to figure out how to approach a topic of such...delicacy.

"Yes? Go on." He rubbed the pad of his thumb back and forth across the tip of my clit. When I arched up, seeking a firmer contact, he snatched his hand away.

"He's been kinder. Less arrogant. More—I don't know exactly—more deferential. He asks me my opinion about recipes. He even let me plan the last segment myself, everything from the appetizer to the dessert."

"I've noticed the change myself. A positive development, given your career goals. But that's not what's making you blush, Ms Wong."

No, I was blushing — at least partly — because he had wiggled one slick finger into my rear hole. "No…um… Oh, Harry, please…"

"Continue, slut, if you don't want me to get out the paddle!"

"Ah…well, he has also been touching me. Just casual touches, you understand — touches that could be accidental. His hand will graze my arm — or my thigh. Or he'll back into me when we're in the kitchen together."

"He has a great ass, doesn't he?"

"What?" My head shot up.

"I'm not gay, don't worry. But I'm not blind either. Monsieur le Chef has fine, round, muscular buttocks. And I've seen the way you look at them. I almost expect saliva to drip from your mouth."

"Harry!" Was I really so transparent? Had anyone else noticed, or only my insanely intuitive and observant lover?

"I'm only teasing, love. Anyway, I adore the fact that you're so — how can I put it politely? — easily aroused. Which is why I'm making you tell me this."

I was silent. Mortified. My cheeks burned like the coals in a hibachi.

"Remember the paddle, Emily…"

"Okay, okay. Yesterday I was in the dressing room, removing my makeup after the show. He knocked and called my name. I didn't think anything of it, just got up and let him in. I figured he'd had an idea about next week's menu. As soon as the door closed, though, he was on his knees, at my feet. Like that first day, when I'd spiked the *choux*."

"Mmm." He wormed his finger deeper into my back passage. Meanwhile, he brushed his other palm over my pubic hair.

My pussy clenched at the maddening delicacy of that touch. How was I supposed to concentrate on the story?

"And?" he prompted.

The bizarre scene was etched into my memory. Etienne had knelt before me, eyes cast down, patrician features composed and serious. His thick auburn curls gleamed. His Hermès cologne had tickled my nostrils. He hadn't said a word, just waited with his head bowed, gorgeous and vulnerable. The bulge in his tailored trousers had spoken for him.

My nipples had snapped to attention. My panties started to dampen. "What is it, Etienne?" I'd asked, though I'd known perfectly well what he wanted.

"Ms Wong." It was the same warm, cultured voice that had helped make him the most popular TV chef currently on the air. One could still hear the echoes of his Provençal childhood in the precise consonants and rounded vowels. Every iota of arrogance, though, was gone, replaced by an astonishing humility. "I think you know. Let me serve you. Please."

Oh, the fierce heat that had shot through me at those words! The sense of power! Because this was real, not some aberration birthed by my grandmother's traditional aphrodisiac. At that instant, I'd known I could command Etienne Duvalier to do more or less anything—certainly, anything that involved sex—and he would obey.

That realization was intoxicating. I imagined that well-coifed head buried between my thighs, licking me to one glorious orgasm after another. I pictured myself straddling him as he lay on the floor, trussed up and straining against my ropes, with that erection pointing toward the ceiling. I thought about dragging his pants to his ankles and spanking that bubble butt with my hair brush, until he moaned and pleaded for mercy.

"Emily! What happened next?" Harry's voice pulled me back to the present. He removed his fingers from my orifices so that he could stroke his cock.

My moan of disappointment made him chuckle. I watched in fascination as he gathered pre-cum from the bulb with his thumb and smeared it along the shaft. Was my tongue hanging out?

"Earth to Emily! The story, girl!"

"He—um—he told me he wanted to 'serve' me. And—" I swallowed again and steeled myself to go further. "That turned me on."

"I'll bet it did!" Harry appeared to be completely unperturbed by my revelation. "So what did you do? Did you make him eat you out? Or fuck you?"

"Talk about a mind in the gutter!"

"Don't play Miss Prim with me. I'll bet you thought about it, didn't you?" He reached down to give my nipple a savage twist. "Well, didn't you?"

"Yes. Yes, I did, and a lot of other things too."

He was jacking off in earnest now. I wanted to help, to swallow his rod and suck until he flooded my mouth with his jism, but of course, tied as I was, I could barely move. Somehow I didn't really mind. A weight had lifted from my spirit. Harry knew I wanted Etienne. He didn't care. No, that wasn't right. He did care. He appeared to be exceptionally interested in my sordid revelation. But he wasn't angry or upset, as far as I could tell. And I didn't have to keep the secret anymore.

Meanwhile, the combination of my confession and my recollections had aroused me to the point that I thought I might climax from the mere sight of Harry spraying his cum all over my bound, naked flesh.

He was close. His hips jerked. His breath came in short grunts. "So—uh—what—did—you—uh—do—uh-uh—oh…?"

"I made him unzip and show me his cock."

"Oh, yeah…!"

"I squeezed it. I dug my nails into his flesh until he had tears in his eyes. I told him if he came, I'd beat him with a wooden kitchen spoon."

Harry's cock looked bigger and harder than I'd ever seen it. Far from making him jealous, my admission seemed to make him hornier than ever. "And—uh-uh—did he—uh—oh—come?"

"No, he was a good boy. But I told him I might beat him anyway."

"Oh—baby!—ah…"

I was tied hand and foot, but I felt echoes of the power I'd experienced in Etienne's presence. I might not be able to use my mouth to get Harry off, but I could use my mind.

"After I sent him away, I kept thinking about his cock and his butt. I fucked my pussy raw."

"God—oh God!"

"With the handle of my hairbrush."

"Arrgh…!"

The last detail—true, as it happened—was 'the wine barrel that sank the junk', as my grandmother would say. The raunchy image tipped my lover over the edge. Cum exploded out between his long, capable fingers, a hot rain that spattered my thighs and belly. His features contorted in a grimace of ecstasy.

Joy welled up in my chest like helium. Harry slumped onto my immobilized body, seemingly drained by the force of his climax. His weight was pure pleasure.

Somehow, though, he mustered the energy to reach between my splayed legs. He caught my pulsing clit between his finger and thumb.

That was all it took to send me flying into glorious release. I floated on a cloud of bliss, free of worry, guilt and shame — secure in the knowledge that I was loved, no matter how twisted my desires.

Chapter Two

"I'm so confused, Harry."

Harry popped the last bite of his croissant into his mouth and licked black currant jam from his fingers. Of course the sensual gesture made my well-used pussy moisten once more. Did he do that deliberately? Or was it just another example of our chemistry?

"Confused about what?" He drained his espresso and set the cup down on the tray.

He'd untied me and now we were having a late Sunday breakfast in bed. Very late—my alarm clock told me it was close to two p.m. We were going to miss the matinee of that new French film at the Lumiere. Again.

As Harry circled my engorged nipple with a still-sticky fingertip, I realized I didn't mind.

Leaning back among the pillows, I let him play with my body. I could have sworn I was sated but before long, the familiar ache had returned, the sense of emptiness that could only be relieved by Harry's cock—or one of the outrageous substitutes we'd purchased together. I closed my eyes with a sigh of delight, giving myself up to my extraordinarily talented lover.

He hooked my pubic curls and gave a light pull, adding a sharp edge to my languid pleasure. "You were saying, Mei Lee? Why are you confused?" His attentive gaze made it clear he expected an answer.

I struggled to organize my thoughts—not an easy task when given that he had two fingers inserted between my pussy lips, stroking and burrowing into my folds.

"Well…before we met, I would never have thought I'd enjoy—well, you know—the things we do."

He arched an eyebrow. "Things? Be specific, please."

After all this time together, he could still make me blush. And I knew it amused him to see my pale cheeks grow pink with embarrassment.

"Come on. You know what I'm talking about. Spankings. Being tied up. Submission." I sat up straighter, seeking a bit of dignity. "I've always been assertive to the point of being bossy. Nobody would ever believe that I could be a submissive. I can't believe it."

"But it seems to be true," he commented, punctuating his statement with a hard twist to my nipple.

Lightning shot from that tender nub down to my equally swollen clit.

"You love it when I use you. Even the pain."

I nodded. "So after three months with you, I'm getting used to the idea that I'm sexually submissive. Then I find myself getting turned on when I order Etienne around. What's going on? I don't know whether I'm really a top, just pretending to be submissive, or really a bottom who happens to like the idea of dominating her boss."

Harry leaned in for a fruit-flavored kiss. Meanwhile, he kneaded my breasts like bread dough, further leavening my arousal. I flung my arms around his neck and pulled him closer, grateful for the moment to be unbound so that I could run my palms over his smooth shoulders and down his solid back. His mouth swept me back into a state of dizzying lust. By the time he released me, I'd almost forgotten what we'd been discussing.

"You worry too much, love." Harry ran his fingers through his tangled locks then stretched out on the bed next to me. "Why not just express your desires, wherever they lead you?"

"You know the way I am, Harry. I need to understand. I like to be in control of myself and the situation."

With sudden strength, he caught my wrists in one of his big hands and dragged my arms over my head. Would he bind me again? Did I want him to? Did it matter?

He straddled my hips and settled his butt on my pelvis. His half-hard penis bobbed against my abdomen. "You're not in control when you're with me, and you seem to like that just fine." Still grasping my wrists, he bent to lick along my neck to the hollow of my throat.

As I relaxed into the sensations, he popped up to snag my earlobe with his teeth.

"Ow! Harry!"

The sting dwindled when he nuzzled the sensitive spot just below my ear. As I'm sure he expected, my clit twitched in response. I arched up, trying to grind my pelvis against his bum. He raised himself to a half-kneel, breaking the contact between our skin, while still holding me more or less immobilized. His cock was now fully engorged. Barely a foot from my hungry mouth, it wept pre-cum onto my chest. I whimpered and struggled against his inexorable grip. I really didn't want to talk anymore. I just wanted him to fuck me. Again.

My Master had other ideas, though. He smiled down at my writhing frustration.

"Based on my experience, some people are one hundred percent submissive. Others are one hundred percent dominant. In more cases than you'd expect, though, it depends on the dynamics between two individuals—the interplay of personalities and fantasies. One person might make you want to surrender. Another might bring out your toppiness. The technical term is 'switch', but personally, I think it's just human nature."

"But, Harry—"

He cut off my argument with another kiss, hard and wet. It left me considerably more docile.

"There's something about Etienne that brings out your dominant side, Em. Nothing wrong with that."

"But why? I'll admit I've had sexual fantasies about him. But never in my wildest dreams did I imagine anything like this."

"You might be responding to his fantasies. He sees you as a powerful woman—gorgeous, desirable, worthy of his devotion. And that's what you become in his presence." Letting go of my arms, he wormed his way down my body until the slick tip of his erection nudged at my pussy lips. "In fact, that's what you are, Emily—at least partly.

I parted my thighs, hoping to tempt him inside. "And I'm partly your slave as well."

"Just partly?" He drew his hips back, rescinding the tantalizing promise of his cock.

I almost wept.

"I thought you were mine, to use and command. If that's not true…"

I squirmed beneath his weight. "Harry! Come on!" I was desperate. "I'm yours, you know that. I'll do whatever you want. Just fuck me now. Okay?"

"Pretty demanding for a little sub, aren't you?" Even as he teased me, though, he slipped his lovely hardness deep into my sex.

I clenched around his bulk and felt him swell further. He was everything I wanted—and more. We rocked together, in a sweet steady rhythm that soon brought me to the brink of yet another climax. *How does he do it?* I wondered, as premonitions of release shimmered through my body. *How does he know exactly what I need?*

He could keep me on the edge forever—I knew that from experience—dangling my orgasm in front of me like a ripe fruit hanging just out of reach. This time, though, he didn't hold back. He hammered into me, driving me closer to coming with each furious thrust. His stone-hard cock grazed my cervix on the inbound stroke and dragged across my clit on the outbound, in a fiery alternation of pain and pleasure. I opened myself and let him take what he wanted.

We came together, in a groaning, thrashing frenzy. The breakfast tray tumbled off the bed, scattering remnants of eggs Florentine and strawberry mousse all over the carpet.

Gradually the waves of bliss died away. Only then did I notice the mess on the floor. I was too dazed with pleasure to really care.

"Ah, love. You never disappoint me." Harry rolled onto his back and stretched, showing off his lean, strong limbs.

I grinned at him, totally satisfied with the state of the world. "I try to please, Sir."

"Don't mock me, girl. I'm just itching for an excuse to try out that paddle."

"Do you need an excuse, Sir?" I knew I was asking for trouble. We normally didn't bother with that sort of epithet. He just asked me to do things, and I obeyed.

"You're right, I don't. But I'm too tired to punish you now."

"Later then?" I snuggled up to his firm body, my cheek resting on his shoulder and my breast filling the warm hollow under his arm. He buried his nose in my hair then kissed my forehead.

"Perhaps. You sound a bit too eager. Meanwhile, I have an assignment for you."

"Yes, Sir?"

My fake deference earned me a vicious pinch to my nipple. I gasped at the sudden pain. Harry chuckled. "I want you to top Etienne."

"What?" The alarm in my voice was no pretense.

"You heard me. Use him. Punish him. Take him as far as he'll let you go."

"But..."

"I thought you wanted to please me."

"I..."

"This is what I want. Turn Etienne into your slave."

Yesterday had been an accident, a fluke—an unintentional lapse. Could I deliberately dominate the suave, self-possessed Frenchman? Did I dare?

"And of course I want you to tell me every detail."

I reared back to look him in the eye. "You're kidding."

"Not in the least. Those are my instructions. Will you obey?"

I didn't answer — not directly — but we both knew I'd do what he'd commanded. "You're one kinky bastard, Harry Sanborne."

My lover just smiled. "Baby, you have no idea."

* * * *

"I distinctly remember requesting *fresh* cream." Etienne held out a pint carton toward Roth. "Read the expiration date."

The androgynous intern clutched his — or was it her? — narrow shoulders as if he were freezing. Behind the steel-rimmed spectacles, his green eyes were wide. "Um — June seventeenth, sir."

"And what is today's date?"

"June sixteenth. So you see, sir, it's not expired..."

"Close enough. You've been with the network for how long, Roth? Two months?"

"Nearly four."

I'd rarely seen an individual look as chastened as the poor youth. Her — or was it his? — lower lip trembled, as if tears were imminent.

"More than long enough to know how I feel about my ingredients, wouldn't you say?"

The intern just nodded. Etienne thrust the cream in Roth's direction. She shrank away.

"You Americans don't seem to realize just how much the flavor depends on always using the very freshest, highest quality foods available. Go return this and get me some *fresh* cream instead. At least a week before expiration, understand?"

"Yes — yes, sir." Roth skittered off to obey, all spiked hair, piercings and studded leather. I caught myself wondering whether the S&M touches in that costume were anything more than the latest fashion.

Damn Harry! He'd really affected my imagination!

Etienne turned to me with an indulgent smile. "Sorry about that, Mei Lee. We'll have to wait until that idiot returns before we can tackle the *crevettes au cognac et beurre blanc*. However, we can get started on the *lotte a l'Imperatrice*. I picked out the fish this morning, down at the Pier 33 wholesale market. You have to get there by five a.m., but it's well worth the effort. I was able to find some lovely scallops for the *coquilles St. Jacques* as well."

Our menu for tomorrow's show focused on seafood—a suggestion of mine that Etienne had heartily endorsed. We typically tested all the recipes the day before, as a sort of rehearsal. As we bustled around the studio kitchen, me cleaning the shrimp, Etienne mincing garlic with the precision of a robot, he seemed as confident and at ease as ever.

Meanwhile, I was sweating, even though the brightest lights were off. My jeans felt too tight and my crotch was embarrassingly damp. I hadn't been this nervous since that first fateful broadcast when I'd slipped Etienne some of my grandmother's aphrodisiac and temporarily turned him into an eager slave, groveling at my feet.

I shuddered to remember. Yet in some sense, my ill-planned attempt to win the favor of Etienne Duvalier was responsible for my current success.

Two shows a week for the past twelve weeks—that made this the twenty-fourth time Etienne and I had shared the spotlight on Toutes Saveurs Francaises. We'd adapted to one another's styles and come up with a standard routine. Viewers apparently loved seeing the distinguished and stylish French chef obeying me, so when we were on the air, I took the lead. Unfailingly polite, almost obsequious, he addressed me as 'Ms Wong', as he hastened to carry out my instructions. I'd always find something to criticize in his culinary knowledge, cooking techniques or diligence in following my orders. The audience adored seeing him repentant and apologetic. Once or twice I'd told him I didn't like his shirt— although in fact he was always impeccably dressed— and made him remove it on camera, as I had during our first show. Those were the segments that got the very highest ratings. Women simply drooled at the sight of his naked, muscular torso. I didn't make him strip too often, for fear that the gimmick would lose its impact.

On the show, we were Ms Wong and Etienne, Mistress chef and her obedient assistant. Off stage, though, one could almost believe it was all an act. Instead of Ms Wong, I became Mei Lee, a temporary employee and junior partner. Etienne was almost laughably serious in his role as the head of the Tastes of France channel. He alternately charmed and terrorized the staff, imposing his perfectionist standards and his reverence for traditional French cuisine upon us all. Indeed, I'd come to appreciate his extensive experience and his sensitive taste buds. And he had become a bit more open to my culinary experimentation, though he still frowned on adding Asian ingredients to French mainstays.

I had begun to think that Etienne's behavior under the influence of the caterpillar fungus had been aberration, some bizarre effect of neurotransmitters running rampant rather than a true expression of his desires. I'd attributed the changes in his manner with me to be a simple reflection of increasing familiarity and perhaps growing respect.

That had been before yesterday's scene in my dressing room.

And now I was under orders from Harry to coax Etienne into submitting once again.

How in the world was I going to manage this? Despite our public display of power exchange on the air — regardless of what had happened yesterday — I still found my elegant and imperious boss a bit intimidating. Yesterday he'd come to me, but now I was playing the black stones, as they say in *weiqi* — it was up to me to make the first move.

The problem preoccupied me throughout our test session. I cooked on autopilot, reducing the *beurre blanc*, poaching the scallops, buttering the mold for the monkfish, thinking all the while about Etienne's pale, slender cock and muscular buttocks. The kitchen was redolent of fried shallots, black pepper and tarragon. Etienne's *coquilles* were picture perfect. I knew the flared shells piled with wine-poached scallops and mushrooms smothered in melted Gruyère would taste as delicious as they looked. I scarcely noticed any of these appealing stimuli.

My stomach twisted into knots, but not due to hunger. When Etienne's back was turned, I snuck a sip of the cognac, trying to bolster my courage. Meanwhile, my boss — my prey — appeared to be completely unaware of my inner turmoil.

Finally we finished. We perched on stools in front of the work counter, sampling our creations. Etienne licked his lips and favored me with an indulgent smile.

"The *lotte* is exceptional, Mei Lee. We've never featured this dish before — I think the audience will love it."

"Um — thanks. The scallops came out very well, too."

"Fresh ingredients make all the difference. But of course you know that."

I just nodded, chewing a mouthful of shrimp and trying to buy time. The clock above the stove read four-thirty. I wasn't scheduled to meet Harry until seven.

It was now or never. If I let the net slip, the fish would flee.

I hiked myself off my seat and squared my shoulders. "Etienne." I tried to pitch my voice a bit lower than usual, to inject a note of gravitas that I normally lack.

My delectable boss looked up, fork halfway to his mouth. His winter-blue eyes widened as he took in my expression. His slight hesitation in answering told me I'd caught his attention.

"Um—yes? What it is it, Mei Lee?"

"Ms Wong," I corrected him, astonished by my own daring.

He swallowed visibly—not a mouthful of food but an obvious lump in his throat—as the truth started to dawn. "Ah, yes, I mean Ms Wong. Is something amiss?"

"That depends on you, Etienne. Come with me to my dressing room."

"Ah—now?" He cast a glance around at all the food then down at his half-empty plate.

"Never mind the mess. *You* can clean that up later. Right now, I want you in my dressing room. Is that clear?"

The chef nodded and rose from his stool. A quick glance at his crotch told me my altered manner was already having some effect. Deliberately trying to convey my certainty that he'd follow, I turned my back on him and headed for the cubicle where I normally changed for the show. It was too small for more than a clothes rack, a couple of shelves, a vanity with a mirror and two chairs. The walls were nothing but thin plywood, but it would have to do.

I unlocked the door, flipped the light switch then stepped inside.

Etienne was right behind me. He hovered in the door frame, as if afraid to step over the threshold.

I settled myself in the more stable of the two chairs.

"Come in. Lock the door behind you."

Panic flared in his eyes and I thought for a moment I'd lost him. Then he swallowed again and obeyed.

A sense of triumph rushed through me, making my pulse race. "Turn around and let me look at you, Etienne."

The debonair host of Toutes Les Saveurs stood before me, eyes cast down and hands clasped in front of his bulging crotch. Panting, his pupils dilated, he made me think of a thief caught in the act of committing a crime. A very horny thief.

"What shall I do with you, Etienne? You're obviously very aroused. Aren't you?"

"Ah—yes. I mean, yes, Ms Wong."

"Why are you in this unseemly state?" I settled back in my chair and crossed one leg over the other, trying for a casual manner. This position had an additional advantage, too. I could squeeze my thighs together and stimulate my throbbing clit.

"I...um... I'm not sure."

"What should I do with you, then? Yesterday you burst into my room and begged to be allowed to serve me. Is that still what you want?"

It was hard for him to admit—I could see this—without the libido-enhancing effects of Gran's powder. He wanted to pretend he was still in charge.

His eyes flitted around the cramped room, as though he was seeking some excuse, some escape. But his need was greater than his shame. He sighed, finally, and gave in to his desire.

"Yes, Ms Wong. I want... I want you to use me for your own pleasure." His voice began with a quaver, but grew stronger as he proceeded. "I want to be your slave, if you'll have me."

My slave! If someone had asked me three months ago if I wanted a sexual slave, I would have laughed. Never, in all my thirty years, had I considered such a notion. Now, though, his words turned me to hot, quivering jelly. Dozens of filthy scenarios flooded my mind. I could scarcely decide which one to try first.

Start with something simple. Like a basic white sauce.

"Hmm. Do you think you deserve that? To serve me? To be my slave."

"Uh—I don't know, Ms Wong. But I'd like to try. When you touched me yesterday... *Mon dieu*, it was so marvelous..." Naked yearning showed in his eyes.

Sympathy welled up inside me. I pushed it aside. I had to be strong. Stern. Maybe even cruel.

"Hush. Do you think I care about your pleasure?"

Chastened, he remained silent as I'd bid him to do.

"Let's use that mouth of yours for a more useful purpose than whining about your desires."

I kicked off my shoes. The clatter made him jump. Standing, I unbuckled my belt, unzipped my jeans then shimmied them down over my hips. His eyes grew wide as I exposed my silk-covered mons, and his nostrils flared. I was hardly surprised. My musky scent rose to fill the enclosed space.

After draping the denim garment—already quite damp between the legs—over the back of my chair, I stripped off my drenched panties. Stepping up to him, invading his personal space, I thrust them under his nose. At the same time, I grabbed his swollen cock and squeezed.

He groaned—whether in anguish or ecstasy, I couldn't tell.

"Do you like the smell of my pussy, Etienne?"

His cock swelled further in my hand, answering without words. Etienne just nodded.

Backing away, I seated myself, spread my thighs, and draped them over the arms of the chair, opening myself to the air and his worshipful gaze.

"Kneel between my legs, Etienne. Eat me until I come. Let's see if you're really worthy to be my slave."

The lanky Frenchman was on his knees almost before I'd finished giving the order. He stroked the inside of my thighs with reverent fingers. The delicate touch felt divine, but I couldn't allow him to know that.

"Just your mouth, slave. Keep your hands behind your back. Imagine I've cuffed them there."

He'd been keeping his gaze averted, humble and deferent, but before he bent to execute my command, he raised his eyes to mine. In their ice-blue depths I saw a flicker of *something*—something that both warmed me inside and turned up the volume on my arousal. Gratitude, maybe? Or complicity?

Whatever it was, it burned away my last shreds of hesitation.

I slapped his face, harder than I would have believed I could. "Did I give you permission to look at me? Your only task right now is to give me pleasure. You're nothing but a mouth—a human sex toy. And I warn you, if you don't make me come within five minutes, I'll toss you aside like a vibrator that's run out of batteries."

He didn't need a second command. He dove into my pussy and sucked my clitoris into his mouth, drawing hard on the little bud. I couldn't bear the intensity, or so I thought—the pleasure so raw it bordered on pain. When he slid away from my clit to stab his tongue into my channel, though, the swollen nub screamed for new stimulation. I grabbed his head and dragged his mouth back to that demanding little bead of flesh.

"Stick to my clit! Give me your tongue! Your teeth! Eat me, damn it. Eat me like I'm the most delicious meal you've ever tasted!"

I clamped my thighs around his head and humped his face. I didn't know if he would even hear my exhortations, but his mouth was busy, his lips firm, his tongue long and flexible. The pleasure built. Fingers buried in his thick, wavy hair, I moved him this way and that, grinding my pussy against that proud Gallic nose. The tension of imminent climax wound tighter in my pelvis. He'd only been at work for few minutes, but I was already close.

Etienne was skillful, I had to admit, though his techniques differed radically from Harry's. Harry's approach to cunnilingus was deliberate, totally conscious, each movement chosen for maximum effect. With Harry I felt each motion, like separate brush strokes painting a masterpiece of pleasure. Etienne was wilder, less controlled, propelled by a seemingly instinctive hunger. He burrowed deep into my cunt—licking, nibbling, sucking, taking my flesh in great mouthfuls. I couldn't say which man I enjoyed more. Before long, I stopped comparing, borne away by the rising tide of sensation in my pussy.

Still, thoughts of Harry lingered on the edge of my awareness. I'd done as he'd ordered. I'd made Etienne my eager slave—at least for the moment. I was in charge here. My satisfaction was all that mattered, yet at the same time I'd overcome my fear and acted according to my Master's dictates.

The paradox aroused me beyond belief. Releasing my grip on Etienne's hair, I lay back, spread my legs wide, and let him drive me over the edge. I didn't need to strain for release. It was Etienne's job to take care of that for me. I surrendered to his urgent mouth. As soon as I let go, the climax hit, a swell of bliss that rose from my depths and drowned me.

I screamed, shaking under Etienne's continuing attentions. Ripples of delight pulsed from my center, radiating through my body. Little by little, the waves subsided. Then Etienne nipped my clit with those perfect teeth and another climax swallowed me.

A sharp knocking roused me from my post-orgasmic languor. "Emily! Are you okay? I heard you screaming."

Harry!

"Oh, by the Wise Ones... Yes, I'm fine, fine. Just a second!"

Etienne watched me, still on his knees, his cheeks wet with my juices. The ghost of a smile twitched at his well-shaped lips. "Get up," I whispered. I threw him a box of tissues. "Clean yourself up!"

"And did I please you, Mistress?" he asked, *sotto voce*. "Will you be wanting me to serve you again?" He looked far too proud of himself to be a proper slave.

Harry rattled the door knob. "It's locked," he called. "Can you let me in?"

"Just a minute!" I struggled to pull my jeans up over my sticky thighs. I had no idea what had happened to my panties. I lowered my voice and tried to sound convincing. "As for you, Etienne—I was quite disappointed. You need serious training."

He bowed his head in seemingly honest distress. "I'm sorry, Mistress. I'll try to do better next time."

I finally managed to get my pants over my hips. I zipped up, trying to seem decisive and powerful. "I don't know if there will be a next time, slave."

We both knew I was lying.

Chapter Three

"Coming!"

I pulled myself together the best I could then unlocked the door. Eyebrows knotted with worry, Harry peered into the cramped space. When he saw Etienne—who looked remarkably cool and self-contained—he broke into a knowing grin.

"Ah, Etienne—I didn't realize you were in here with Emily. Conferring about tomorrow's show?"

"Of course, Harry. What else?" Duvalier's voice was like ice water.

What else indeed? I envied Etienne's composure. The heat of the blush painted my cheeks. My heart rate hadn't yet returned to normal after my shattering orgasm and I was short of breath, as if I'd just completed a marathon.

"Why'd you lock the door, Em? Are you two cooking up some kind of new secret to entertain the audience?" Still hovering in the doorway since there really wasn't room for him in the dressing stall, he turned his attention to me. His nostrils flared, and I guessed he was picking up the scent of my recently exposed pussy. I wanted to drop through the floor.

"Uh—it wasn't locked—it just has a tendency to stick." I hoped Harry would forgive me the face-saving lie.

Etienne shot me a grateful look.

"Oh, right. But why did you scream?"

By the gods, he was a merciless tease!

I cast my eyes around the room, desperately seeking inspiration. The studio had taken over half a block of remodeled Victorian row houses. Dust bunnies gathered in one corner, where the wooden floor met the outside wall. "Cockroaches!" I blurted out. "There was a cockroach, climbing up my leg!"

"Really? Oh dear." Harry pretended to believe me. "I'll have to call in the exterminators again. Definitely a problem in these old buildings. Anyway, I'm glad you're not hurt or anything. That was quite a squeal."

He was struggling not to laugh. I wondered if Etienne could tell. Even if the chef noticed, though, he'd never let his knowledge show. Cool, calm and collected, that was Etienne Duvalier in a nutshell. At least in public.

"Did you want something, Mr Sanborne?" Etienne swept an errant auburn lock back from his brow and stepped up to face Harry.

Harry was the taller of the two men, by a few centimeters, but Etienne broadcast the impression that he was totally in charge. Nevertheless, Harry didn't act in the least cowed.

"I just got word from upstairs—Mr Elliot wants to see you both. Right away."

Oh, no! Roger Elliot was chief executive for the Foodie Network. I'd met him a couple of times, but he rarely intervened directly in the running of Tastes of France channel, which was Etienne's baby.

This couldn't be good. Had someone overheard my encounter with Etienne the previous afternoon? The thin walls of the dressing cubicles meant that was a distinct possibility. What would happen if the network learned I was having sexual interactions, on the job, with my boss? I saw my career plans sinking like an over-loaded merchant's junk sailing into a typhoon. Why, oh why, couldn't I just resist temptation? I couldn't expect Harry to save me this time...

"Did Roger tell you anything about the reason?" Etienne flicked an invisible speck of lint off his ink-black Yves Saint-Laurent shirt and took another decisive step forward. This time Harry retreated to let him pass.

"Not a thing. But he's called me in, too, so it's probably something related to your show."

I released the breath I'd been holding. Harry's summons meant this couldn't be about Etienne's and my little interlude. But the close call highlighted the risks I'd been taking, indulging my lust here at the studio, where anyone could discover me. In the past I'd always managed to keep my work life and my private life separate. Why had I gotten so sloppy?

Harry watched me intently, as if reading my mind. Vivid recollections of our first ferocious, awkward encounter flooded my mind — the hard tiles of the kitchen floor beneath my back, the rigid length of Harry's cock buried in my hungry pussy, the mingled scents of sugar, sweat, sex and the insatiable need that made me forget everything else. Incredibly risky, no doubt. Still, that afternoon had been the beginning of the most outrageous, and most fulfilling, relationship in my life. I couldn't honestly wish it hadn't happened.

Together we climbed the three flights to Mr Elliot's office suite, which was located in a glass-walled penthouse constructed upon the building's flat roof, back in the days when that sort of architectural desecration had not yet been outlawed. Etienne led the way. I couldn't help admiring the flex of his world-class buttocks as he mounted the stairs in front of me. Meanwhile, I knew Harry, bringing up the rear, was watching my butt jiggle under my jeans. I could feel his eyes like lasers. As usual, I started to get wet in response to his lustful scrutiny. Elliot's secretary – Jonathan? Joshua? – a fashionably-dressed young man who looked like he divided his leisure time between the gym and the waxing-salon, showed us in to the CEO's office.

Roger Elliot rose from his ergonomic chair to greet us. His baby face and teddy bear physique were deceiving. He had the sharp mind of a master businessman, plus a decade of experience in broadcasting to back that up. I'd heard that he could be ruthless when the occasion required it, although I'd never witnessed that in person. Today, however, he wore a broad smile as he spread his arms as if to embrace us all.

"Etienne! Ms Wong! My top-rated stars! Allow me to congratulate you. Toutes les Saveures has broken the network's rating record. And our subscriber base has jumped by fifteen percent since Ms Wong joined the show."

"Harry deserves some of the credit," Etienne pointed out with a graciousness that surprised me. "The whole thing would fall apart without his hands-on management."

"I know that. Well done, Harry. And as for you, Ms Wong—"

"Call me Emily, please!"

"Sorry, Emily—I'll do that. I'm just so used to hearing Etienne using the formal mode of address with you... A brilliant stroke, I must say, making the formidable *enfant terrible* of the cooking world into your eager, humble assistant. I love it, and so do the viewers." Elliot chuckled.

Etienne showed not the slightest hint of embarrassment. I was impressed.

"Sit down, all of you. I've got more exciting news."

Breathing a sigh of relief, I followed his suggestion, as did the rest of the group.

"As I said, the show is going great. However, we all know how fickle an audience can be. People are so easily bored." He shrugged, as if to suggest that any audience who tired of Etienne and my antics had little taste. "We have to innovate constantly, to give them something new to amuse them."

Anxiety flickered through me. What did he have in mind?

"So we've decided to kick off the upcoming season with something new—a series of episodes recorded on location in France."

"*Mon dieu*! That's a marvelous idea!" The master chef's excitement was obvious in his eyes, his voice, his overall demeanor. "With Paris as a backdrop, our recipes will be so much more meaningful..."

I'd rarely seen Etienne so enthusiastic, aside from when he was eating my pussy.

"Not just Paris." The CEO clasped his pudgy fingers together on the polished desk top and leaned forward. "We're thinking that you should visit a variety of locales, presenting the regional specialties in each one.

Bouillabaisse in Marseille. *Andouillettes* and *cervelle de canut* in Lyons. *Boeuf en daube* and *ratatouille* in Avignon. *Crêpes* in Brittany."

Saliva gathered in my mouth, though I'd been sampling Etienne's and my test dishes less than an hour before.

"I want to send the whole crew — camera and sound, makeup, costumes. With you, of course, Harry, to keep them all in line. And I'm thinking we shouldn't focus entirely on cooking. We can intersperse the kitchen segments with shots of Etienne and Emily enjoying the sights together — maybe cash in on the travel-hungry crowd as well as the foodies. Not to mention all the romantics who are already convinced the two of them are a couple."

I glanced over at Etienne. He wouldn't meet my eyes.

"Sounds more like a vacation than work," Harry commented.

"Well, you all deserve a bit of a reward. But we'll get our money's worth from you, don't worry. Location shoots tend to be fraught with problems. I expect that you'll have all sorts of obstacles to overcome. For one thing, the French are renowned for being obstructionist."

Etienne sniffed audibly, his mouth twisted into a scowl.

The executive chuckled. "Just teasing, Etienne. I'm sure your compatriots will bend over backward to welcome you. Still, working on location can be tough. You have to be ready for anything."

"I'd like to make sure we schedule at least one show in St Rémy de Provence," said Etienne, his face brightening. "My home town. And we shouldn't miss

Bordeaux—*agneau de lait du Pauilliac* and *confit de canard...*"

"I'll leave it to you three to figure out the itinerary and the menus. By next week, if possible."

"Next week!" Harry shifted in his chair. "That'll be a challenge."

"I have confidence in you, Harry. I'd like you to leave by the beginning of July. You could devote two, or even three, weeks to the trip. You send back each segment as you shoot it and we'll air some of them right away."

"I don't know. We still have four shows to produce for this season..."

"I'll ask Jonathan to give you a hand. He can manage the travel arrangements, hotel bookings and so on."

Hotel bookings! Up to that point I'd been listening to the conversation with a mixture of relief and excitement. I was grateful that the meeting with Elliot had nothing to do with the private interactions between Etienne and me. Meanwhile, the trip sounded like a great opportunity to see more of France. I'd been mostly stuck in Paris during my years at the Cordon Bleu. Finally, I agreed with Roger Elliot's assessment. The on-location shows were a great idea for building our audience. The trip was bound to boost my career.

The mention of hotels, however, brought me back to reality. Harry, Etienne and me in close quarters, day after day after horny day? How would we manage? As Confucius said, 'Study the past to define the future'. My recent past made it clear that I had little ability to resist the lure of the flesh.

My relationship with Harry was the lesser problem. Although we didn't broadcast the fact, most of our co-workers had some idea that we were...um...dating. They didn't know about the velvet blindfold or the chrome-plated handcuffs or the cute little cat o' nine tails we'd found in Leather Masters—some of which I was certain Harry would bring to France—but as long as I kept quiet in the bedroom, they didn't need to know. I suspected Harry would be happy to gag me if he thought I was too loud. That somewhat scary notion generated a faint queasiness in my stomach and a wet fluttering between my thighs.

Etienne was another story altogether. Having sampled my dominance, he'd want more—I was certain of that. Would I be able to refuse him? As unlikely as a clear day on The Peak! Besides, Harry had, in effect, ordered me to top him. "Take him as far as he'll let you go," my lover had commanded.

After this afternoon, I couldn't begin to guess how far that might be. I had no idea how far *I* was willing to go. However, a disturbingly large number of possible steps occurred to me. Exposure, though, could ruin both our careers. How could I be sufficiently discreet when the whole crew would be traveling with us? How could I satisfy my Master's demands, Etienne's fantasies and my inexplicable craving for power, when the whole world was watching?

My first inclination was to find an escape route. I listened with half an ear to the three men as they discussed staffing and equipment, schedules and expenses, all the while running through the possibilities. I could try to convince Roger Elliot that the whole notion was a bad idea. I doubted I'd succeed, since I didn't believe that myself. I could feign illness, but I guessed they'd simply postpone the trip until I 'recovered'. And how could I lie to Harry, in any case?

Perhaps I could claim that the Belvedere had canceled my leave and wanted me back on the job immediately. The ruse would get me out of this situation, certainly, but at the expense of leaving Harry and Etienne behind. That would be 'torching the rice to discourage the locusts', as my grandmother would say. I pictured my lonely life back in Hong Kong, without either of the two men who'd given me so much pleasure and satisfaction.

Unbearable thought!

No, somehow I had to take the ox by the horns and deal with the challenge of submitting to Harry and dominating Etienne under everyone's noses, without giving away our secrets.

It was going to be quite a trip.

Chapter Four

"You are going to *fǎguó* with two different men?" Gran shook her head. The video signal lagged a fraction of a second behind the audio, so that her lips didn't sync with her voice. It made me think of a poorly dubbed movie.

"This is work. I don't have a choice."

How had she figured Grandmother out, anyway, that I had some sort of relationship with both Harry and Etienne? I Skyped with her regularly—she was always eager to hear about the people and events in my life in Gold Mountain—but I could swear I'd never told her Harry was my lover and I was certain I'd never even hinted there was anything going on with Etienne. She would never in a million years understand the weird dynamics that drew us together.

She'd sensed something, though, sniffed it out with that sharp old nose of hers. "The handsome one—the chef—he's wealthy too, right?"

"Without his glasses, Harry's just as good looking," I replied then bit my tongue.

"But not rich." She folded her arms across her chest. Her floral blouse looked feminine and a bit old-fashioned, but her powdered face was set in a stubborn frown. "Forget the producer, First Granddaughter. Pursue the chef. He's powerful and strong-willed—I can tell from watching him on the Internet. He will be a stern but loving husband. He will take good care of you."

My mind flipped back to my latest session with Etienne. I'd summoned him to my apartment one evening—no more risky meetings in the studio, if I could help it. He'd arrived exactly on time, but I'd claimed he was late and spanked his glorious bare ass until it was as red as Chairman Mao's little book. Then I'd forced him—though given his eagerness to comply, the word hardly fit—to lie on the carpet while I rode his cock to a shuddering climax. I'd been tempted to let him come. The look on his face when I'd threatened to deny him that release—pained yet ecstatic—had changed my mind. I'd sent him home with his swollen, purple cock coated with my juice and forbidden him to touch himself until we met next.

Later that night, I'd regaled Harry with all the details, my own butt pink from the impact of his palm.

"Film him," my master had ordered, tweaking a nipple. "Set up a webcam. I want to see it all."

"What? Without his permission?" I'd squirmed away from him in real horror. "I can't do that. It's totally unethical."

"You'd refuse me?"

The sadness in his voice almost made me agree.

Then he'd given me a reprieve. "Ask him if you can take videos. I bet he'll agree. It will make him even hotter, to think that you're recording his degradation."

"But—what if he asks who's going to see them?"

"Tell him the truth. He still won't refuse."

I hadn't had the chance yet to test Harry's intuitions. But I had a suspicion he'd turn out to be right.

I pushed these thoughts from my mind. Knowing my grandmother, she'd notice my flushed cheeks and quickened breathing.

"Anyway, we leave tomorrow, and our itinerary has us moving to a new city every few days. I probably won't have time to Skype again until I get back to the US."

"You couldn't stop here on the way?" Her slack cheeks crinkled into a pleading smile. "I have something I want to give to you."

I laughed. "Hong Kong is not exactly on the way between the America and France!"

"But I miss you, First Granddaughter."

"I miss you too. I'll be home in January for the New Year's festival."

"Bring the chef with you. Your parents want to meet him."

"Grandmother, I'm not about to marry Etienne!" If I were going to settle down with anyone, it would be Harry. Etienne was just a... Well, I didn't know exactly what Etienne was to me. Certainly not fiancé material, though. But then, was a guy who whipped me and tied me up a good choice for a husband?

"Well, you should." She patted her gray bun and shook her head, making her jade eardrops sway. "Young people! They never listen to their elders."

"Did you listen when your family didn't want you to marry Grandfather? As I recall the story, you defied your own father and ran away with a penniless poet, instead of accepting the young man Great Grandfather was grooming to take over...uh...the business."

She gave me a gap-toothed grin. "That was different. I was wise beyond my years."

"I cannot claim your wisdom, but remember the words of Confucius: 'The cautious seldom err'. I'm not going to make a commitment until I'm sure I've found the right man."

"Well, I can hardly argue with that. I wish you a safe and productive journey, First Granddaughter. Be careful. Think with your head – not your loins."

I wasn't fooling her. "Thank you. I will call you when I return. Bye."

"Oh, wait a moment! Do you need me to send you more *dōngchóngxiàcǎo*?"

"Oh – no, definitely not!"

She smiled at my vehemence. Was I really that transparent?

"I just wanted to make sure."

* * * *

"Oh! That tickles!" I jerked as Harry brushed the feather duster over my bare buttocks. He had arranged me in one of his favorite positions, on my belly with my hips elevated by a pillow. Tonight he'd also spread my legs and tied my ankles to the corners of the bed – for greater accessibility, he'd asserted with a cheeky grin – though he'd left my arms unbound.

"Oh, please – oh, no!" His fluffy instrument of torture whispered its way along my rear crevice then fluttered against the sensitive skin of my inner thigh.

"Harry...oh...oh...no...ah..."

I writhed, trying without success to escape the maddening brush of the feathers. My frantic struggles ground my pubis against the supporting cushion, further stimulating my already aching clit. If only he'd stop teasing! I was desperate to feel him inside me again.

"Be still, slut!" He landed a solid slap on my bum. The sting provided a brief, welcome relief from the unbearable tickling. "Or would you prefer the strap?"

"I think I would, to be honest."

"Well, to be honest, *I* enjoy seeing you squirm. You look delicious." He traced the feathers up my spine.

I couldn't help myself. I reached behind me to snatch the irritating duster away from him and toss it to the floor. "Oh, Emily, you'll pay for that! What a naughty sub you are!"

Instead of punishing me, though, he straddled me and trailed a line of tantalizing, wet kisses up my back. Settling his familiar weight on top of me, he nuzzled the spot between my shoulder blades. Lovely heat shimmered through me. His cock wedged itself into the crevice between my rear cheeks. Constrained both by my bonds and his body, I shifted awkwardly on the pillow. I had to get that lovely bulk lined up with the entrance to my pussy.

"Oh no you don't!" Harry reacted by scooting up higher, so that his cockhead pressed into the curve just above my butt. "Who's in control here?" He nipped my shoulder.

"Ow! You—but..."

"Who decides when you get fucked?" Was he really annoyed? I couldn't tell.

"Ah—you do, Harry." I tried to relax and lie still, as he'd commanded. He'd give me satisfaction, sooner or later. He always did.

"Maybe I should just make you wait..." His actions didn't match his scolding tone in the least, though. Raising his hips and reaching between his legs, he adjusted his cock until the head bumped against my raging clit.

"God, Harry... Please..."

With one smooth stroke, he slid into my soaked cleft. "On the other hand, why should I put off my own pleasure, just to punish you?"

I gloried in the sudden sense of fullness. Harry always knew what I needed. "Oh — oh, thank you...oh!" Each powerful thrust drove my mound into the pillow. The indirect pressure complemented the direct sensation of his hardness sliding over my inner walls. In minutes he had me hovering on the brink of climax.

How could I resist him? He might lead me along new and scary paths, but every one led to pleasure.

We came together, my wild wailing mingling with his grunts as he emptied himself inside me. Afterward, he slumped down onto my back, his evening stubble pricking my tender skin. His arms stretched out along mine, with our hands clasped.

"I can't just be strict with you, Em," he murmured. "I want you too much."

"You're strict enough. I have the marks on my ass to prove it." I twisted my head and strained backward. "Kiss, please..."

Once more he granted my desire.

We relaxed back onto the mattress, our limbs entwined. "Have you dominated a lot of women, Harry?" I was suddenly curious. For some reason I'd never wondered about this before.

"Just a few. It takes someone special to bring out that side of me."

"Oh?"

"Yeah, I can't top just anyone. I have to feel a connection, a sense of trust. It's not a game for me, the way it is for some Doms. It's tough to find a woman who'll open herself to me the way I need."

"So that's why you came to San Francisco?" I laughed. Even in Hong Kong, Gold Mountain is well known as the S&M capital of the world.

Harry caught my earlobe in his teeth and pulled. "Minx! Of course not. I came here for my career, just like you."

"Someday you'll have to tell me about your first sub."

"Would that turn you on, baby? I'll bet it would." He licked his way along the line of my shoulder. "But honestly, no woman in my past can compare to you. No one."

"I... Well, you're special to me, too, Harry." Why was it so difficult for me to say it? I'd never felt anything like the joy he kindled, just by his presence. But I still wasn't sure how much my feelings depended on our obvious sexual compatibility. And I didn't want to commit myself until I knew. I didn't want to make a mistake that would hurt everyone involved.

Possibly sensing my uncertainty, my lover didn't reply. He lifted my hair to nuzzle my nape. Sparks leaped in my pussy. Everything he did to me turned me on.

"Hey, what's this? I never realized you had a tattoo."

I froze for a moment—did he notice?—then made my voice casual. "I've had it since I was a child. It's for protection." The truth, but not the whole truth. I didn't want to scare him away.

"Very cool dragon! Too bad it's hidden away. The workmanship is fantastic."

"Well, as I said, it's not intended as decoration."

"So it's a traditional design? Some kind of oriental secret?"

"Something like that." I tried to change the subject. "I hate to kick you out, Harry, but it's pretty late and the plane leaves at ten in the morning. I don't know about you, but I'm not packed yet."

He planted one last kiss on my shoulder then rolled and busied himself untying my ankles. "I hate to say it, but you're probably right. Anyway, we'll have lots of time together on the trip. Lots of adventures!"

"Given your filthy mind, I can just imagine the kind of adventures you're thinking about!" I tossed him his clothing.

"Given *your* filthy mind, Em, I'll bet you can!" He paused while buttoning his shirt to gaze at me.

I could see the wheels turning. Meanwhile all I wanted to do was tear that shirt off again and fasten my lips on his tempting pink nipples.

I grabbed my robe and belted it around my waist. I had to resist temptation. "What are you thinking about, you pervert?"

"Tattoos, actually. About tattooing my initials on your ass. That would be a pretty clear sign that you were mine."

The notion sent a queasy thrill racing through me. Would I let him do that? Part of me was horrified at the notion of such a permanent step. Part of me found the notion of being so irrevocably claimed incredibly arousing.

"Oh sure! Why don't you just brand me, like some cattle!"

"Now there's a thought...see what I mean about your mind?"

I threw a pillow at him. "Go home and pack! I'll see you tomorrow."

"Okay, okay. I'll pretend you're the boss for now. But later…"

He swept me into his arms and took control, his lips sealing to mine. Here at least I could surrender. As he devoured my mouth, a sweet fever rose in me, burning away my doubts. The heat still lingered after he'd released me and closed the door behind him.

Chapter Five

"You're sleeping with him, aren't you? At least, that's what everyone says."

Etienne kept his voice low, to avoid being heard by the crew fiddling with their equipment a few meters away.

"Uh — well — not exactly sleeping..." I stared into my cappuccino, then up at the café umbrella, then over toward the gleaming dome and spires of Sacre Coeur across the square. Anywhere but into his wounded eyes.

"Do not play the innocent with me, Mei Lee. You know what I'm saying. You're involved in a sexual relationship with Harry, are you not?"

I ventured a peek at him from under lowered lids. He seemed less distressed than I'd expected.

As usual, Etienne Duvalier looked as scrumptious as his own cooking. We'd come up to Montmartre to shoot one of the travel-oriented segments Roger Elliot wanted. Wardrobe had dressed us both in the French national colors. Etienne wore navy trousers, a crisp white shirt with sleeves rolled up to display his burnished forearms, and—believe it or not—a cherry red beret. On someone else, this crowning touch would have been ridiculous, but the chef wore it with such flair it seemed a part of him. His eyes, reflecting the deep blue of the mid-summer sky, were warmer than usual. A light breeze stirred his russet locks. He sipped his espresso and I glimpsed his pink tongue, which had so recently been rooting in my pussy.

The memory bolstered my courage. I squared my shoulders, flicked a brioche crumb off the front of my crimson blouse, and met his gaze. "Yes—yes, I am. But that has nothing to do with you."

The half-truth made my earlobes burn. Since the scalding scene in my dressing room, Harry had continued to grill me about my interludes with Etienne, and I found myself concocting ever more extreme trials for my eager submissive, in order to amuse my master. Not that Etienne appeared to mind, of course. He'd met every escalation of my demands with an enthusiasm that was almost frightening.

Uncharacteristically pensive, Etienne nibbled his *mille-feuille* for a moment before he continued. "And does Harry—ah—serve you, as I do?"

Searching the tourist-packed square, I located Harry, in a huddle with Marty, and Mack, our head camera man. They'd shot two sequences already, one of Etienne and me wandering past the rows of street artists that lined the cobbled plaza, the other interacting with the *garçon* here at the café. I guessed they were arguing about what to take next. As if he felt my eyes upon him, the producer looked up and flashed me a cocky smile. Even at a distance, that proprietary look could melt me like ice cream atop *crêpes flambées*.

"No, we don't have that kind of relationship," I answered after a moment, with total honesty.

"But he does fuck you, right?" A bolt of heat buzzed through me. I'd never heard Etienne speak so crudely, even during our 'sessions'.

"Ah—um—yes, he certainly does."

"Lucky man," Etienne muttered. He sawed off a huge chunk of pastry and shoveled it into his mouth. Now he wouldn't meet *my* eyes.

I covered his hand with mine. "I'm sorry, Etienne. I don't want to hurt you. But I can't lie to you either. Harry and I are—well, we're very close."

"Since before—before that first time, on the show...? Before me?"

"A bit before, yes." That might have been Etienne, I realized, if Harry hadn't walked into the studio kitchen first. How the gods love to laugh at our expense!

My boss, co-star and slave polished off the final bite of his sweet. "Well, I can hardly blame him, can I? It's not that surprising that we should both find you irresistible." He shrugged and brushed a wayward lock of hair off his forehead. All at once he looked much younger than his forty-odd years.

"I don't know about that..."

"Believe me, there's something about you—I really can't fathom it. I've tried to figure it out, and failed miserably. All I know is that when you're around, all I want is... Well, you know what I want, Ms Wong."

He favored me with a rueful smile then gave my hand a quick squeeze. His manner felt more affectionate than lustful, but I read familiar, naked want in his face.

I could drop my purse under the table. Make him pick it up. And while he was on his knees, he could slip those slender, aristocratic fingers into my pussy...

I was already damp from our unusually frank discussion. The sudden notion of Etienne crouched at my feet only made me wetter.

The man in question watched me with such avid attention that I wondered if he could read my thoughts. I squelched the naughty images, reminding myself of my vow to be discreet and not jeopardize my apparently flourishing career.

My culinary star was rising, as demonstrated by our ratings. Then there was this all-expenses-paid trip to France—quite a perk. All I had to do was control my libido, at least in public. It should have been easy. But the lovely Frenchman sitting across from me, so debonair and so vulnerable, was a terrible temptation.

"I really am sorry." I didn't know what else to say. "I guess you must be jealous."

Why was I apologizing to him? I was supposed to be the one in charge.

"Less than you might think," he answered, with an enigmatic half smile. "Far less than if you'd told me you played the Mistress with him as well."

My cheeks burned. We'd never discussed his passion for surrender before. Outside of one of our scenes, he acted the role of Gallic martinet with the same flair as always.

The change made me very nervous.

"We're fortunate to have hit such perfect weather," I babbled. Indeed, the cloudless blue bowl of the sky and the mild, benevolent sunshine made the iconic scene look like some picture postcard. "Harry told me the cameras aren't really intended for outdoor use..."

"Mei Lee." The severity I heard in his voice contrasted with the yearning I still read in his eyes. "Don't change the subject."

Chastened, I pushed the crumbs around on my plate.

"May I come to your room tonight?"

"Uh—tonight?" I searched frantically for some excuse that would not wound him too deeply. Tonight I was promised to Harry.

With the confusion of our arrival and the hectic preparations for our Paris show the previous day, I'd slept alone for the past two nights. Tomorrow we would move on to Lyon, but not until after lunch—no six a.m. alarm like the past two mornings. My Master had guaranteed we'd have a special evening.

"Or do you have other plans?" Etienne nodded toward Harry's approaching form.

Before I could answer, the producer sank into the third chair at the marble-topped table, wiped his sleeve across his brow then signaled to the waiter.

"Iced tea with lemon, please…"

The clean-shaven young man gave him a look of haughty incomprehension.

I stepped into the breach. *Thé glacée avec citron, s'il vous plaît.*

The *garçon's* eyes widened in surprise at my near-perfect accent. With a curt nod, he disappeared back into the shadowed interior of the café.

Harry chuckled. "Thanks, Emily. I'd be lost here without you." Stretching out his long legs under the table, he tipped his chair back. "You two have it easy. It's hot as hell out there in the middle of the square."

"Well, we *are* the stars," I teased. "But I don't find it too warm."

"Try lugging an ENG camera on your shoulder for half an hour and see how you feel."

"I thought that was Mack's job. Anyway, if you think this is hot, you should try summer in Hong Kong. Thirty plus degrees and ninety-five percent humidity!"

"Hmph!" Etienne pushed his chair away from the table and rose to his feet. "Not my preferred climate at all."

You see, Grandmother? He's not the one I should bring home to meet the family.

"Excuse me for a moment." The chef followed in the waiter's footsteps, presumably seeking the toilets. I found myself straining to catch a glimpse of his crotch. Perhaps he was on his way to relieve himself in a different way than the obvious. However, he turned his back before I could gauge his level of tumescence.

"Ahem!"

I swiveled back to face Harry, feeling guilty as a kid who'd filched a pork bun behind his mother's back.

"What have you been up to, Emily? You're blushing."

For the ten millionth time, I cursed my pale skin. But then Harry could read me even in the dark.

"Nothing. Etienne and I were just...um...just talking."

"About what?"

He didn't touch me, but I felt the force of his implacable will. He crossed his arms over his chest—he was wearing a red polo shirt that was just tight enough to show off his delicious pecs—fixed me those espresso-brown eyes, and waited for me to succumb.

I stared into my empty cup. I really didn't want to share the content of Etienne's and my recent conversation. It seemed too intimate, too personal. On the other hand, I owed Harry at least the same honesty that I'd given to Etienne.

"Ah—well, we were talking about you. About you and me. And about Etienne's...uh...needs."

"Excellent! It sounds as though he's becoming a bit more comfortable with the whole idea."

I nodded. I found discussing the chef's masochistic desires in the broad light of day to be deeply disconcerting, but most likely it *was* a healthy sign.

"And?"

"And he wants to come to my room, to 'serve' me. Tonight."

"Perfect!" Harry rubbed his hands together like some cartoon villain. If he'd had a mustache, he'd have been twirling it. "Tell him he can come. No, *order* him to come."

"But—what about us? You promised you'd come to my room tonight. Every time I look at the brass headboard on my bed, I get excited..."

"I'll be there, love."

I didn't like that evil grin of his at all. Well, I did like it—perhaps too much, because I remembered the other times I'd seen it decorating his kissable mouth—but it definitely had me worried. "Harry? What are you planning? I don't want this to blow up in our faces. We're stuck here with Etienne for the next two-and-a-half weeks."

He swung an arm around my shoulder and pulled me into a smoldering kiss. I forgot my concerns, at least for the duration. "Don't you trust me by now, Emily? Nothing is going to blow up in our faces. We're just going to take the next logical step in our relationship."

Chapter Six

The elegance of my room at the Hotel Fantasie de L'Opera compensated to some extent for its modest size. The green and gold brocade of the bedspread matched the upholstered desk chair and the curtains. Gold-fringed tiebacks held the drapes on either side, revealing lace sheers. Outside the tall windows, a wrought iron balcony protruded over the narrow street. The bed, which occupied most of the room, was barely double width, but piled high with fluffy feather pillows. Art Deco curlicues of gleaming brass twined at the head and foot.

Before I'd met Harry, I would have admired the furnishings for the quality of the materials and the exceptional taste that had influenced their selection. Now all I saw were bondage possibilities—the headboard, the steel rings securing the tiebacks, even the balcony rails. The notion of being secured outdoors, exposed to everyone in the building opposite, as well as any pedestrians who just happened to look up, quickened my pulse and drenched my pussy. Surely Harry wouldn't dare to use me in that way—but deep down I knew that if the idea had crossed my mind, he'd no doubt considered it the moment he'd seen the room through the connecting door that led to his.

I hope he can control himself, I mused, as I dried myself after my shower with a thick, rose-scented towel. *We can't afford to jeopardize the tour.* Compared to Americans, the French were moderately relaxed about sex, but even here public indecency was likely a crime.

If he ordered me out to the balcony, though, even in my current state of complete undress, I knew I'd obey. That knowledge made me wetter still.

After wrapping the towel around my body, I stepped over to the window and loosened the ties. The drapes fell closed, hiding that disturbing and tempting architectural detail. I glanced at the alarm clock by the bed. Nine-fifty. Etienne was scheduled to arrive in a mere ten minutes.

Should I dress? Or receive him in the nude, to make his torture more acute?

I settled on the red silk corset Harry had bought for me—and had insisted I bring on the trip—with its tiny matching thong. I'd let Etienne drool for a while before I allowed him to get a look at my charms. I didn't lace it as tightly as Harry would have, but the way the garment clasped my flesh still made my breath come fast and shallow. My breasts tumbled out from the half cups that embraced them, my nipples plump with anticipatory arousal. Sheer black stockings fastened to the attached garters and my dressy black heels completed the costume. I dusted my eyelids with gold glitter, painted my lips crimson and slicked my hair back from my forehead with a bit of gel.

The woman who stared back at me from the gilt-framed mirror on the bathroom door looked nothing like the fresh-faced, wholesome-looking young chef I was used to seeing. She looked severe—powerful—even a bit frightening. I was a creature from some kinky fantasy. Etienne Duvalier's fantasy, to be exact.

The soft knock came as if in answer to my thoughts. I seated myself on edge of the bed, thighs crossed, dangling one spiky shoe, in what I hoped was an alluring pose.

"Enter."

The door swung open on soundless hinges and the chef stepped inside. He'd removed the suit he'd worn to dinner and was now clad in black sweatpants with a bright blue stripe down each leg, with a matching sweatshirt. I'd never seen him dressed so casually.

It didn't matter what he wore. He always looked good enough to eat.

"Ms Wong."

I caught the glint of lust in his eyes as he took in my costume, an instant before he lowered his eyes in perfect deference. Should I scold him for the minor lapse?

"Good evening, Etienne. Flip the deadbolt. I don't want to be disturbed."

After locking the door, he slipped out of his shoes, as I had taught him, then remained standing near the door, awaiting my next instructions. His arms hung in front of him, one hand grasping the other. His chest rose and fell with his rapid breathing. The loose jersey of his outfit could not hide the substantial bulge at his crotch.

I let the suspense build, giving him plenty of time to wonder what I'd require from him tonight. He shifted his weight from his left foot to his right and back. The fingers of his right hand tightened around his left wrist. His lips pressed together into a thin line, as though he were afraid of what would emerge if he should open them. His nostrils flared as he picked up my scent and a faint flush painted his chiseled features.

I could see his excitement and his fear rising together, one feeding on the other. The subtle physical cues seemed obvious. I suddenly understood why Harry found me so transparent.

The seconds stretched into minutes. I continued to study him, reading the signs of his growing need. My arousal tracked his, eating into my patience. "Strip," I commanded finally, unable to wait any longer.

Without the slightest hesitation, he drew the sweatshirt over his head and revealed the glory of his lightly furred chest. Unsure of what to do with the garment, he looked to me for guidance.

"The floor will do. I have plans for the chair."

He tossed the shirt aside like some rag, then pushed the sweatpants down his corded thighs to his ankles and stepped out of them. His eagerness made me grin.

"No undershorts, Etienne? What a nasty little man you are!" I swung myself off the bed and strode to face him, swaying on my heels.

His cock rose from its nest of auburn curls, hugely swollen, trembling with his every breath. I pinched the taut skin covering the bulb and was rewarded by a gasp. Gathering pre-cum from the tip, I smeared it across his pursed lips. He shuddered with what might have been disgust, but didn't resist.

"Perhaps I need to give you a pair of my panties. Silky, frilly ones, with lots of lace. You'll wear them for our next show. Shall I do that?"

I stalked around him, admiring his bronzed skin and the lean muscle that rippled beneath. I knew Etienne loved to eat almost as much as he loved to cook, but you'd never believe that from his athlete's body, which was firm and sleek, without an ounce of fat. He stood at attention, shoulders squared and back straight. I ran my fingernail down his spine and smiled at his shivering response.

Paler then the rest of him, his magnificent ass swelled from his narrow waist, with matching dimples on either side of the shadowed crease. I wanted to fondle that astounding butt, to mold and massage each perfect orb, to press my lips against the silky skin. To worship it, in short. Instead, I landed a vicious slap on the right globe. My palm stung with the force of it. Undeterred by my own pain, I smacked the opposite cheek. The flesh wobbled slightly with the force of my blow, and pink blotches appeared on the creamy background. I spanked him again, on the same side. He bit back a moan.

"On your hands and knees, slave."

Almost before the words had left my mouth, he assumed the required position.

"Crawl to the chair. Quickly now!"

I gave him a push with my foot, pricking at him with my heel and making him yelp. He really didn't need any encouragement. It took only a few seconds for him to traverse the small room to the desk in the corner. He huddled by the chair, head down and ass up, waiting for my next command.

I could drape him over the chair seat and give him a serious spanking. Last time, though—two days before we'd left for Paris—I'd really walloped him, using the paddle Harry had purchased for me. I knew from personal experience how much that hurt. In fact, I was relieved to see that the marks had faded. Perhaps tonight I should let him off without a beating.

But then, would *he* be satisfied with that? In the twisted logic governing this relationship, compassion might be viewed as cruelty.

I sank into a crouch next to him with my butt resting on my heels. As my thighs parted, I caught a whiff of my pussy scent. I leaned closer, to make sure he could smell me too. Gathering a handful of his hair, I yanked his eyes up to meet mine. The undisguised adoration I saw in their blue-gray depths flooded me with warmth.

"So what should I do with you, Etienne?"

He swallowed hard. "Whatever you want, Mistress. Use me however you wish."

"But what do *you* want? Do you want me to tie you up?" I jerked my hair-filled fist, making him wince. "Or whip you?"

"If that pleases you, Mistress."

"But what about you?" I captured the erection bobbing against his flat belly and squeezed so hard he sucked in his breath. "Shall I bind your cock tight with my stockings, so that you can't come no matter how much you need to? Attach my hair clips to your balls and nipples? Grease up the handle of my hairbrush with soap and force it into your ass? Is that what you want, Etienne?"

His lips parted. His cock swelled and jerked in my hand.

"Don't come. If you come, I'll send you away. Just tell me what you want the most."

His eyes fluttered closed, as though he couldn't bear the challenge in mine.

I tugged at his scalp. "Look at me. I'm ordering you to speak."

"I—ah—yes, Mistress. Yes…"

"Yes what?"

"I—I want you to do that— I want you…"

Moisture dampened my hand, leaking from the head of his cock, which I still held in a near-brutal grip.

"Which? Which one?"

"All of it—all— Oh my God, please…" His entertainer's voice, normally so well-controlled, was choked and ragged.

I knew only too well what he was feeling, that exquisite blend of shame and lust that came from being forced to admit one's unspeakable desires. Harry had wrung similar confessions from me on many occasions.

A hot, sweet wave of triumph washed over me, a heady sense of my own power. I had brought him to this state. He was mine—my prize and my plaything.

The thought was almost enough to make *me* come.

Later, I told myself. *Lots to do first.*

I rotated the chair so that it faced the bed. "Up on the chair, Etienne. I'm going to make your dreams come true."

With gratifying speed, he settled his bare butt on the brocade seat. I worried for a moment about possible damage to the fabric. "If you mess up the upholstery, Etienne, I'll make you lick up every drop, understand?"

He nodded, so eagerly that I wondered if he'd deliberately sully the furniture, just to endure the consequences.

"Reach down to grab the back chair legs. That's right."

I squirmed past him—the room really was tiny—letting my stockings brush his knees. Over at the window, I detached the tiebacks from their hooks. The cords were about half a meter long and a few centimeters thick, braided from some sort of smoothly woven fabric. More than strong enough, I guessed, to restrain a man, especially one who wasn't going to fight too hard.

Back at the chair, I looped one of the cords around his left wrist and forearm and secured him to the left leg of the chair. "Too tight?" I glanced up, into his gleaming eyes.

He shook his head.

"Ankles."

I didn't need to elaborate. He understood my intentions perfectly, bending his knees at an acute angle so that his ankles pressed against the front chair leg. I wound the other end of the first tieback around hot flesh and polished wood, until he was immobilized hand and foot on the left side. The fringe at the end of the tiebacks draped over his instep—a nice artistic touch.

Squeezing past him again, this time with my back to him, so that my bare ass grazed his cock, I bound his right arm and leg in the same manner.

I'd never been particularly good with knots. I'd learned a lot, however, during the past few months with Harry.

After kicking off my shoes, I sat cross-legged on the bed across from the chair, examining its bound occupant. Less than a meter separated us. I could see the sheen of sweat on my captive's forehead, the clear droplets gathering at his slit then dribbling down his shaft. My position exposed the thoroughly soaked crotch of my silk thong. Etienne licked his lips. His cock twitched as though he'd been hit by an electric shock.

"Now that you're tied up nice and tight, I think I'm going to punish you. You deserve it—begging me to invite you to my room then showing up dressed like the slut that you are…"

I crawled up toward the head of the bed, giving him a good view of my bum and opened the drawer of the table next to the bed. I'd been too afraid of customs inspections to bring much in the way of sex toys, but I figured I could improvise.

Pulling out a pair of lacquered wood chopsticks, I held them up for Etienne to see. His perplexed expression made me chuckle.

"Were you hoping for a flogger, maybe? Or some clamps? You'd be surprised how versatile these can be…"

Perched on the edge of the bed once more, I leaned forward and caught one of his pink little nipples between the tips.

"Oh…"

Maintaining an iron grip, I pulled. I've been using *kuàizi* since I was three. I know how to hold on to a grain of rice or a morsel of meat and not let go.

"Ow! Oh, *mon Dieu!*"

"Don't complain now, Etienne, or I'll have to gag you."

I moved to the other nipple, grabbing and twisting. Ever obedient, Etienne swallowed his cry of pain. The first nipple stood up smartly, fatter and redder than before.

"I've read that chopsticks can be used as nipple clamps." I snapped the wood against the nub I'd assaulted first. He flinched, but his cock was harder than ever. "You capture the nipple between the two sticks then loop rubber bands around the two ends to force them together." Actually, Harry had told me this, one night when he had me spread on his kitchen counter with clothespins biting into my labia. The thrill had pretty much neutralized the pain. He hadn't yet tried the chopstick maneuver on me. I suspected he'd get around to that at some point.

"By moving the rubber bands closer to the center of the parallel sticks, you can increase the pressure."

"Ah — ar — ah…"

"But I find chopsticks also work well when you don't happen to have a cane or a crop." Using the two chopsticks like miniature switches, I struck both nipples at once. Then I snapped at his thighs with the sticks, first on one side, then the other, moving closer to his erection with each stroke. "And they're very portable." Red streaks appeared in the wake of my blows, nicely parallel lines decorating his tanned skin.

How could I be doing this? And enjoying it? Because I *was* enjoying myself, I had to admit. I loved marking him, the sense of power and ownership it conveyed. I loved the notion that he'd endure this kind of pain, just to please me. If I were honest with myself, I'd have to admit that I loved seeing the proud and domineering master chef humbled. I recalled those first few days on the set, when he'd dismissed my culinary creations as faddish and unauthentic. Now I had him eating out of my hand, figuratively and literally too, if that was what I wanted.

Etienne was whimpering now, squirming against his bonds each time the lacquered wood made contact with his flesh. I paused, mere centimeters from his cock, and brushed his hair out of his eyes.

"Should I stop? Is it too much?" I knew that if I lashed his swollen penis, the sting would be far more intense than from my blows to his thighs. I peered into his face, reading both terror and desire.

"Uh—it's up to you, Mistress." He wanted to know what it would feel like, I could tell, but he couldn't admit it. This time, I wouldn't force him to confess.

"Hmm. Well—how about one stroke on each side then. You mustn't come, though. If you do, I'll make you very, very sorry. Understand?"

He nodded. I planted a brief kiss on his ripe lips as a reward. He was really so sweet, so vulnerable, so giving. He opened and thrust out his tongue, rude and forward. I just laughed and pulled away.

"You know you'll pay for that, Etienne."

"Yes, Mistress." The sparkle in his eyes belied his deferent tone of voice. Some slave! But how could I complain?

"Are you ready? Take a deep breath…"

I flicked my wrist and snapped the chopstick against his quivering cock. His breath hitched, but his eyes stayed locked to mine.

"Good boy," I murmured. "One more." I was tempted to hold back with this last blow. His expression changed my mind.

"*Sacre bleu…*" he hissed. He jerked in his bonds. His cock surged like a rocket and for a moment, I was certain he'd lose control.

I pictured my lovely red corset, splattered with his cum. The image was so erotic I almost hoped he'd fail. By some miracle of will, though, he managed to hold on.

"Very good. Very good indeed." I wanted to cradle him to my chest, to shower his auburn head with kisses, but I knew I had to stay in character. Being stern was difficult, though. I felt extraordinarily blessed by Etienne's submission. Was this the way Harry felt when he dominated me?

"You've acquitted yourself admirably. As a reward, I'm going to entertain you."

I sank back onto the bed, hiked up my bum and pulled off the thong, exposing my damp pubic curls. Etienne followed every move.

"You want this?" I held up the wet ball of silk.

He gave me a weak grin and a sheepish nod.

"You're such a glutton for pussy. Open wide, then." I stuffed the odiferous wad of cloth into his mouth. It wasn't big enough to seriously gag him, but I knew he'd be drowning in my scent.

Making a pile of the pillows behind me to support my upper body, I settled back onto the bed. I definitely wanted to be able to see his face—and his cock. I spread my thighs, bent my knees and pulled my heels up toward my ass, then reached between my legs to part my lower lips. They were fat, slippery and sensitive. When I drew my thumbs along the inner surface, electric pleasure arced to my core.

"Ah... See how horny I get, ordering you around?" I slid two fingers into my channel, gathering moisture. With the other hand, I teased my suddenly insistent clit, circling the bud and prodding it gently. I didn't succumb to my need for rough friction, not yet. Instead I played with myself and with Etienne, trying to keep my motions languid and graceful—putting on a show that I knew would drive my audience to desperation.

"You'd like to be doing this, wouldn't you?" I lifted one breast out of my corset and swirled my slick finger around the aching nipple. When I brushed my palm over the ruddy nub, my pussy clenched around my other hand. "Ah—oh—!"

"Ahm-mmm," Etienne agreed.

"If you behave very well, I might let you. I might sit on your face and grind my cunt against your mouth until I come all over you. And then I'll make you walk around all day with pussy juice smeared on your cheeks... Oh, yes..."

The images kept rolling in my mind, but I was too far gone to describe them to my audience. As I danced my fingers over my clit and probed my cunt, one lascivious idea after another swam through my consciousness. Etienne suspended from the ceiling, while I striped him with a bullwhip. Etienne bent over a chair so I could work a plug between those luscious cheeks then blister them with a cane. Etienne holding a dildo between his teeth and delving into my pussy, while Harry spanked me with the studded glove he'd described in such loving detail. Harry forcing his cock into my mouth while instructing Etienne to lick my rear hole...

Eyes screwed shut, I'd totally forgotten I was being watched. I was locked in a fugue of fantasy, rocking against my fingers, driving them deep into my channel. I humped my hands and imagined Etienne's tongue, Harry's cock, Harry's fingers, Etienne's cock — everything at once, hard and fast, pain and delight twining together in a whirlwind of sensation.

I swelled, shuddered and burst, overwhelmed by the confluence of physical stimulation and uncensored imagination. Bliss raced from my center in undulating waves. I didn't know who I was, where I was, whether I was still alive or burnt to a crisp by the searing heat of my own desire. I collapsed back into the nest of pillows and drifted away, after-shocks of pleasure still shuddering through me.

"Arhm. Mmph."

Etienne! I had to get up, remove his gag, untie his limbs. I had no idea how long I'd been laid low by my ferocious orgasm. Even as I prodded myself mentally to get up and help him, though, I couldn't quite get my limp body to obey me.

"Rmmph."

Come on, woman! Get your ass out of bed and help the poor man.

"There you go. Better? She really had you trussed up, didn't she?"

What?

"Ah — *mon Dieu*! My fingers were starting to get numb. Thank you, Harry."

"Harry?" My eyes flew open. I jackknifed into a sit. "What are you doing here?"

Etienne perched on the edge of the chair, rubbing his wrists. I noticed he was still hard. He'd maintained control despite my exhibition. Impressive.

Harry stood beside him, idly shifting a scrap of red that I recognized as my thong from one hand to the other. The door connecting my room with his was ajar. I could have sworn it was locked...

He favored me with a grin that held equal parts of affection and mischief.

"Hello, love. I promised you I'd be here tonight. And you know I always keep my promises."

Chapter Seven

"I should probably leave." Etienne rose from his chair, his penis still rampant with unrelieved need. "If you will excuse me..."

He tried to go collect his discarded clothing, but Harry's sturdy form obstructed his path.

"Just a moment, please." Harry turned to me, grinning like the perverted fiend he was. "That's really Emily's decision, isn't it? What do you say, love?"

"Huh?" I swept my hair out of my eyes with sticky fingers and looked from one man to the other in disbelief. This couldn't be happening. It was just too embarrassing.

I hadn't completely recovered from that devastating orgasm. My pussy tingled and my clit felt huge and tender. When I struggled to sit up, I found my rubbery arms would barely support me. "What do you mean?"

"Etienne obviously likes taking orders from you."

The chef blushed a bit, but otherwise maintained his admirable composure.

"I'm sure if you told him you wanted him to remain in the room, he'd gladly obey."

Etienne flashed me one of his brilliant TV star smiles. Did he actually *want* to stay? To watch Harry fuck me? Wouldn't that be torture, to see me taken by someone else?

But Etienne enjoyed being tortured, at least by me...

I searched Harry's face, trying to figure out what *he* had in mind. "I don't know — I mean, tonight — you said you had special plans..."

"Oh, I do, don't worry. For instance I brought these..." Reaching into the pocket of his baggy trousers, he brought out a pair of hand cuffs. He stepped closer to the bed and dangled them in front of me. "Like them?"

I sucked in my breath and my stomach did a back flip. "Harry! How could you? What about Customs inspection?"

"Props. We're in the entertainment business, right?" He tossed the cuffs on the bed. "Though actually, those curtain ties you so cleverly discovered might be even more effective. Lie down again, with your arms above your head, and we'll see."

Desire and habit conspired to make me obey. With astonishing speed and skill, Harry wrapped my wrists in the silky cords and secured them to the headboard. I let him move and position me like some doll. Already I'd started to sink into a trance of submission.

"Ahhem." Etienne cleared his throat. "I'll go then and give you two some privacy."

"Emily?" Harry gave me one of those looks — the ones that turn me into a puddle of lust. "Do you want 'privacy'?" He captured one of my nipples between his thumb and forefinger and gave a sharp twist.

Pain spiked then shifted to a sweet throb that had me hoping he'd do it again. Extracting a spring-loaded clip from those capacious pockets, he surrounded the swollen nub with its jaws. I gasped as the metal bit into my skin. Rivulets of fire raced from my breast to my drenched pussy. My other breast felt naked and needy, craving symmetrical sensations.

"Tell Etienne what you want, woman."

I glanced over at the tall Frenchman, elegant and self-assured despite his rearing cock and the livid marks from my beating that marched in a regular pattern along his thighs. A half-smile hovered on his lips. What was he thinking? Did he understand that I craved Harry's domination the same way Etienne craved mine? Would that undermine the balance of power between us? Would he still do as I asked, now that he'd seen my secret, submissive side?

There was only one way to find out.

"Stay, Etienne." It was difficult to put the necessary authority in my voice, bound to the bed as I was and given the way Harry was abusing my poor breasts. "Sit down and watch. But don't—ow!—touch either me or yourself. Not unless I give you permission."

Harry tugged at the clamp, ramping up the intensity. Meanwhile, he tickled my skin with the other clip, a silent, delicious threat. I focused my will and my gaze on Etienne. *Never mind that I'm Harry's slave. Are you still mine?*

"Yes, Mistress. Whatever you say." He seated himself, placed his palms on his thighs—well away from his cock—and turned his full attention to the scene unfolding on the bed.

Hot satisfaction flooded through me. The bite of the second clamp added a dark current of intoxicating pain. Still clothed, Harry straddled my waist and gazed down at me with obvious delight. The bulk of his erection pressed against my corseted torso. I ached to have that hardness inside me. Liquid trickled from my sex, soaking the lovely brocade of the spread. Would the hotel charge us for damages? Harry flicked the two clips, waking new crises of sensation and erasing the momentary worry. I moaned in anguished need.

"Too much, love?"

I shook my head. If I spoke, Etienne would hear the yearning in my voice.

"What do you want, Emily?"

Oh no. Please don't make me beg.

He bent to kiss me, forcing his tongue into my mouth. When I responded, he bit my lower lip, just enough to sting, then pulled back, sitting on his haunches.

"Oh— Harry…!"

"Shall I beat you? Use my belt on that wet, swollen pussy of yours?"

Oh, by the gods! With Etienne watching?

When he swung himself off the bed, I thought he was about to make good on his threat. Instead he spread my thighs wide and roped my left ankle to the foot board.

"Excuse me—if I could just get by here—"

Harry squeezed past Etienne to the other side of the bed and with a couple of firm tugs secured my other ankle. Now I was completely helpless, bound hand and foot, at the mercy of the most sexually twisted man I'd ever met.

A man who said he loved me and who cared about my pleasure at least as much as his own. I could scarcely complain, could I?

"There. That should hold you nicely, while Etienne and I do our worst..."

Etienne? Did they plan this? Would they dare?

I was suddenly furious. I cared for them both, but I didn't appreciate being the victim of their sexual conspiracies.

"What do you mean? What do you have planned?"

"Does it matter? You'll do whatever I ask, won't you, sweet?"

That shut me up. Because it was true. I didn't know which burned hotter, my lust or my anger. Sometimes I hated myself for being so compliant—even though submitting to Harry turned me on more than anything else I'd experienced.

Over to my right, between the bed and the windows, Harry shucked off his shirt and dropped his pants. Like Etienne, he'd neglected to wear anything underneath. The sight of his solid, muscular body and eager cock dispelled the last of my annoyance.

With a flourish I knew was deliberate, he drew his leather belt from the loops of his trousers and draped it over the headboard.

I shuddered with terror and arousal.

"That's better."

He stroked his erection once or twice, making my mouth water, then smoothed the hair off my forehead and pressed his lips to mine. I opened to him, welcoming a bit of tenderness. Tonight he tasted of the Burgundy we'd shared at dinner. His familiar scent— a mix of natural musk and nautical aftershave— engulfed me. His cock brushed my naked thigh, leaving a wet trail of pre-cum. My pussy ached for want of that hardness.

As we kissed, he wiggled the clamps anchored to my nipples. Even the slightest movement sent bolts of agony sizzling down to my sex, where somehow they morphed into searing pleasure. Bizarre as it might seem, I found myself close to climax.

"I think you've worn these long enough. Take a deep breath, now."

I knew what to expect. He'd clamped my nips before. Still, memory doesn't do justice to the torment when the blood surges back into the formerly compressed flesh.

He loosened the first clamp gradually. Despite his care, I couldn't stop myself from whimpering as the ache built and built, almost unbearable.

"Mistress?"

The raw concern in Etienne's voice muted the pain. I struggled to gain control of my voice.

"Don't worry. I'm fine."

"Good girl," Harry told me. "Now the other."

I braced myself. Pain struck like lightning as he flipped the device off the battered nub. At the same time, he thrust three fingers into my pussy and thumbed my clit. Raw sensation drove me over the edge. A helpless victim of pleasure, I howled and thrashed in my bonds, my pussy convulsing around his hand.

Little by little, the storm abated. I sank back into the pillows, embarrassed, exhausted and grateful.

"Hope we didn't disturb the people in the next room," Harry chuckled. "Probably I should have gagged you."

"*You're* staying in the next room. Anyway, it's too late now."

"Well, I doubt that's the only orgasm you're going to have tonight. Am I right, Etienne?"

"Very likely," the chef observed, with his characteristic dryness.

"But what about you, M Duvalier? I'd guess you'd like some relief yourself."

"That's up to Ms Wong to decide." How could Etienne be so calm, after what he'd just witnessed?

"Emily, don't you think Etienne deserves a reward? He's followed your orders to the letter."

"Well…"

"For instance, I imagine he'd love to come in your mouth. Wouldn't you, Etienne?"

"I—I couldn't—wouldn't presume…"

"Unless she ordered you to do so, of course."

"Yes, yes—of course, if Ms Wong wanted to suck on my cock, I'd be eager to oblige."

"What do you say, Emily?"

I listened to this exchange, amazed by the casual manner in which my two lovers discussed this bizarre situation. Once again I suspected collusion. At this point, however, I didn't care.

Harry knew me well. The first orgasm—all right, the second, counting the one I'd given myself while performing for Etienne—had whetted my appetite for more. My whole body simmered with arousal. I knew it would be easy for Harry to bring me to a fierce boil.

Etienne still sat where I'd placed him, on the chair at the foot of the bed. His smooth, solid shaft, as elegant as the rest of him, arched up toward the ceiling. I'd wanted to taste him many times over the past few weeks, but my dominant role had more or less prevented me from acting on that impulse.

Now Harry had given me the chance.

Shackled to the bed, still tingling and weak from my last climax, I struggled to project the necessary authority. "Get up here, Etienne. On the double. I want you on your hands and knees, facing away from me—that's right, knees on the pillows, on either side of my head. That way I can admire the stripes on your ass while I'm devouring your cock."

I'll admit, it was difficult to muster an appropriate level of authority when I was bound hand and foot, effectively powerless. Etienne didn't seem to mind. He obeyed as rapidly as if I'd been standing over him with a crop in my hand.

His glorious ass hovered above me. I watched the muscles shift under that soft skin as he maneuvered his way into position. In fact all signs from his last beating had faded, but I could imagine the rosy streaks that I'd inflicted, not to mention the stripes I'd leave in the future.

Arousal had tightened his scrotum, drawing his balls up close to the base of his cock. The tender stretch of skin behind them gleamed with moisture. The swell of his rear cheeks mostly hid the dark whorl of his anus. If I'd not been bound, I could have pulled those cheeks apart, to insert a finger, or a tongue...

I dragged my attention back to the present. His cock reared up toward his belly, at an awkward angle. I wasn't going to be able to take the whole thing—the geometry wasn't right—but I could lick and tongue him, and generally drive him crazy.

"Crouch down. Bring that cock of yours closer."

He did what he could. The smooth head brushed my lips, leaving salty traces behind. I stuck out my tongue and lapped at the tip. A shudder trembled through his limbs.

"Don't you dare come! Not until I give you permission. Until I command you."

"Yes, Mistress."

His rigid shaft butted against my nose. I tilted my head, struggling to capture at least the plump cap between my lips. Aware of my difficulties, he lowered his torso and canted his hips back, so that his cock pointed closer to the vertical. Straining up, I managed to engulf the first few centimeters of that delicious column.

His taut skin was as smooth as greased glass. He tasted, bizarrely, of vanilla. The odd angle pressed his cockhead against the back part of my tongue. I curled the tip around to flick the sensitive ridge on the underside and trace the shallow cleft that always made me think of ripe peaches. Closing my mouth around his sweet flesh, I sucked with all the power I could muster.

Etienne's hips jerked involuntarily, driving his cock deeper. I almost gagged as he filled my throat. *We'll have none of that*, I warned him mentally. *I'm in charge here*. I could scarcely give him orders when my mouth was stuffed with his penis, but when I clamped my teeth down on his swollen rod—not too hard, but with enough force to hurt—he got the message and backed off.

I resumed my suction, alternating with tongue-play and occasional nips. He held his body as still as he could, giving me the control I wanted. I felt the tension in his muscles as he worked to maintain his awkward stance. Transferring more weight to his bent forearms, he rested his cheek against my satin-clad abdomen, just below my breasts. His soft chest hair tickled my throbbing nipples.

It wasn't easy or natural. For some reason that made it even more erotic. Despite being tied hand and foot, I felt a delirious sense of power. If Etienne had been facing me, I could have swallowed him to the root, but that would have offered him too much freedom of movement. It would have been far more difficult to control him.

This contorted presentation of his cock to my mouth required more discipline, more finesse. I cast my eyes up at the gorgeous globes of his ass looming above me, the muscles tightening each time I drew him deeper or raked my teeth along his length. His cock twitched and jumped upon my tongue. He must be close — even Etienne's self-control had limits. I sucked harder, determined to make him spill into my mouth and disobey me. I'd get to taste his cum now and to punish him later.

The mattress shifted with Harry's weight as he crawled between my splayed thighs. Focused on the delightful sensations involved in teasing Etienne, I'd temporarily forgotten my diabolical Master. All at once I remembered how vulnerable I was, my pussy gaping and exposed. Did he have his belt with him, as he'd threatened? Fresh moisture trickled from my cleft at the thought, further soaking the poor bedspread. I swallowed hard and Etienne's cock convulsed, on the very verge of exploding. Now, though, my attention was elsewhere.

Stiff leather dragged along the inside of my thigh. I moaned around the flesh plugging my mouth, torn between fear and desire. Now Harry addressed the other thigh, using the scratchy edge of the belt to waken my senses. My clit pulsed, hot and hard. I imagined it glowing, like a live coal in a brazier. One touch and it would burst into flame.

"Ah, love. You're drenched. You must be enjoying your feast of cock. And now you want the belt, too! Don't deny it. You want me to whip your hungry pussy. You're such a glutton!"

The bed shook as he changed position. My view obscured by Etienne's ass and balls, I couldn't see Harry, but my mind painted a vivid picture of his lean, naked body, kneeling all too close to my tender, unprotected flesh, raising the belt above his tousled head.

I held my breath, lips slack around Etienne's shaft, waiting for the first terrible kiss of leather strap — fearing my lover's assault as much as I wanted it.

Catching my tension, Etienne stilled as well. Salty moisture gathered on my tongue.

The moment lengthened. My heart pounded as though I'd run up half a dozen flights of stairs. Dizzy from lack of oxygen, I sucked air into my lungs. At that instant, Harry let loose.

But not with the belt, as I'd expected. Instead he drove his stone-hard cock into my gaping sex. He used all of his considerable strength, but there was no pain. I was wetter than wet. His luscious, familiar bulk stretched me to the limit, filling me to the brim.

Relieved, grateful, overwhelmed by unalloyed pleasure, I overflowed. I tumbled headlong into a cataract of brilliant sensation, shuddering around Harry's magnificent cock. He didn't stop for an instant, didn't hold back. I strained against my bonds, my hips tilting up to meet his ferocious thrusts. He gripped my thighs and pounded into me, pushing me back up the slope to climax and over the precipice yet again.

I screamed as I came, my voice muffled by Etienne's cock Perhaps the vibrations were too much for Etienne to bear. Perhaps the shuddering reality of my climax sparked his. Whatever the reason, he finally let go, flooding my mouth with bitter cum.

I sputtered and coughed, almost drowning in the warm flood of his jism. Quick to note my distress, he pulled out, his last spasms scattering white droplets over my chin and throat. He swung his body off mine just in time for me to see Harry throw back his head and howl.

Deep in my center, I felt Harry swell and loose a flood of cum, bathing me in delicious heat. A final orgasm shimmered through me, rich and sweet as custard. As I closed my eyes against the nearly unbearable pleasure, I caught a glimpse of Harry's smile.

The cat who snuck into the pigeon coop never looked that satisfied.

Chapter Eight

"This bed really isn't big enough for three people."

Trying to avoid tipping someone onto the floor, I worked to extricate my arm from underneath me. I lay on my right side, facing the windows, sandwiched between two wonderfully muscular male bodies. Harry had stretched out facing me, his head pillowed on his right elbow, his arm around my waist. His belly pressed against mine and his half-erect cock nestled between my sticky thighs. Etienne spooned me from behind. He was well on the way back to being hard as well, his pre-cum dampening the crevice between my ass cheeks. He had worked his left arm under mine, so that his hand gently cradled my breast.

I hadn't told him to fondle me that way. I hadn't even given my permission. On the other hand, I hadn't forbidden it, either, and I had to admit his touch felt delicious. After Harry had untied me, the three of us had collapsed together, exhausted by our mutual passion. For a long time, no one had wanted to move. Now however, I was starting to feel restless — and horribly embarrassed.

Harry leaned in to kiss me. "I agree. In Lyon we'll make sure to get a king. Next time I'd like to have a bit more room."

"Next time? Harold Sanborne, what makes you think there's going to be a next time?"

I pretended shocked indignation. I suspect I was not very convincing.

Harry chuckled and rolled over on his back, almost landing on the carpet. He stretched with lazy grace then folded his arms behind his head. His cock pointed at the chandelier, taunting me.

"Come on, Emily! Are you trying to tell me you didn't enjoy yourself?"

I gave his erection an energetic squeeze in lieu of answering.

Etienne nuzzled my neck—blast it all, he'd found that spot, too!—and murmured into my ear, "It might be presumptuous of me to say so, Ms Wong, but you seemed to be experiencing significant pleasure."

My, he was getting cheeky. What had happened to my obedient slave?

When he rolled my nipple between his finger and thumb, I found it difficult to concentrate on that question.

"Of course, we'd never do anything without your consent." Harry's velvet-brown eyes sparked with mischief. "You're the boss."

"Consent? I didn't consent to—this!" My limbs were too entangled with theirs to make the sort of dismissive gesture my protest required.

"You didn't exactly object." Harry captured my other nipple—Etienne was still massaging the first—and delivered a moderately vicious pinch that made me wince, then tingle with renewed need.

"But you two—you conspired against me, didn't you? Etienne, you didn't seem the least bit surprised when Harry showed up!"

"Well, you told me yourself that you and he were lovers." The chef released my breast and feathered his way down my belly in the direction of my rapidly moistening pussy.

I tried to ignore the sparks he kindled when he brushed his fingertips over the damp curls shielding my sex. Gathering every ounce of will I could muster, I tore myself away from his caresses and pulled myself into a sitting position. I glared at the chef lounging beside me, trying to reclaim my authority. "Tell me the truth. Did you and Harry plan this three-way scenario?"

Etienne and Harry exchanged a meaningful look. Their coziness suddenly infuriated me.

"Damn you both! I'm not some piece of meat to be carved up between you!" All at once I wanted to get out of this too crowded bed. I wanted to throw on my clothes and storm out of the room in righteous indignation. To do so, though, I would have to clamber over Etienne's magnificent body. It would be difficult to avoid touching his resurgent erection.

"Calm down, Emily." Harry's hand clamped around my wrist and I knew I wasn't going anywhere. "We did confer about tonight, I admit. We agreed that sharing you was the best approach to a situation that was bound to become awkward very soon."

"Awkward? Things were going very smoothly. You dominated me. I dominated Etienne. Everyone was happy."

"*You* weren't happy, love. Admit it. You felt guilty and confused. When you were with Etienne, you felt as though you were betraying me. Meanwhile

Etienne's devotion had you worried about his reaction when he learned you belonged to me."

He was right, of course. I remembered my *tête à tête* with Etienne at the café that afternoon. I'd been terribly concerned about his reaction to the news about Harry. Meanwhile when Harry had made me recount my exploits with Etienne, I'd always tried to conceal my excitement, to play down the thrill I got acting the role of his Mistress.

"You've got nothing to hide now." With his lanky frame, mussed hair and crooked grin, Harry almost looked like a teenager. A very horny teen, considering the substantial erection bobbing hopefully at his groin. He flipped back onto his side and fixed me with a slightly fuzzy gaze. He was irresistibly cute without his glasses. "Everything's out in the open."

"But it's all so—complicated!" As usual, my objections began to melt in the warmth of his smile.

He danced his fingers up my outstretched thigh and my pussy clenched in anticipation.

"On the contrary, I think this considerably simplifies the situation—Ms Wong." Etienne's voice was deferential, but I read a mirror of Harry's mischief in his expression. "I serve you. You serve Harry. Each of us gets what he or she wants."

"There's no more need for secrets, love. Or for surreptitiously administered enhancements to the libido, either…" Harry slipped a fingertip between my moist lips and grazed a fingernail across my clit.

My annoyance paled next to the flare of pleasure kindled by his touch. Before I could clamp down to hold his hand in my crotch, however, he'd snatched it away.

"Oh no!" I groaned, fighting arousal and disappointment. "You told him…?"

"I had my suspicions in any case. It doesn't matter. Your methods might have been dubious, but I'm grateful for the results." Etienne glanced down at the livid marks from my beating, a set of parallel strips leading up his lean thighs toward his rearing cock. "I might never have had the courage to act on my desires if not for your—um—intervention." His voice held quiet pride.

"You don't have to be ashamed or embarrassed," Harry added. "All we want—both of us—is to satisfy you. To please you and make you happy. Can't you just accept that?"

Harry hooked an arm around my neck and pulled me down into lush kiss. His tongue was assertive as ever, yet I caught a hint of uncertainty in his manner. Under his brashness, he worried that I'd reject the solution he and Etienne had worked out. If I did, would I choose him, or the suave, glamorous chef?

I relaxed and let him plunder my mouth, offering reassurance via my physical surrender. His hands roamed over my body, visiting all the sensitive spots he'd discovered in our months together. There was no pain now, only bliss, pouring from him into me.

Warmth pressed against my back. I smelled vanilla and thyme. Etienne's fingers joined Harry's, tracing along the top of my corset. He stroked the tender flesh under my arm, making me shiver, then let his palm wander down my side to the curve of my hip. His uncharacteristic boldness increased the thrill of his touch. *You'll be sorry,* I thought, giddy with desire, as Harry continued his hungry kisses. *I'll trash your butt until you can't sit down.*

Etienne knew he'd be punished. We both knew that was part of his motivation.

Only part, though. I felt the hair lifted off my neck, the moist, gentle pressure of Etienne's lips between my shoulder blades. The eloquence of that simple gesture almost brought tears to my eyes. I eased my lips away from Harry's, beaming him a look I hoped was full of love. Then I swiveled to offer my mouth to Etienne.

The chef accepted my kiss with the eagerness of a starving man. He opened to the probing of my tongue, letting me drink my fill of him. I tasted the walnut mousse he'd sampled earlier at L'Auberge de Francois-Martine and the Courvoisier he'd used to wash it down. Under it all, I caught a hint of some half-bitter flavor that reminded me of rainy autumn afternoons in Jardin les Tuileries. As I kissed him, I realized I'd been craving this since the first day he'd graced me with that haughty smile.

While his mouth was subservient, his hands became increasingly more brazen, palming my breasts and thumbing my nipples, then sneaking down to tease my lower lips. Meanwhile, Harry was busy unlacing my corset. I hadn't appreciated how much the garment had constrained me until he managed to slip it off, somehow without breaking the lip-to-lip connection between Etienne and me.

I paused to draw in a lungful of the sex-scented air and looked from one man to the other. Had Harry minded my kissing Etienne? Did Etienne think I was rejecting him for Harry?

Both of my lovers wore broad smiles. Relief washed over me. The last vestiges of guilt evaporated. And I was too horny to be embarrassed.

"What...what about male ego?" I gasped, as Etienne's fingers delved into my cleft and found my clit. "I thought—oh, yes!—thought that you all see other guys as threats, challenges to your masculinity..."

Harry urged me onto my hands and knees and buried his face between my thighs. He slithered his tongue into my channel while Etienne continued to stroke tingling nub at my center. A new climax gathered deep in my pelvis—I'd lost count of how many times I'd come, by this point—encouraged by the wet shock of Harry's tongue circling my rear hole.

"Other guys," Harry replied, taking a breather before returning to lick me into a further frenzy.

"Not us," Etienne agreed, diddling my clit with one hand while stroking his gorgeous erection with the other. I imagined that lovely cock pounding into my cunt. I could make those fantasies real. All I had to do was ask.

"We'd rather share you than lose you, love." On his knees behind me, Harry ran his cockhead along my slick crevice, then pushed inside, filling my pussy with delicious, familiar hardness. He waited, letting me adjust to the welcome intrusion. I closed my eyes, focused on the bliss rippling through me.

Satin-soft skin brushed my lips, leaving a residue of moisture. My eyes flew open to find Etienne kneeling before me, presenting his cock for my consumption.

His eyes shone, blue as a summer sky. "If I could be so bold..."

I lunged forward and swallowed the whole sleek length of him. Etienne trembled on my tongue, but didn't move or thrust, awaiting my instructions like the good submissive he was.

I sucked hard, my nose in the musky tangles of his pubic hair. His fists clenched by his sides, he fought his natural inclinations.

Sweet — so very sweet...

Harry drove deep, taking me over. The sensations dragged my attention back to the tantalizing ache building in my core. Yet another climax shimmered in the near distance, with Harry pushing me closer with every thrust.

Lovely, bossy, kinky, sensitive Harry, who claimed me as his slave only to devote himself to my pleasure.

I must have been a saint in a previous life, to deserve such luck in this one.

Chapter Nine

"'Silk worker's brains'? Are you joking, Etienne?"

"Not at all. You've never encountered *cervelle de canut*? A Lyonnais specialty, and quite delicious, I might add."

Morning sunlight poured through tall windows into the demonstration kitchen of the École Supériore de Cuisine Lyonnais, the site for our show that afternoon. Seated side by side at a butcher block table, Etienne and I pored over drafts of menus and recipes. I was trying to ignore the effects his closeness had on the speed of my pulse and the humidity of my pussy.

"Er—do you really think our American audience will be interested in brains?" We Chinese have a reputation for eating almost anything—I have a particular fondness for *zhafeichang*, deep fried pork intestines with sweet bean sauce—but I knew that Westerners tended to be more squeamish.

"No brains are actually involved, Mei Lee. The dish is based on *fromage blanc*, seasoned with fresh herbs, shallots, olive oil and vinegar. Very savory, I assure you, and unique to the Lyon region."

"All right—whatever you recommend."

Etienne shot me a sharp look, as though he found my acquiescence surprising. Today he looked devastating, as usual, in a blindingly white dress shirt tucked into narrow black jeans. He had rolled up his sleeves. The red-gold hair dusting his forearms was very distracting. I knew how soft it was.

"We'll do *quenelles de brochet*, Lyonnais potatoes of course, *salade Lyonnais* with bacon and poached egg, and *marrons glacés* for dessert. Do you think that's enough?"

"For an hour-long show? Plenty. I've never made the *quenelles*, though."

"You'll find them straightforward. Baked fish, bread crumbs, egg yolk, a standard cream sauce—quite simple."

I'd sampled *quenelles* the previous evening, while dining at a classic *bouchon* with Harry and Etienne and thought them a bit bland. To be honest, though, I hadn't really paid much attention to the food for which Lyon was renowned. My senses were too dazzled by the proximity of my two lovers. Although I'd consumed only one glass of the robust Beaujolais presented by the rotund proprietor, I'd felt totally intoxicated, joy bubbling through my veins like champagne.

My mind wandered, reviewing the marvels of the last twenty-four hours.

After the astonishing night with Harry and Etienne in Paris, the routine details of traveling felt completely unreal. Along with the rest of the crew, we'd piled onto the bus for the four hour drive to Lyon. I'd shared my seat with Lisa, not wanting to encourage any gossip. I'm afraid I hadn't been very sociable. I'd been preoccupied with recollections of the night's pleasures. Whenever we'd stopped for a bathroom break, I'd felt the eyes of both men following me. I'd spent the entire trip in a fever of anticipation.

Once we'd arrived and settled into the hotel, they'd whisked me away to the narrow, cobbled lanes of the medieval Old Town. We'd roamed the streets together, poking our heads into cramped souvenir shops, sampling bits of sausage and cheese, pausing in a café facing the majestic Cathédrale St-Jean to admire the sunset behind the hills of Fourvière.

The golden summer dusk had slipped gradually into a violet evening. Every sensory impression had possessed a sort of magical clarity—the lilt of children's voices as they'd kicked a ball around the cathedral square, the twittering of starlings wheeling above the tiled roofs, the saliva-inducing smell of grilling pork emanating from the open doors of traditional bistros, the anise flavor of the Ricard that Etienne had ordered for Harry and me. The warmth of the balmy night and the heat coming from my lover's bodies. *I'll remember this all my life*, I'd thought, gazing at them in the deepening gloom.

They'd kept touching me. A brush of casual fingers against my thigh. An arm encircling my waist. A powerful hand, clasping and squeezing mine. We'd spoken of superficialities, the history of the city, the show the next day, which restaurant we should choose for dinner. The silent messages we'd exchanged had dealt with different topics all together.

We'd walked to the rustic *bouchon* arm in arm in arm. The shopkeepers' smiles as we'd passed had been indulgent. Our outrageous arrangement felt natural, right. And even as the exquisite sights, sounds, scents and tastes of the evening had engraved themselves upon my soul, I had not been able to keep my thoughts from the night to come.

It had been everything I'd imagined, and more. We'd come together after midnight, in Etienne's room, which true to Harry's promise held a bed more than adequate for the three of us. Still, Harry had taken me first in front of the tall window overlooking Place des Terraux, with the curtains open and all the lights turned on. My hands braced against the window frame, I'd arched my back as he'd entered me from behind. The fear of potential exposure had only sharpened my pleasure.

Later, I'd straddled Etienne on the bed and 'forced' him to fuck me, while Harry had watched. I'd half expected Harry to claim my rear hole—to share my body in the most intimate way possible.

"Not yet," he'd told me, guessing my thoughts as he so often did. "No, this time I just want to see your face as you come. I can't think of anything sexier than that."

"In that case, you'd better make me come, and come hard," I told Etienne, twisting his nipple until he groaned.

"Of course, Mistress," he'd replied with a beatific smile, and had proceeded to do exactly what he'd promised.

Etienne's scolding brought me back to the sunny kitchen.

"Mei Lee! Pay attention. I understand that you might be tired." His scowl softened into a conspiratorial half smile. "However, we're on a tight schedule here. We've only got a few hours to pull this meal together."

"Sorry. You're right." I brushed invisible crumbs from my jeans and put my throbbing clit out of my mind. "What were you saying?"

"You'll do the fish and the potatoes. I think that's well within your abilities." He paused. "Do you agree?"

"Ah—yes, yes, of course." A little thrill shimmered up my spine. He was sexy when he was bossy.

Who was I kidding? He was always sexy.

The crew was scheduled to start shooting at two p.m., five a.m. in California. That would give the network plenty of time to edit the video before the Toutes Les Saveurs broadcast at four p.m. Pacific Time. After taping the show, Etienne and I were supposed to head to Croix-Rouge so the team could get some touristy footage of us in the *traboules*, the famous network of passages and stairways created by Lyon's nineteenth century silk industry. The evening we'd have free for—uh—personal time.

Why was it that every avenue of thought led me back to the two men who now shared my bed? I forced myself to concentrate on the ingredients and procedure for the *quenelles*. No sooner had I got my pulse down to normal, though, than my other lover burst into the kitchen.

"Etienne, Emily—I'm afraid there's been a change of plans."

Harry appeared even more disheveled than usual, with his black locks falling into his eyes and his wrinkled sport shirt half in, half out of his chinos.

Etienne looked up from the skillet where he was frying thick slabs of bacon. "Oh? What's going on?"

Harry waved a piece of paper in front of our faces. "Just got a fax from the Cordon Bleu Marseille.

They've rescheduled our four p.m. slot tomorrow to ten a.m."

"Ten in the morning? Are they *folles*? How are we supposed to be ready by then?" Etienne grimaced as though he'd eaten a bad oyster. "Who's responsible for this ridiculous imposition?"

"Chef Marcel Choffard, head of the school. I gather he needs the kitchen for some event later in the day."

"Choffard! Hmph. I'm sure this is deliberate. He has always been envious of my success." Etienne shook his head in disgust then agitated the pan as if he were grilling his rival in the hot oil. "What about the day after tomorrow?"

"Fully booked. Anyway, we've got reservations in Avignon for Thursday. If we stay an extra night in Marseille, we'll mess up the rest of our schedule."

"*Merde.*" The Frenchman turned off the gas then neatly flipped the crispy *lardons* out of the skillet and onto absorbent paper. "We'll have to leave this afternoon, right after the show."

"Tonight," Harry countered. "Elliot really wants those shots from Croix-Rouge..."

My spirits sank as my anticipated night of sensual excess evaporated. Then I realized Etienne was truly upset. I knew him well enough to understand his concerns. He wanted—no, needed—every show to be perfect. And it was going to take a minor miracle to plan a menu, purchase ingredients, and produce the Marseille segment, given our time constraints.

I placed what I hoped was a comforting hand on his shoulder. "Don't worry. You and I can work out the details of what we'll be preparing on the bus tonight. Then Harry can send Roth out, first thing tomorrow, to buy what we need at the fresh market, while you and I get organized in the kitchen."

"You know I prefer to select my own ingredients, Mei Lee."

I almost laughed at his aggrieved tone, until I saw the real distress in his face.

Body heat seeped through the crisp cotton of his shirt. I had a startling, dangerous urge to pinch his nipple. I bet that would distract him from his compulsive preoccupation.

I resisted the temptation. "Don't sulk, Etienne." My voice came out sharper than I'd intended. "As Mr Elliot said before we left, one must be flexible when traveling. Let Roth do the shopping. No one will know."

"*I* will know." Twisting out of my grasp, he grabbed a red capsicum and began carving it into razor thin slices.

I gripped his wrist, halting his movements, and stared into those ocean-blue eyes. "Etienne, let it go."

A little shudder ran through him as he realized what was going on.

"That's an order. Do you understand?"

He lowered his gaze to the juicy pile of sliced peppers. "Yes."

"Yes what?"

My knickers grew damp at my own daring. Harry watched our exchange, an enigmatic smile playing on his lips.

"Yes, I will let it go—Ms Wong."

* * * *

Against all odds, we actually did manage a near-perfect show. Roth must have learned a bit from his mentor, because the fish, clams, mussels and prawns he chose for the bouillabaisse were fresh and succulent enough to satisfy even Etienne's exacting standards. The aioli I whipped up had a lovely tang that just balanced the richness of the olive oil and egg yolk. That creamy golden dip conveyed a certain decadence on the crisp baby carrots and steamed asparagus we served with it. *Ratatouille* seasoned with raw basil and thyme, and chocolate honey mousse completed our Provençal menu, which we and the crew had consumed with gusto after the cameras had stopped rolling.

Etienne had smiled like the Mediterranean sun as he'd led viewers through the steps in creating these delectable dishes. I'd let him take center stage for once, acting the part of his loyal assistant — although I did double the prescribed portion of garlic in the aioli, with excellent results. This was, after all, his home turf. Born in the village of Saint-Rémy-de-Provence, between Avignon and Nîmes, he'd grown up eating these simple, exquisite foods.

Instead of being exhausted after the show, as I should have been given our one a.m. arrival at the hotel, I sizzled with energy. I guess I was running on a hormone high.

The afternoon schedule called for a tourism segment filmed at the Château d'If. The sixteenth century fortress and notorious prison off the coast was now one of Marseille's major attractions. A brisk sea breeze rifled my hair as our boat emerged from the Old Port into open water. Etienne and I stood side by side at the rail, watching the forbidding gray walls of the citadel grow taller as we approached.

He'd donned a tailored spruce green jacket for the trip, which brought out the reddish highlights in his hair. Meanwhile, wardrobe had me wearing a hyper-feminine, floral patterned summer dress that fluttered around my bare thighs. It didn't suit me at all, at least in my opinion. In addition, it protected me from neither the ferocious sun nor the biting wind.

I wanted to cuddle up to the inviting male body next to me, to feel Etienne's warmth and breathe in his citrus cologne. The cameras were trained on us, though, so I didn't dare. I felt Harry watching, too, in the background. *He* wouldn't mind if I gave in to temptation, of course. I wouldn't be surprised if he was picturing Etienne's hand sliding under my ridiculous frilly skirt and cupping my ass cheeks, in full view of the crew.

I tried to banish the provocative image. Instead, my overly active mind continued to embroider upon that initial scenario.

Etienne's fingers steal under the elastic waistband of my knickers and down along my rear cleft, brushing across my rear hole before diving into my rapidly moistening pussy. He steps behind me, shielding me from the eyes of the camera crew. Surely they'll know what is going on, though, as he flips up my skirt and rubs his erect cock over my silk-sheathed buttocks. In the real world, the submissive chef would never be so forward – would he? – but in my fantasy, he peels away my panties, unzips his fly, and slides into me without even asking permission.

And Harry? What does Harry do while Etienne is taking such liberties? Producer becomes director. Harry turns and positions us, so Etienne's back is to the rail, his cock still lodged inside me from behind. When Harry has us where he wants us, he tucks my skirt into my belt, drags my knickers all the way to my knees, and crouches down to lap at my exposed pussy.

Oh, by the gods, I'm really turned on now! Etienne stretches my pussy, while Harry teases my clit. Is Harry's tongue encountering Etienne's cock? The forbidden notion just excites me more. And the crew, staring at this tableau?

They're aroused too. All of them, aside from Lisa, are male. Unable to resist the effects of our raunchy performance, they haul their hard cocks out of their trousers. They jerk themselves off as they watch the stars of Toutes Les Saveurs fulfill hungers of a more carnal sort.

Lisa acts shocked at first, but before long she has one hand thrust into her blouse, massaging her breast, with the other is buried in her panties. Harry brings me to the edge again and again, handling his own hard rod while he tortures me. The slick head grazes my thigh, letting me know that once Etienne has filled me with his cum, it will be Harry's turn...

"You've read Dumas, haven't you?"

Etienne's voice shattered into my daydream, dispelling the lurid images but not my arousal. My thighs were wet as the sea surrounding our craft.

"Ah — what? I'm sorry, what did you say?"

"The Count of Monte Christo? Have you read it?"

"Um, actually, I haven't." Hong Kong's British-influenced educational system did not tend to focus much on French literature. "But I know that the hero was imprisoned in the Château D'If. I did see the movie."

"Read the book. The film — I assume you mean the 2002 version — glosses over too many details." Etienne's smug superiority brought out my inner Domme. I hadn't really punished him in days. Perhaps this evening I'd borrow Harry's belt.

I was about to call him out on his arrogant tone when I noticed his expression. I would not be exaggerating too much if I called it worshipful.

"You're shivering, Mei Lee." His sparkling eyes reflected the deep blue of the waves. "Here, take my jacket."

Before I could protest, he'd removed the garment and settled it around my shoulders. He gave them a quick squeeze that warmed me at least as much as the extra layer.

"It's this silly dress—it's made out of tissue paper." I snuggled into the jacket, which held a trace of his heat and his scent.

"I like the dress." He flashed me a brilliant smile, turning on his celebrated charm. "It's romantic, like something out of a 1940's musical."

My desire to thrash his butt morphed into a need to feel those full lips on my own.

"What's romantic? The dungeons of the Château?" Harry joined us by the railing before I gave in to temptation. As he brushed past to stand on the opposite side from Etienne, he gave my ass a surreptitious pinch through the thin fabric of my costume.

I sucked in my breath at the sudden sting then relaxed as new warmth flooded through me.

"Mei Lee's dress. Don't you think she looks beautiful?"

"She always looks beautiful, whatever she wears. Most especially when she's not wearing anything at all."

"Harry!" I scolded, as a blush climbed into my cheeks. "Someone in the crew might hear you."

"So what? I'm not ashamed of loving you. I'm sure Etienne feels the same way."

"Please! If the network finds out—I don't want to lose this job..."

"You're still more concerned about your career than about me, Emily?"

A quick glance at Harry's face told me he wasn't teasing. "No, of course not..."

"Then why don't you just relax?"

"But the media — Etienne's fans — if the word got out about what we're doing..."

"If word got out, our ratings would likely sky rocket," Etienne commented, arching an eyebrow. "Don't worry, though. Our lips are sealed."

"In all the right places."

"Harry! You're impossible." Despite my embarrassment, though, I couldn't help laughing. How could I be angry when they both so obviously cared about me?

I looked from one of my lovers to the other, shaking my head. "Whatever am I going to do with you two?"

Over my head, their eyes met.

"Oh no you don't!" I tried to forestall more embarrassing conversation. "That was not an invitation for you to share your latest filthy ideas!"

"Filthy?" Etienne's indignation was almost convincing. "What in the world are you talking about, Mei Lee Wong?"

A whistle from the bridge interrupted, signaling our approach to the island. Harry jumped to the dock then extended his hand to help me disembark. Etienne hovered behind me, steadying me on the rickety gang plank. Mack and the rest of the video crew followed, lugging their equipment.

Two squat towers of rough, gray stone confronted us, flanking an arched gateway with an open iron portcullis. "Let's get some pictures of you two by the gate and in the courtyard," Mack suggested. "Then you can climb to the lookout and we'll film you with the old port in the background."

The wind died once we were on land. A cloudless sky the color of Chinese willow porcelain burned overhead. The rugged rock walls, baking under the Mediterranean sun, radiated heat. By the time we finished filming, I was drenched in sweat, despite the lightweight clothing I'd complained of.

The crew took a break, guzzling chilled Cokes in the one shady corner of the courtyard. I wandered off by myself, exploring the dimly lit corridors and peering through windows barred with rusty iron, out to the achingly blue sea.

The fort's cool interior refreshed me physically, but the exchange on the boat still nagged and unsettled me. How did I really feel about Harry? About Etienne? Was there any truth in Harry's accusation about my career? Was I just using them for personal enjoyment? Or to further my ambitions?

Over the past few months I'd let emotion and sensation sweep me away, into a whirlpool of forbidden pleasure. I hadn't really stopped to think at all, not since that fateful day when I'd been inspired to use Gran's aphrodisiac on Etienne in order to win him to my side. It was about time I stopped to consider rationally just what was going on and to decide what I truly wanted.

My orderly mind and my iron will had always been my secret weapons, countering all the stereotypes about soft, compliant Asian women. Business was business. Gran had taught me that lesson, a legacy from my powerful and notorious great-grandfather.

When I'd first gone to Paris and entered the Cordon Bleu, I'd carefully observed the organization and the people around me. I'd noted the particular preferences of each instructor, the type of behavior each one expected, the sort of accomplishments that would win their praise. I'd learned how the system worked, and I made it work for me rather than against me. Not that I hadn't earned my grand diploma. I paid my dues. However, I used my analytical skills and planning ability to maximize my chances of success. Afterward I'd graduated, too, I'd risen quickly in my chosen profession at least partly because I could be dispassionate and logical about my goals and how best to achieve them.

Since I'd arrived in Gold Mountain, though, and met Etienne and Harry, I'd let emotion rule me to what now seemed a shocking extent. *'You are going to* fàguó *with two different men?'* Grandmother's provocative question rang in my mind. If I'd really thought about the trip, analyzed the probabilities and the possible outcomes, I would have found some way to refuse. I remembered my panic when Roger Elliot had unveiled his proposal. *That* had been realistic, not cowardly as I'd labeled it then. But since Etienne and Harry had entered my life, I'd been thinking with my pussy, not my brain.

There was no way this triangle could turn out well. Not in the long term. My carefully constructed career would suffer. Etienne's might, too. And Harry — it was possible that Etienne's attraction to me was mostly sexual, but I knew Harry loved me. The longer I let this go on, the more I'd hurt him. I had to extricate myself from this situation before I did even more damage.

But how could I even think about leaving Harry behind? The notion made me shudder. I'd miss him terribly. Maybe we could both quit Tastes of France, to get away from the temptation of Etienne. Would Harry give up his job for me, though? Was I willing to relinquish my mine? I loved Harry, but wouldn't we start to blame each other for lost opportunities if we sacrificed our careers for the sake of our relationship?

My aimless meandering had brought me to a thick wooden door, hooked open. A sign in French, English,

Japanese and Chinese identified this as the dungeon where Edmond Dantès had been imprisoned. Inside, a single, straight backed chair waited under a vaulted stone ceiling. I sank into the hard seat, worn out by my musings.

How should I play this, now that I'd gotten myself so deeply enmeshed with these two men? I needed to get away from France, and from my two lovers, as quickly as I could, if possible without letting them know that they were the cause. I needed a chance to think, logically and rationally, about the situation, without being distracted by my libido. If I could find an excuse to return to Hong Kong, telling them perhaps a family member was ill...

I shivered a bit at the thought. Do not speak of evil events, lest you create them, Grandmother always told me.

Perhaps Gran would have some ideas. Could I trust her with my lurid secret? She'd never tell my parents, but would she despise me for my slutty behavior? She'd likely be more contemptuous of my impulsiveness and failure to plan.

She loved me, though. She'd forgive me. And quite possibly, with her sharp mind, she might see a solution to my dilemma.

I'd call her tomorrow from Avignon. And for once, I would listen to her advice.

The decision gave me fresh energy. My watch told me it was going on four p.m. We'd probably be leaving soon. The crew, not to mention Harry and Etienne, would be wondering where I was.

"Emily?" Harry's voice boomed through the corridors, as if in answer to my thoughts.

"In here. In Dantès cell."

Harry had to duck to get through the low doorway. "Ah. I should have figured I'd find you in a dungeon." He smelled of sunscreen, sweat and musk. Like Pavlov's dog, I started to get wet in response to the familiar stimulus.

I fought my rising need. "Hi, Harry. I was just about to head back…"

Before I could stop him, he'd clasped me to his chest. "I missed you, love." He buried his nose in my wind-tousled hair, breathing deep then nibbled my ear. "You smell delicious."

I tried to untangle myself from his arms. "I need a shower." My laugh sounded hollow.

"That's why you smell so good. No, actually that's not true. You always smell good. One whiff of your magic scent and I'm hard as a rock."

He wasn't lying. His erection prodded my belly as he ran his hands over my curves and burrowed into the crook of my neck.

"Too bad there aren't any iron rings or bars. You'd look so fetching, shackled to the dungeon wall."

"Harry, come one. Be serious!" Once more I struggled against his embrace, without success. He only held me tighter. He was far stronger than I. My stomach did a dizzy little flip at this realization. "They're probably waiting for us…"

He left off his nuzzling and gazed into my eyes. In the dim cell, his were full of shadows. "Let them wait. And I am serious, Emily. I've never been more serious in my life."

I couldn't avoid the kiss. Honestly, I didn't want to. His mouth sealed itself to mine and his tongue forced my lips apart, claiming me. Lust roared through me, unleashed by the ferocity of his oral conquest. I tasted the sugary residue of his soft drink, the mint of his toothpaste, residual garlic and herbs from the *ratatouille*. His assertive male odor surrounded me, the essence of pure sex. I opened to him and let him take me. I had no choice.

He didn't fondle my breasts or pinch my bottom or insinuate his fingers into my drenched knickers. He did nothing but kiss me, pouring every ounce of feeling into that mouth-to-mouth connection. Without the slightest stimulation, aside from his taste and smell, the firmness of his lips and the probing of his tongue, I found myself trembling on the verge of climax. Irresistible power flowed from him, overwhelming me. Helpless, lost and grateful, I let myself go.

He understood what he was doing to me. He felt my last resistance crumble. My plans, my qualms, my logic all came to nothing when faced with the intensity of his desire. And as I surrendered, the kiss changed.

Now he sipped at my mouth rather than swallowing me whole. His tongue feathered over my lips, coaxing me to let him enter. He breathed into me, warm and sweet, gentle as drifting clouds on a spring day. Holding me close, so close I could feel the heartbeat under his sweat-damp shirt, he bathed me in his devotion.

My sex still tingled and sparked, but now some other sensation swelled in my chest, a rare joy that seemed on the edge of triggering both laughter and tears.

"I love you, Emily." His voice was rough velvet, his lips moist against my cheek. "More than I can ever say. More than I know what to do with."

Tell him, my rational self whimpered, weaker by the instant. *Tell him you're leaving, before it's too late.*

I raised my face to his and offered him my mouth, and the truth.

"I love you, too."

Chapter Ten

"More *merguez*?" Etienne gestured toward a plate still half full of spicy sausage morsels.

"Sorry, but I'm stuffed. Couldn't eat another bite." I leaned back into the nest of cushions and stretched. "I wouldn't mind a bit more *arak*, though, if there's any left."

"Whatever you wish, Ms Wong." Etienne's cheeky grin took a decade off his age.

From one flask, he decanted a few centimeters of clear fluid into my glass then added water from another. The contents turned milky and the odor of anise tickled my nostrils. The sweet burn of alcohol mingled with a childhood memory of licorice as I took a sip.

Harry tore a corner off a circle of pita bread then mopped up the last remnants of the *baba ghanouj*, a savory dip of roasted eggplant and sesame paste. A dozen other dishes, empty to varying degrees, littered the table. "This place is amazing, Etienne. How'd you find it?"

"I used to come here—a long time ago. Aside from the fact that everyone has smart phones now, it's hardly changed since I was nineteen. Still the same hole in the wall, but the food is as wonderful as ever. The true flavors of the Levant."

I'd been a bit surprised that the sophisticated chef would take us to such a frankly scruffy establishment as the Al-Mansour Café. Tucked away in a narrow maze of streets, near the harbor but several kilometers from the tourist district, the café was cramped and dark. There were no chairs. Customers reclined against rather dingy pillows scattered on a threadbare carpet, around low tables of scarred wood. The air was thick with apple-molasses tobacco smoke from the shishas and the aroma of grilled lamb.

The tables surrounded an open area where, according to Etienne, a live band or a belly dancer would sometimes perform. I could hardly believe there'd be room. Tonight recorded music spilled from speakers suspended from the grimy ceiling, full of clipped drum rhythms and wailing clarinets.

"I would have liked to see you at nineteen," I told Etienne. "What were you like?"

"Oh, I was bad news, believe me. Wild. I'd ride my motorcycle to Marseille every weekend and spend two days whoring, drinking and doing drugs. Then I'd drag myself home Monday morning, stinking of whiskey or worse, fall into bed, and sleep for ten hours. My poor mother had no idea what to do with me."

Harry chuckled. "Who would have guessed you'd become a celebrity and a world class chef?"

"Yes, well—let's just say it took me a while to find my true vocation." Etienne's gentle smile brightened the gloom.

"What did you look like back then?" I encouraged him to continue. He rarely talked about his past.

"Scrawny, with bad skin, and hair that stuck up like a broom. I thought I was Jean Paul Belmondo, though."

We all laughed. A customer at the next table, a swarthy young man with a dense beard, shot us a hostile look. I was suddenly very conscious of the fact that I was the only woman in the crowded room.

"Perhaps we should get back to the hotel."

Harry's perfectly innocent statement set my pulse racing.

He squeezed my hand. "It's only ten, but we have another busy day tomorrow."

"And Ms Wong needs her beauty sleep," Etienne teased, running a casual finger along my bare arm and sending tingling ripples down to my sex.

I wondered what the two of them had planned for after our return. Harry had announced at lunch that his room had a big balcony overlooking the port. I didn't want to think about the uses to which he might put that balcony — but of course I couldn't control my imagination.

What are you doing, Mei Lee Wong? my logical side protested. *You're just digging yourself in deeper.*

I closed my inner ears to those protests. Instead, I put my arms around Etienne's neck and pulled him into a passionate kiss. After my encounter with Harry in the old prison, I felt a bit guilty. I didn't love Etienne the way I loved Harry, but I wanted him to understand that I definitely lusted after him.

Etienne submitted almost meekly to my mouth. When I finally released him, he beamed then waved his hand at the mustached proprietor. "Hassan! *L'addition, s'il vous plait.*"

I drained my glass and stood on somewhat wobbly legs. "Ah—I think I need the toilet." I wasn't optimistic about its cleanliness, but I didn't have a choice. I'd drunk rather more *arak* than I'd intended and the taxi ride would be at least twenty minutes.

"We'll wait for you outside." Etienne placed a stack of euro bills on the tray and made a gesture indicating that Hassan should keep the change.

The grateful proprietor was still bowing when I pushed aside the curtains leading to the WC. The dimly lit bathroom was less disgusting than I'd expected. I found toilet paper, albeit coarse enough to scrape me raw, and even a sliver of soap. When I emerged, much relieved, a few minutes later, Etienne and Harry were gone. Ignoring the scowls of some other patrons, I nodded to the proprietor and stepped through another curtained arch into the night.

Buildings of brick, stone and stucco made the street into a shadowy canyon. Overhead there were decorative cornices and wrought iron balconies, remnants of another, more prosperous time, but at the ground level, most had roll down metal shutters, locked tight. Neon-hued graffiti decorated the blank steel panels. Fast food wrappers and crumpled newspaper stirred in the gutters. The temperature had remained balmy but fog had crept in from the harbor, bringing the smell of rotting kelp and giving halos to the scattered street lights.

I didn't see Etienne and Harry at first. I'd expected them to linger just outside the café, but the sidewalk was empty under the weathered, creaking restaurant sign. Alarm spiked in my chest as I searched the deserted street.

Then relief surged through me as I located them, across the street and perhaps a dozen meters away, peering into one of the few shops without a metal grate. I stepped into the road, about to call out to them.

A vehicle—some sort of hulking SUV, black or maybe dark blue—raced past me, going far too fast for the narrow road. I stumbled back onto the footpath, barely avoiding being hit. The car screeched to a halt just beyond Harry and Etienne. The two men turned, clearly startled, as four figures emerged from the vehicle's four doors.

Two of them grabbed Etienne's arms. The others went for Harry.

"Hey! Let me go!" Harry struggled and knowing his strength, I thought for a moment he'd break free.

"*Ta gueule!*" growled one of the thugs, his accent rough and strange. Before I could make a move, he brought the butt end of a gun down on Harry's skull. He slumped in the guy's arms. His assailant tossed his body into the back of the SUV like a sack of dirty laundry.

"*Lâche-moi! Fils de salope! Au secours! Au secours!*" Etienne yelled, squirmed and wiggled like a fish on a line, until he saw Harry knocked unconscious. Then the fight went out of him. The goons dragged Etienne's hands behind his back and bound them in some way, then hustled him into the car on the other side.

"Get your asses into the car," ordered another of the hoodlums—in perfect Cantonese.

Astonishment crowded out my terror. He jumped into the front seat on the passenger side. The other ruffians piled into the back, slamming the doors behind them. The engine roared and the car sped away, rounding a corner and disappearing.

The whole attack took no more than thirty seconds.

I stood there, dazed, for at least another half a minute. I couldn't believe what I'd seen, horrifying and yet all too familiar from the tales of my childhood.

It was real, though. Trash rustled along the sidewalk of the deserted street. The creeping fog stank of death. Harry and Etienne were gone.

Finally, I started to scream.

Chapter Eleven

"They were Chinese," I insisted for the twentieth time. "Not Arabs." I shook my head in disgust at the intransigence of the policeman interviewing me, an action I immediately regretted. Someone had initiated a construction project inside my skull, complete with jackhammers and blasting. I clutched my Styrofoam coffee cup and gritted my teeth until the pounding pain subsided a bit.

"You were in the Arab quarter, Mademoiselle Wong. And we've had a rash of kidnappings by Al-Qaeda-linked groups in the past year." Inspector Rousseau's slow articulation and excessive courtesy showed all too clearly his opinion of the female sex. Fragile. Dependent. Sloppy thinkers. Over-emotional to the point of hysteria. "You must have been mistaken."

"Cantonese is my native tongue, Inspector. I'm one hundred percent certain the men who abducted M Duvalier and M Sanborne were Chinese. Most likely from Hong Kong or Guangzhou."

"You only heard a single sentence, am I correct?"

I sighed. My throat was sore from yelling. My eyes burned from crying and lack of sleep. Worst of all, though, was the tight ache in my chest, like someone was squeezing my heart in his fist. I almost wished Harry and Etienne had been taken by terrorists as the police so stubbornly believed. At least we'd have some notion of what to expect.

"Correct, as I've already told you. The rest of the time they spoke French."

"And by your own admission, you were somewhat intoxicated, were you not?"

"Not nearly drunk enough to confuse Chinese and Arabic, Inspector."

"And of course, you didn't record the license of the vehicle? Or the make and model?"

"The street was dark, they were twenty meters away, and the whole thing was over in an instant. Plus I was in shock." Why hadn't I been more observant? All I could recall was the general shape of the SUV and the chilling voice of the man who'd hit Harry.

"Of course, of course. I understand."

I hated his patronizing tone. But the angrier I got, the more my head hurt.

The dark-haired policeman pulled on his dapper little mustache, scribbled a few more notes then closed the file folder. "Well, I think that will do for now, Mademoiselle. We'll contact you if we have any further information. I assume you'll remain in Marseille for the next few days, *n'est-ce pas?*"

"That's it? That's all you're going to do?"

Rousseau released a weary sigh. "We've faxed the victims' photos to every *gendarmerie* in the country. I've sent a forensic team to rue Longue des Capucins, though given your description of the incident, I don't expect they will find much that is useful. We're tracking the victims' mobile phones, just in case the kidnappers are stupid enough to leave them on. We'll be interrogating the owner of Al-Mansour later today, to see if he noticed anything unusual. In these cases, though, we normally can do little but wait."

"Wait for what?" I had to ask, though I was terrified of his reply.

"Their release, if we're lucky. A ransom request, most likely." He met my eyes and for the first time I saw a hint of sympathy mingled with his scorn. "Possibly the discovery of their bodies."

"Oh, no…! Please…" Someone had kicked me in the solar plexus. I buried my face in my hands, struggling to catch my breath.

"Mademoiselle, I don't want to lie to you. This is the most dangerous city in France. Half the criminal gangs in Europe operate here, not to mention the anarchists, the terrorists and the ordinary petty scum." He sat back in his chair and brushed an invisible speck of lint off his perfectly pressed uniform. "Usually, though, when *les bougnouls*—the Arabs—nick a foreigner, they're looking for some quick cash."

I didn't bother to object. I knew it wouldn't do any good.

"Well, thank you for your, um…help, Inspector." I pushed back my chair, which seemed to weigh a ton. My body felt as though I were the one who'd been beaten on the street. "I hope I'll hear from you soon."

"As soon as we get any news, Mademoiselle. Perhaps you should go back to your hotel and get some sleep."

"Perhaps."

"You'll find a taxi stand just outside the station."

"*Merci.*" My voice was barely audible. I trudged down the hall to the ladies' room, well aware that the inspector was relieved to see me go.

I splashed some water on my face then rinsed out my mouth, trying to wash away the acrid taste of the execrable police coffee. Catching a glimpse of myself in the mirror, I began to understand the inspector's attitude. My skin looked like uncooked bread dough. My hair was in knots and my rumpled clothing smelled of tobacco and stale grease. Strawberry red rimmed my eyes, with green-gray circles from exhaustion underneath. In those eyes burned a desperate fever, a sort of madness. These were not the eyes of a rational person.

No wonder they wanted to get rid of me. I looked a fright.

'*She always looks beautiful.*' Harry's playful compliment rang in my mind. The recollection opened the wounds of terror and loss. Against closed eyelids I tried to picture my rumpled, virile lover. Instead the image of him knocked unconscious and shoved into the kidnapper's truck played, again and again.

Was he badly hurt? Was he still alive? I slumped to the floor, great sobs tearing my chest. How could I go on without him? And what about Etienne? Guilt tarnished my sorrow as I remembered my other lover, in equal danger.

"Hey, can I help?" A female voice, deep alto, full of confidence and concern. "Don't cry. Here, sweetie. Wipe away those tears. They won't do anything to save your man."

She thrust a crumbled tissue into my hand. Obediently, I used it to blot my eyes and blow my nose.

"That's good. Now, let's get you on your feet. You've got to be strong, girl. You can't let them get the better of you."

The woman more or less dragged me to a standing position. I probably couldn't have risen on my own. Blinking away the moisture fogging my vision, I tried to focus on this Samaritan.

She towered over me — she must have been nearly as tall as Harry — and fixed me with startling jade-green eyes. In those eyes I read sympathy and shrewd intelligence. She had a broad mouth, currently stretched in a warm smile, under a straight nose just a bit too long to be perfect. Her short honey blonde hair, clipped to below her earlobes, gave her a no-nonsense look. Her well-tailored uniform hinted at a powerful body with generous curves.

If I were a crook, I definitely wouldn't want to mess with *her*.

"Sor — hic — sorry." I tossed the used Kleenex in a bin next to the sink and stood a bit straighter. I didn't want this Amazon to think I was some sniveling wimp, the way the inspector obviously did. "Guess I do need some rest. I'm not usually like this…"

The policewoman shrugged. "Don't let Rousseau get to you. He's something of a chauvinistic prick — never really listens to a woman. Plus he's obsessed with Islamic terrorists, ever since 9/11."

I tried without much success to smooth the wrinkles from my dress, the same one I'd been wearing at the fort. It looked much the worse for the night's events. "I noticed both of those characteristics. You were listening in?"

"I passed his door on the way to get coffee and happened to catch a bit of your conversation, yes. You looked so beaten down and lost, I couldn't resist stopping. I gather someone was kidnapped? When? What happened?"

"Last night, maybe ten or ten thirty. Both of my — um — colleagues were assaulted and forced into a black SUV."

"Any idea why? Who were the victims?"

"The star of a cooking show from the US and his producer. And honestly, I can't come up with any motive. Etienne's a bit of a celebrity, especially in America, but he's no millionaire. And Harry — well, he's just an ordinary guy. *With a massive cock and a kinky streak a mile wide, but this lady doesn't need to know that.*

I sniffed and swallowed a lump of phlegm. She gave me an encouraging nod. I was starting to feel a bit better. Being taken seriously made a huge difference.

"I wonder whether the kidnappers confused him with someone else," I continued. "They seemed very organized. I don't think it was a random crime."

"Hmm — that's possible. Let's go to my office where we can be more comfortable and talk some more. You done in here?"

I combed my fingers through the disaster of my hair, without much effect, and grimaced. "I don't think there's much more I can do. Let's go."

She flashed me a grin. "I'm Detective Leblanc, by the way. Antoinette Leblanc. My friends call me Toni."

"Mei Lee Wong — or Emily, if you'd rather."

"You'll find I'm not a big fan of formality. Or bureaucratic rules either."

I was glad to discover we didn't need to pass Rousseau's office to reach hers.

"Have a seat, Emily. Want some coffee?"

"Ah — sure. Thanks."

She chuckled, apparently noticing my lack of enthusiasm. "How about a Coke, then? Roughly twice the caffeine of coffee, which you look like you could use. Be back in a sec."

Inspector Rousseau's desk had been piled with paper. Detective Leblanc's was bare, aside from a keyboard and a huge LCD monitor.

I glanced out of the window, which overlooked a busy commercial thoroughfare. Pedestrians hurried by on their way to work. In the café across the street, businessmen breakfasted behind their newspapers. The institutional wall clock told me it was nine fifteen.

Less than twelve hours since Etienne and Harry had disappeared.

My panic started to rise again. I forced it down, taking slow, deep breaths, willing the fear away. I needed to stay calm and focused. If I set my emotions free, I was lost.

"Here you go." The detective handed me a chilled can and a straw.

I took a big swallow. The sugar buzzed through me like some kind of drug. Immediately I felt more alert.

Toni sipped at her own can. "Breakfast of champions," she quipped. "Anyway, where were we? You were saying you thought the attack was planned?"

"I'm sure of it. They came speeding down the street, right to where Harry and Etienne were standing, and simply grabbed them. They had guns all ready—at least, I saw one gun—and some sort of restraining devices as well."

"Plastic handcuffs?"

"Maybe. I couldn't really see. I was across the road, maybe half a block away."

"Get a look at any of their faces?" She leaned forward, elbows on the desk.

I shook my head, my spirits plummeting again. "Not really. It was pretty dark, and mostly they were facing away from me. They all wore dark clothing, business suits I think." Why hadn't I paid more attention? I'd been too shocked to exercise my usual powers of observation.

"But you told Rousseau the attackers were Chinese."

"I'm sure of it. One of them gave an order in Cantonese. The others obeyed right away."

"Hmm." The policewomen sat back in her chair for a moment, then typed a few lines on her keyboard. "Maybe this is Triad business."

Just the mention of the dreaded Chinese gangs sent a chill down my spine. "Triads? Here in Europe?"

"Honey, crime has gone global. The Russians, the Chinese, the North Koreans, the Mafia, the Yakuza— these days everyone wants a piece of the pie." Key clicks filled the pause in her speech. "Here's an informer's report, dating from two months ago, about the Iron Hammer Triad and some major drug shipment, in transit from the Golden Triangle to the States." She typed some more. "Just that isolated item, though. Seems that the informer has disappeared…"

The Iron Hammer! Hong Kong parents used tales of their cold-blooded ferocity to scare kids into behaving. Especially in my family. "If you're not good, the Iron Hammer will get you." If Harry and Etienne had fallen into their hands… I didn't want to follow that thought to its logical conclusion.

"But why would a Chinese gang be interested in a French chef?" I wondered aloud.

"Maybe they thought he was someone else, like you said in the bathroom. Got any photos of the victims?"

I pulled my phone out of my purse and navigated to a shot of Etienne I'd snapped just before yesterday's show. "This is the chef. Etienne Duvalier."

"Oh—he's quite a hunk, isn't he?"

I couldn't help but smile. "His fans think so."

"He looks really familiar."

"He's quite well known in the US. Do you get Tastes of France network here?"

Toni's eyebrows arched. "You think the French public is going to watch an American cooking show? But I could swear I've seen him before…"

"Maybe on YouTube?"

"No, no—just a second. Let me download this to my hard drive…and then let's try my new face matching program…" Her fingers flew over the keys. "Takes a bit of time—there's some serious computation going on here…"

My eyes drifted closed. My head pounded. I didn't care who had taken Harry or why. I just wanted him back.

"Ah! Of course! Le Requin!"

Her exclamation dragged me out of my exhausted funk. "What?"

"You're not going to believe this. Come take a look."

I circled the desk to stand beside her and glanced at a row of photos on the screen, photos of an all-too-familiar, though younger, face. The Gallic nose, the auburn curls, the cocky grin—it had to be the handsome, stylish TV star I knew so well. In one picture, though, he wore a baggy, striped shirt that looked like a prison uniform. And another, despite his flirty half-grin, was unquestionably a mug shot.

"Etienne has a criminal record?" He'd told us he was wild, but I hadn't expected this.

"These aren't photos of Etienne Duvalier, Emily. This is Jean Le Requin—Jean the Shark—one of the most notorious gangsters in modern France."

"You're kidding!"

Toni shook her head. "It's Requin all right. No wonder I thought I recognized your chef. I've never met Requin in person, but he's been on our most wanted list ever since I joined the force six years ago."

Suddenly it all made sense. "So the Triad guys thought Etienne was this Le Requin and grabbed him."

"*Peut être*. Why, though? The different gangs usually stay out of each other's way. Each one's got its own territory, its own rackets. Like I said, they all want a piece of the pie, but they tend to explicitly divide it up. Less messy that way."

I stared at the image of Jean Le Requin, seeking answers. The resemblance was astonishing, but when I looked more closely, I noticed small differences between his face and Etienne's. The gangster's features were more aquiline, with more prominent cheek bones. His eyebrows were bushier and not quite so arched. He had a mole near his left temple and a small scar on his chin. His eyes showed the biggest contrast, though. His lips curved into a seductive smile, with just a hint of mockery—the exact smile I'd seen on Etienne's face when he was lecturing me about some culinary detail. But the laughter didn't reach Le Requin's eyes. Those eyes were empty of any warmth, any empathy or joy. They were the eyes of a ruthless, desperate, possibly violent man—a man without scruples. Etienne's eyes had never been so cold.

"I'll bet the Shark got greedy and stole something that belonged to the Hammer. Or maybe he did it just for spite." I could easily believe the man in those photos would take risks just to amuse himself and piss off the competition. "I wouldn't be surprised if he hates the Chinese, too. He probably sees them as muscling in on his territory. I'll bet he wanted to teach them a lesson. And now the Triad people want revenge."

"That's a lot of speculation, Emily, based on nothing but the guy's photos."

I shrugged. For some reason I was sure I was right. For better or worse, I knew something about how the Iron Hammer operatives might think. But of course I couldn't tell Toni about that.

"I'm good at reading people." I sank back into my chair, trying to connect the ideas floating in my weary brain. "Anyway, by now the Triad certainly will have figured out their mistake—that the man they snatched is not, in fact, their target. What do you think they'll do to Etienne and Harry?"

"Maybe the Chinese will release them." The detective's face grew somber. "Or maybe they'll kill them."

Kill them! Though I'd expected this answer, I couldn't handle hearing it spoken out loud. Yesterday I'd been wasting mental energy on sexual fantasies. Now my lovers might lose their lives! The room whirled around me. My stomach churned. Sudden blackness descended.

"Put your head between your legs, Em. That's right. Breathe. You've got to breathe. In. Out. In. Out. Good. That's a good girl…"

Toni's strong hand gripped my shoulder, keeping me from toppling off my chair. Gradually the horrid vertigo subsided. I blinked hard, trying to focus.

"What—what happened?"

"You nearly fainted."

"What? I've never fainted in my life." Shame washed over me. How could I be so weak?

"It's not surprising, hon. You're very upset. You might even be in shock. I can tell you really care about this Etienne." She held my gaze for a moment, curiosity sparkling in her green eyes. "And this Harry guy, too."

"Yeah," I murmured. "I do."

"Go home, rest, get some sleep. Meanwhile I'll dig into your case, see if I can find anything more recent about Iron Hammer — or about Le Requin."

"Thanks, but don't you have other work to do? Other cases to attend to? Inspector Rousseau made it clear that this was his jurisdiction…"

"Inspector Rousseau is an Islam-obsessed fool. And I do what I want. I told you, I'm not big on protocol. You need my help. Give me your mobile number."

Mute and helpless, I obeyed. I was horribly weary, but I knew that every minute increased the danger for the two captives. Toni helped me to my feet and handed me my bag. "I'll call you this afternoon." With a firm hand on my back, she guided me to the door.

I glanced out of the window again, at the normal world. It seemed another planet, one from which I'd been banished forever. The women leading their children along the sidewalk, the men with their noses in the business pages — they were totally alien to me.

Inspiration struck like the proverbial lightning. I sucked in my breath.

The detective noticed. "What is it? Feeling faint again?"

"No, no, nothing like that. I had an idea." I pushed past her, back into the office, and gestured at the computer. "Does Marseille have a Chinese language newspaper?"

"I don't know. Probably. Let me check." She sat down behind the desk once more, her fingers whizzing over the keys. "Yeah. Two in fact. They've even got websites. But I can't understand a word."

"I can." Standing beside her desk, I scanned the home page for the *Shi Yuan Times*. They published daily, and sure enough, they had a classified advertising section. They even had a form for online orders, but unsurprisingly, Toni's computer couldn't enter Chinese characters. I grabbed my purse and extricated my phone.

Toni looked puzzled but intrigued as I spoke in Mandarin.

"*Huay.* Shi Yuan Times? I want to place an advertisement. Yes, in Chinese. 'You have our men. We want them back. What do you want? Call 067-743-2109 and let us know.' Exactly. Thank you. I want to run this for the next three days. Please charge my credit card."

I gave the operator my card number and hung up, smiling for the first time in hours.

"What are you doing, Emily?"

"Teasing the tiger."

Chapter Twelve

Toni walked me down to the curb and put me into a taxi. Despite the caffeine and the sugar I'd recently consumed, my eyelids felt weighted with lead. I sank into a half doze, only to be roused by the cheery chirp of my mobile.

That was quick. Frantic, fighting my drowsiness, I rummaged in my bag. Of course the phone had sunk to the very bottom. *Please, please, don't hang up!*

I didn't recognize the caller's number. As I stabbed at the screen to pick up the call, though, I realized it couldn't be the kidnappers. The evening edition of the *Shi Yuan Times* didn't hit the newsstands until five p.m., though the operator had told me the website would be updated by three.

"Emily? We've been frantic! Where are you?" Lisa's voice held a touching level of concern.

"In a cab, headed back to the hotel."

"Ah. You must have had quite a night!" Amusement replaced the worry in her tone. "Well, the bus to Avignon leaves at eleven, so I hope you and Harry don't need much time to pack." She paused. "Um—is

Etienne with you, too? We haven't been able to contact him either."

I swallowed the bile that rose into my mouth. The show, the crew — I'd completely forgotten about them. "Er — ah — no. Something's happened…"

"Something? What? Are you okay?"

"They've been kidnapped. Etienne and Harry."

Lisa sucked in her breath. "Kidnapped? That's like — oh God! Who? When? Are you all right?"

"More or less." My trembling voice belied that statement. I paused for a moment to collect myself. "Four thugs in an SUV grabbed them last night, as we were leaving a restaurant." I forced down my panic as I remembered the awful sight of Harry being knocked out. "I've been talking to the police since then, first at the scene, then at the station."

"But why? What did the cops say?"

"The inspector in charge wants us to wait until the kidnappers get in touch."

"How long?"

"He didn't know. Anyway, I don't agree." *The longer we wait, the higher the probability that they'll be hurt.* I kept the thought to myself. I didn't want to alarm poor Lisa more than necessary.

"What are you going to do, Emily?"

"Take a shower, first. Get a bit of sleep. I really can't think in my present state."

"But — what about the show? About Avignon?"

I shook my head, trying to banish my weariness. With Harry and Etienne both out of the picture for the moment, it appeared that I was now in charge of the Tastes of France team.

"Uh — can you please contact the Académie Culinaire and explain the situation? Tell them we need to cancel — no, reschedule — our spot. Say we'll call them again tomorrow. Roth should have the phone number."

"Sure, no problem." There was an expectant silence on the other end of the line.

"I'll phone Mr Elliot when I get back to the hotel. We'll see what he has to say. See you soon."

"Okay. I'll wait for you in the lobby."

"Fine. See you shortly."

I peered out of the taxi window. I didn't know Marseille well enough to estimate how far I was from the Old Port where we were staying.

The driver had mahogany skin, a hooked nose, black hair and a full beard. I caught what looked like suspicion in his eyes as he watched me via the rear-view mirror. Did he understand English? Was he really taking me to the hotel? Was it possible he was connected to the gang who'd abducted Etienne and Harry?

This was the most dangerous city in France, according to Rousseau. I needed to stay on my guard, to pay attention to every detail around me.

Surreptitiously, I scoured the back seat area until I located the taxi registration number and texted the information to Lisa's phone. Just in case.

However, just as I pressed 'send', the cab rounded a corner and the bristling masts of *le Vieux Port* came into view. The driver pulled up before the balconied façade of the Hotel Neptune.

"Fourteen euros," he announced in gruff, strongly accented French. He didn't smile, but I was so happy to have arrived safely that I handed him a twenty and waved for him to keep the change.

As promised, Lisa awaited me, along with Marty, Mack, Roth and the rest of the crew — nearly a dozen people in all. I had barely trudged through the leaded glass door when they all crowded around me.

"Emily! Are you hurt?"

"What happened?"

"Bastards!"

"Want some coffee?"

"What are we going to do?"

"Here — sit down, sit down…"

"What did the police say?"

I sank onto a velvet upholstered sofa and raised my palm for silence. "Thanks for your concern. I'm not hurt, just very, very tired. The police are investigating. The inspector told me we'd probably receive a ransom demand soon."

"Ransom! Mr Elliot's not going to like that."

"He's not going to like any of this, Marty." *Especially the likelihood that his star is in danger.* "I'll call him as soon as I've showered. I need to clear my head. I don't think I could be really coherent right now."

"Want me to send up room service?"

I hadn't even thought about breakfast, but now I realized that I was starving. "Oh, Lisa — that would be fantastic."

"Eggs? Croissants?"

"Whatever. Just be sure to include a pot of strong coffee."

* * * *

Clean, full of *omelette aux fine herbes* and almond brioche washed down with two double espressos, I felt slightly more human. The soft bed heaped with feather pillows called to me, but I knew I had to contact Roger Elliot before it got too late. Ten-thirty a.m. in Marseille meant it was one thirty in the morning in San Francisco. My boss might still be awake.

I got through to Roger on the first try. Somehow I managed to explain the situation without breaking down. Every time I remembered that gun slamming down on Harry's skull, I felt like bursting into tears, but I didn't want to get a reputation as a cry baby.

"It sounds as though you're on top of things, Emily. At least as much as can be expected."

"I don't know. I should have been paying closer attention..."

"Don't beat yourself up. Save your energy for whatever comes next."

I shuddered, only too aware of his meaning. I guessed he was as concerned as I was about Etienne's and Harry's well-being, though perhaps for different reasons.

"What about the show? The tour?"

"We'll do reruns for the next few days, until the situation becomes clearer. You say the police expect a ransom demand?"

"Yes—but they think the kidnappers are Arabs, maybe terrorists. I'm certain that's not true." I'd told Roger about the Cantonese-speaking leader of the gang, but not about my classified ad. Only Toni knew about that. Instinct and experience both told me to reveal my plans to as few people as possible.

"Well, we'll see. The network will pay whatever they ask, by the way. We've got insurance to cover this sort of eventuality."

"You have kidnapping insurance?"

"Well, we have an extremely broad policy that covers Etienne's health and safety. After all, where would we be without him?"

Where indeed? "Well, that's one thing we don't have to worry about."

"Right. Look, get some sleep—I can tell you're exhausted. Not that I'm surprised. Call me tomorrow, or sooner if you have any news, all right?"

"Right." I stifled a yawn. "Thanks, Roger."

"Thank *you*, Emily. I'm so glad we've got someone as responsible and intelligent as you out there to handle this. Someone with a level head."

A level head? I grimaced at the unintentional irony. If I'd truly been the rational, dependable woman Roger imagined, I wouldn't have come to France in the first place. Etienne and Harry would be safe and sound in San Francisco. And I'd probably be back in Hong Kong, working to forget them.

"Good night. Talk to you soon."

"Night."

At last I could succumb to the lure of the bed. I tumbled onto the mattress without removing my robe or drawing the curtains against the midday brightness. The coffee I'd drunk didn't stand a chance of keeping me awake. Even my fears, the images of my lovers, beaten and bloody, were not enough to counter my bone-deep weariness. I was asleep more or less the instant my head hit the pillow.

Chapter Thirteen

I woke abruptly from a nightmare full of lust and terror. My heart slammed against my ribs. Dried tears crusted my eyes, making them hard to open. At the same time, tell-tale stickiness coated my inner thighs. The details of the dream had fled, leaving nothing more than a vague recollection of arousal and a sense of dread.

I was grateful not to remember more. Some superstitious Chinese believe that dreams foretell the future.

Gran always dismissed that notion. "Dreams are windows into the rooms you keep locked," she'd say. "They're messages from your secret self, not from the gods."

I didn't want to peer too closely into that shuttered room.

I stumbled into the bathroom—after all that coffee and Coke I had a rather urgent need—then stepped back into the shower, turning the tap to cold. The chill water did the trick, bringing me to sputtering wakefulness and dispelling the dark atmosphere of my slumbers.

Toweling my hair, I padded back out into my room, just in time to hear my phone.

After talking to Roger, I'd left it on my bed table. I took the call on the third ring.

"Hello?"

"*Huay.* Did you place a notice in the Shin Yu Times?" The man on the other end of the line spoke educated Mandarin, but with a southern accent.

My pulse was loud in my ears. When I switched the handset to my left ear so I could grab a pencil, I noticed my hand shaking. Still, I managed to keep the fear out of my voice as I replied in the same language. I didn't want him to know I was fluent in Cantonese.

"Yes, I am responsible for the advertisement. It seems as though you've made an unfortunate error, esteemed uncle. We would like to assist in remedying this awkward situation."

"In what way can you assist us?"

"We can take charge of your unwanted guests, while guaranteeing silence." I glanced at the incoming number—a land line, with a Marseille area code. I jotted the number down on the pad provided by the hotel.

"Who are you?" The man spoke brusquely, as though he was accustomed to giving orders. "What organization do you represent? Are you associated with that cursed bastard The Shark?"

Should I share my secret, use it for leverage? No, not yet. "We are merely a group of private citizens, sir, who do not want to cause you any difficulty. Return our men and we will forget all about your error. The police will forget as well."

"Phew! The police do not concern me. I am curious about you, young lady. The men we picked up, by mistake as you surmise, are barbarians. You, however, are obviously *zhongguoren*. Furthermore, you somehow knew that we were as well, or you would not have posted your advertisement in Chinese."

"I was there when you abducted them, esteemed uncle. I saw you."

The man paused as though considering this.

"We did not see any woman."

"That does not surprise me. I was well hidden."

"Could you identify us? Did you already speak to the police?"

"I went to the police to ask their help. They insisted that my friends had been taken by Arab terrorists."

The man at the other end issued a short bark of laughter. "As I suspected, we have little to fear from the police."

"Perhaps, although I have quite a bit more evidence now that you have contacted me." I paused for breath. "However, as I told you before, I have no desire to make problems for you or your organization. Simply release my friends, and I will keep my mouth closed."

"Since you obviously want them released, why should we comply without receiving anything in return?"

At last. I'd never expected them to just let Harry and Etienne go for free. Of course there would have to be some sort of transaction. That was the nature of the business.

"You receive my silence, sir."

"Your speech cannot hurt us."

"Are you certain, esteemed uncle? You do not know who I am, whom I know, or what resources I command. The Marseille police are idiots but Interpol is a different matter."

The Triad boss — if that was what he was — paused as if to consider my statement.

I pressed my advantage. "However, we may be willing to offer you something tangible in trade for the two hostages. That is, of course, assuming they are alive and unharmed."

"They are fine — so far."

"May I speak to them, in order to verify this?"

"Later. In any case, I doubt that you could come up with the price for their release."

"Do not underestimate me, uncle. How much do you want?"

"It is not money that we require, but something else."

"Yes? What?"

"Something was stolen from us, something very valuable. We all have our superiors to whom we must answer, lady, and mine are extremely unhappy about this loss."

"Tell me more, please. Perhaps I can recover this item for you."

The man's chuckle held not the slightest shred of mirth. "You think that you can succeed where we have failed? That is highly unlikely."

"Uncle, as I noted previously, you know nothing about me or my connections. Nor, I might mention, does the thief. What is this item that was stolen from you and who is responsible?"

"The thief is a French ruffian known as Jean the Shark, a petty criminal whose arrogance has made him overly ambitious. Last week he made off with more than twenty kilograms of raw opium. Our opium, already committed to a very demanding customer." The man sighed. "That loss has caused us far more trouble than the little mistake with your friends. After all, they can be easily disposed of."

I swallowed hard. My hunch had been completely correct, but I hardly felt triumphant. How in the world was I going to get hold of a shipment of drugs, presumably in the possession of one of France's most notorious gangsters? Still, I had to try. I've never been someone to back away from a challenge.

"If I find the Shark, get back the opium and return it to you, will you set the captives free?"

"You're very confident, young miss." He paused.

I waited for him to continue, expecting that he'd agree. After all, what did he have to lose?

"Very well," he said at last. "I accept your bargain. Return our goods and we will release the Frenchman and the American." The man's voice was cordial now, even friendly. "Within the next week, please."

"We will do our best, uncle. But what if we cannot recover your stolen property within that time frame?"

"You appear to be a clever young lady. I will assume you already know the answer to that question."

The terror from my dream returned, choking me. Frozen to the phone, I struggled to find my voice. When I finally managed to speak, my calm tone astonished me.

"Very well. Let me speak to the hostages. The American first."

"They're not here. I'll have them call you within an hour at this number. Will that satisfy you?"

"That should be adequate. If you take much longer, however, I will go to Interpol."

He rung off without comment. The alarm clock by the bed read four p.m. An hour. That should just give me time to call Toni.

Chapter Fourteen

The detective answered on the first ring. "Emily!"

She'd obviously stored my number in her mobile. I found that reassuring.

"Hey, Toni."

"*Et bien?* You sound much better. Did you sleep?"

"Some."

"*Superbe!* Look, I've been doing some research on Le Requin..."

"I just talked to the kidnappers."

That stopped her cold. "Really? How...?"

"My ad in the Chinese paper. They phoned me, just as I hoped they would."

"And your friends? They're safe?"

"According to what the caller told me, yes. To prove it, he agreed to let them call me, soon. I thought maybe you might want to trace the call when they do."

"I doubt that will be useful. They'll probably just toss the SIM afterward."

"Probably. Anyway, you might check this land line." I recited the number I'd scrawled on the pad by the bed. For a minute all I heard were key clicks.

"Public phone. I figured as much."

"Where?"

"Centre Bourse shopping center. That would be packed at this time of day."

"Well, at least we know the gang hasn't taken them far from Marseille."

"Not yet, at least. So what's the bottom line, Emily? How much do they want to release your friends?"

"It isn't money they want."

"Huh?"

I explained about Le Requin and the stolen drugs.

"Exactly as you guessed! You're brilliant!"

"Doesn't do me much good, does it?"

"Never mind. We'll figure out where they're hiding, somehow. I've got some nifty search tools I can try..."

"No—we can't. I promised. I told them I would get the shipment back for them. In return, they'll let Etienne and Harry go."

Toni let her breath out in a whistle. *"Folle!* Absolutely crazy! Do you have any appreciation for who you're dealing with, girl?"

I shuddered. She had no idea. "I grew up with gory stories about the Triads."

"Then you should know better than to get involved. Let the police handle this."

"The gang leader swore he'd kill them if I go to the authorities. I believe him. Besides, this is officially Inspector Rousseau's case. You think I should trust *him* not to screw up?"

The patter of fingers on the keyboard filled Toni's silence. "He's got an APB out for certain known terrorist figures," she continued after a moment.

"Other than that, his report recommends that the police suspend action until the kidnappers tip their hand."

"Well, they have, but in not the way he expects." I wiped my sweaty palms on my robe. "Look, I'm going to deal with this privately. I'm Chinese. I have some idea how these guys think. Somehow, I'm going to find Le Requin, get hold of the opium, and deliver it to the Iron Hammer."

"Somehow? How?"

"I'm working on that." In fact I didn't have the slightest clue how to go about accomplishing any of these objectives. But I didn't intend to let that stop me. "I'll put together a plan."

"Like I said, you're nuts." I could imagine Toni shaking her head, her lips pursed in disapproval. "But I can tell from your voice that I won't succeed in convincing you. So what can I do to help?"

My mood brightened a bit. Detective Leblanc would make a valuable ally. Still I felt obliged to make at least a token protest. "You sure you want to get involved? You could lose your job, working without orders, going behind Rousseau's back."

"Nobody tells me what to do, Emily. You should have realized that by now. I'm going to stick with you on this, whether you want my assistance or not."

"Okay, okay! I get the message. So what do you know about Jean Le Requin?"

"Well... He's forty-two years old. Born somewhere in Provence, we think. We don't have much information about his background. First conviction and incarceration was at the age of twenty, for petty theft. His next arrest involved a much more ambitious crime—relieving some Indian diplomat's wife of her jewels. Since then he's been in and out of jail, but mostly out. He's wealthy enough to afford excellent lawyers. He's suspected in at least a dozen open cases of larceny, smuggling, fraud and blackmail, as well as two murders, but we don't have enough evidence to firmly tie him to any of them. Very frustrating! If we found him, though, we could at least haul him in for questioning."

"Hmm. What else? Do you know where he lives?"

"He has a town house in Paris, a country place near Arles, a condo in Nice, perhaps half a dozen other properties around France. Probably places outside France, too."

"You know all this, but you can't arrest him?"

"He might be called The Shark, but he's slippery as an eel. He always seems to be one step ahead of us. He's as clever as he is ruthless."

My spirits sank back into the gutter. If the police had people as sharp as Toni and still couldn't get hold of Le Requin, what made me think I could? "So, he's smart, rich, handsome, and without scruples. Does he have any weaknesses?"

Toni chuckled. "The usual French vices. Beautiful women, food and wine, fast cars."

"Well, I'm a gourmet chef. Maybe I could whip up something to tempt his discriminating palate."

"You're gorgeous, too. I don't mean to insult you, but you might be able to use your looks to some advantage. Apparently he's partial to Asian beauties. A while back the gossip magazines had a big spread of him escorting the reigning Miss Thailand to the Paris Opera and the Grand Prix."

Something gnawed at the edges of my consciousness, some buried thought struggling to surface. "The famous auto races?"

"Yeah. He's a huge fan. In fact, two years ago, he raced his own Porsche in Monaco, right under the noses of the authorities."

"Sounds like an arrogant bastard." Distracted, I searched my memory, trying to coax the tickling sense of relevance out of hiding.

"Oh, definitely. And I gather he revels in that image. He's not your usual retiring criminal. He seems to adore seeing his name in the papers."

The papers. Something I'd read yesterday, in the hotel lobby, while waiting for Etienne...

I had it. "Isn't there supposed to be some sort of race soon—in the next few days? In Nice?"

I listened to Toni's fingers dancing across her keyboard. "You're right. The Grand Prix de Nice starts the day after tomorrow. First time they've held a street race in the city in more than fifty years. They're expecting a big crowd, including movie stars and celebrities—and lots of press coverage."

"Do you think Le Requin might attend?"

"It's certainly possible. But how will you find him?"

"I'm going to bet that he'll find me. But I'm going to need your help."

"What can I do for you, Emily?"

"Take me shopping. If I'm going to hook a world-class criminal, I'll need a better wardrobe."

Chapter Fifteen

I wrapped up my conversation with Toni as quickly as I could, agreeing to meet her at the rue Saint Ferréol at six. Then I dressed in clean jeans and a striped knit top and sat down to wait for the Chinese to call.

My mind whirled. What could I do to attract Jean's attention? I brought up the browser on my iPad to search the web for pictures of the gangster and his Thai beauty queen. In five minutes I had half a dozen. The media loved The Shark.

As I might have expected, Miss Thailand was exquisite, slender and willowy, with a cascade of midnight black hair down her back. How could I compete, with my sturdy peasant build, however curvy, and my practical bob?

She always looks beautiful. I could almost hear Harry's voice in my ear. In fact, I could imagine his delicate tongue tracing the inner whorls and feel him nibbling at the lobe. The virtual sensations were enough to quicken my pulse and dampen my crotch. At the same time, a fist of pain clutched inside my chest. I missed him so very much.

I glanced back at the images of my target. Perhaps Le Requin's uncanny resemblance to Etienne would make it easier for me to act the part of the femme fatale. Indeed, I could scarcely believe the man in the photos was *not* Etienne. With his arm hooked possessively through that of his lovely companion, he shepherded her through a crowd of bright, blurry faces.

Even in a still snapshot, Jean conveyed a sense of energy and power. He peered into the distance, his face animated—eyes wide, eyebrows arched, mouth open as if about to offer some opinion. The Asian woman at his side, far shorter than he was, gazed up at him with something like worship.

He's used to being adored, I thought. *He expects it.* Perhaps I could use that.

The chirp of my phone startled me out of my reverie. The alarm clock told me it was exactly five.

"*Huay,*" I answered in Mandarin, not sure who to expect at the other end of the line.

"Mei Lee?"

A warm tide of relief surged through me. "Etienne! How are you?"

"Fine, fine—aside from a bit of rope burn, I'm perfectly all right."

"Is Harry okay? Can you tell me where you are? Can we talk freely? Do your captors speak English?"

"Yes, no and I don't know." Etienne's voice carried a trace of his habitual impatience. "Harry has completely recovered from being knocked out, as far as I can determine."

"Thank the gods!"

"I have no idea where we are. We were blindfolded during the trip here. However, I suspect we're not far from the sea. There's a kind of salty tang to the air, even indoors."

"So you might still be in Marseille. The boss of the gang called me from Marseille."

"As I said, I don't know. The thugs who grabbed us speak French to me and expect me to translate for Harry's benefit. They use some dialect of Chinese among themselves. But it's possible they understand English and are trying to hide the fact. Harry and I converse in English of course."

"Right. And they keep you bound?"

"Just our wrists, which isn't too uncomfortable."

I squelched the temptation to make some comment about his enjoying that aspect of his captivity. My delight at hearing his voice had made me a bit giddy.

"And I must admit they are feeding us very well, all sorts of Chinese dishes I've never tasted before."

I grinned to myself. Despite the dire situation, Etienne didn't sound too traumatized.

"Glad to hear you won't starve, Etienne. Meanwhile, hold on, keep your eyes open for – uh – opportunities. And don't give up hope. I'm doing my best to get you released."

I expected some dismissive remark in response, some comment on the folly of a TV chef trying to take on an international crime syndicate.

I was wrong.

"I have complete faith in you, Ms Wong. And I hope to see you soon. I miss you."

"Same here, Etienne. It's wonderful to talk to you."

Tears gathered at the corners of my eyes. I blinked them away.

"Take care of yourself, Mei Lee. Don't risk your own safety on our behalf, agreed?"

"Ah — I'll be careful. I promise." I wasn't exactly lying. I did plan to be careful.

"Good girl. Here's Harry."

I took a deep breath, swallowing a sob. This was far more difficult than I'd envisioned.

"Em, love! How are you?"

"Silly question." I forced out a chuckle. "I'm racking my brains to come up with a plan to set you two free. But what about you? How's your head?"

"I've got a lump the size of an ostrich egg, but otherwise no ill effects. Hey, I'm tough. When I was a linebacker for Indiana State, they called me Hard-headed Harry."

This time my laugh was real. "You sound awfully cheerful for a guy who's been kidnapped."

"I'm talking to my lover. What do you expect?" His voice became softer and more intimate. "The worst aspect of this whole situation is being away from you, imagining you in my arms, worrying about you. You have no idea how much that hurts."

"Oh, I do. Believe me, I do."

Memory overwhelmed me, painfully vivid snippets from our short, intense relationship. That first luscious kiss in the studio kitchen, redolent of almonds and sweet cream. The first time he'd bound me, under the stars up on Twin Peaks. I remembered caresses and spankings, equally welcome when delivered by his talented hands. I recalled his extraordinary ability to sense what I needed before I knew myself. With utter certainty, I realized that he loved me as no one else ever had in my entire life.

And unless my crazy, improbable plan succeeded, I might never see him again.

"Em? You still there?"

Damn these tears.

"Yes, of course — I'm just trying to stop fantasizing about you."

"Don't stop. Keep me in your thoughts. That's the only way I can bear this."

Love and sorrow tore me in two. Someone else took over the line before I could respond.

"That should be enough to convince you that your associates have not been harmed, young lady."

The first few syllables of Mandarin flipped my mind into the logic of that language, like a game of chess played in metaphors. "Thank you for keeping your word, esteemed uncle." Somehow I kept the trembling out of my voice.

"We'll expect news of our shipment soon, then. As I indicated earlier, we can give you one week. After that point, your associates will become too inconvenient for us to maintain."

"I will do my best to reclaim your property. How can I contact you when I have it in hand?"

"Leave a message at the following number."

I scribbled down the number he recited and read it back to him.

"I will be in touch as soon as I have any news, uncle."

"Good. Let me remind you also not to involve any law enforcement officials — either local or international — in this matter. If you should do so, the next time you see your associates they will be floating in the waters of the Old Port with their throats slit. Do you understand?"

"Yes, esteemed uncle. I understand."

"Excellent. Good luck, young miss."

The phone went dead. I tossed it onto the bed and finally surrendered to my tears.

Chapter Sixteen

I didn't have time to think too much about the implications of the phone call. The hotel called me a cab and I headed for my rendezvous with Toni. By mutual agreement, we didn't discuss the kidnapping in public. Instead, the statuesque detective led me from one glittering boutique to the next, offering surprisingly astute advice on which outfits I should acquire. I say surprising because her own no-nonsense style suggested she had little personal interest in fashion or glamour. She'd shed her uniform for a pair of cargo pants and a Che Guevara T-shirt that confirmed my suspicious about her curvaceous figure, but indicated a certain disdain for haute couture.

"The teal suit would be best for the race itself," she suggested. "It drapes beautifully, and the color makes your skin look like porcelain."

"You don't think it's too formal for a sporting event?" I looked over my shoulder, admiring the way the narrow skirt accented my bottom. It fell to the middle of my knee in a nod to propriety, but the back had a kick pleat that revealed a lot of thigh under the right circumstances—a good thing, too, since walking would have been difficult otherwise.

"You want to stand out, don't you? To catch his eye?" Her approving grin made me wonder whether her interest in me went beyond the platonic. "It's a bit old-fashioned, too. Traditional. French men are suckers for classic elegance."

"Oh really? You're an expert?"

"I should be...after three French husbands!" She chuckled at my obvious disbelief. "Yes, it's true. I keep hoping I'll find someone who appreciates me the way I am. My husbands thought I was too masculine, too bossy and independent. They all wanted Catherine Deneuve."

"Who is a blonde with aristocratic features, not a China girl with slanty eyes and a tiny nose!"

"Come on, Emily—you do know you're beautiful, don't you? Anyway, we've already established that your target is attracted to Asian women."

I slipped off the fitted jacket to scrutinize the filmy white blouse I wore underneath. It was translucent to the point of indecency. My everyday bra showed through clearly. "The top seems a bit extreme, though. I mean, if we're going for a classic look..."

"Contrast, Emily. Contrast. Keep him off balance. Make him wonder. Are you a lady or a slut? He'll be desperate to find out. Though I do think we'll need to pick up some new lingerie for you, to complete the look."

I doffed the suit and handed it to the clerk along with my credit card, wondering briefly whether the network's insurance policy would cover the costs of my augmented wardrobe. Then Toni shepherded me down the block, to a window where mannequins adopted poses both suggestive and demure, attired in various frothy confections of satin, lace and even feathers.

No one makes lingerie like the French. It's a national passion. Gazing at the garter belts, brassieres, bustiers, corsets, brazen thongs, frilly boy shorts, slinky night gowns and diaphanous peignoirs, I felt like a kid with a sweet tooth peering into a pastry shop. Every item whispered of sensual encounters. The soft, clinging fabrics gleamed in the muted lighting. I could almost feel the silky texture against my skin and imagine how the delicate garments would transmit body heat to a lover's fingers.

Harry would adore this. The thought kindled a bittersweet smile. If only he were here to help me choose. We'd done some shopping together in the leather district, but San Francisco couldn't begin to compete with this place, in variety or in elegance.

"*Bonsoir, Mademoiselles. Bienvenue à la Vie Douce.*" The plump, matronly shop owner bustled over to greet us. The Sweet Life! How appropriate. "How can I help you, ladies?"

Toni took the lead. "My friend has a special engagement coming up, with a very special guy."

The proprietor broke into a knowing smile at Toni's wink.

"She needs some under things—a couple of bra and panty sets—that will really impress him."

"What sort of mood do you want to project?" the shop owner asked. "Innocent? Romantic? Daring?"

"More in the daring direction, but classy," I replied. "And least one set should be white or something similar, since it will be visible through my blouse."

The older woman surveyed me with unnerving attention. I had the feeling she rarely needed the measuring tape that hung around her neck. "I have exactly the thing," she announced at last. "You're an eighty-five C, am I correct? And ninety centimeter hips?"

"Perfect." Clearly we were in the presence of an expert.

"Sit, please. I'll be right back." She disappeared into the back of the shop, repeating my dimensions to herself.

Toni wandered from one display to another. She paused before a figure clad in a full-length corset of forest green satin and ran her index finger along the boning. "I like this one..."

"Really?"

With her cropped hair and mannish clothing, she didn't seem the lingerie type, although I could see that the vibrant hue would flatter her buttery complexion.

"Oh, yes. It would go so well with my thigh high black boots. And my crop."

What? Before I could ask her to clarify, the shop owner returned.

"Try this one, Mademoiselle." She gestured toward a curtained cubicle, handing me an exquisite pushup brassiere. Champagne-colored silk covered the underside of the cups. The upper hemispheres were fashioned of creamy lace. In terms of coverage, it looked fairly conservative. However, when I put it on, I saw that the lacey panels hid nothing. My nipples were more than obvious through the delicate tracery. They tightened into ruddy points as I admired the way the magnificent garment accentuated my curves.

I might not be a beauty queen, but I had to admit this bra shifted me closer to Miss Thailand's class.

Although the matching silk panties were cut high at the leg, they fully covered my bottom, clinging like a second skin. I approved. Thongs might look hot, but they were pretty uncomfortable. I didn't know whether to be shocked or amused when I discovered the garment had a split crotch. What did that say about a woman?

That she was a slut looking for sex, of course. And that *was* the message I wanted to convey to Jean Le Requin, the fact that I was available for a carnal encounter. What would I do, though, if the wandering cranes came home to nest and I actually ended up in bed with the gangster?

The notion scared me. I couldn't let that happen. True, he resembled Etienne so strongly, sharing all of the chef's delectable hotness. However I was willing to bet my diploma Le Requin didn't have a submissive bone in his body. Indeed, his appearance was far more Dom-ish than rumpled, bespectacled Harry. Unlike Harry, though, who would never truly hurt me and who used pain only as seasoning to intensify the pleasure, Le Requin looked like he had a vicious streak. He'd be the sort of Dom who delighted in making a woman suffer, who wouldn't pay any attention to questions of consent or safe words.

I would not have sex with The Shark, period.

But what if I were forced to do so, to save my lover's life?

"How does it look, Emily?" Toni's voice pulled me back to the present.

"Um—pretty amazing."

"Can I see?"

The eagerness in Toni's voice made me wonder once more about her sexual interests. And had I really heard her say 'crop'?

"Sure. C'mon in." The dressing room was more capacious than I'd expected, in line with the exclusivity of the shop, I guess. In a moment Toni had ducked through the curtain to stand next to me, gazing at my reflection in the gilt-framed mirror.

"Wow! The Shark doesn't stand a chance!"

"I hope you're right."

"And here's what Madame Mirasolle suggests to go with the cocktail dress..." She handed me a one-piece garment of black satin and mesh, with under-wired half-cups and red satin garters. "She's got seamed silk stockings, of course. Taupe, with scarlet ribbons around the thighs."

"Nothing innocent about this," I joked. Could I really wear something so blatant?

She crossed her arms over Guevara's face. "Put it on. Let's see if it fits."

Heat climbed into my cheeks. Normally I'm not the modest type, but her focused gaze made me nervous. "Ah—give me a couple of minutes, okay? This dressing room's a bit crowded."

"Oh, come on, Emily. It's just us girls here. Do it."

The authority in her voice sent a little thrill racing through me. Her bossiness reminded me of Harry. Wouldn't he love this outfit? I could vividly imagine his reactions. It was a good thing I planned to buy the champagne-colored set, because the flimsy strip of cloth between my legs was growing a bit damp, even through the paper shield I'd been given to protect it.

Obeying Toni's command, wishing she were Harry, I peeled off the bra and panties and handed them to her. With some difficulty I wriggled into the strapless black costume. As I settled my breasts into the satin cups, I tried to avoid my swollen nipples, without success. A bolt of sensation zipped down to my sex. I sucked in my breath.

"Something wrong?"

I met Toni's gleaming eyes in the mirror. "No, no—it's just a bit tight."

"Not too tight, at least in my opinion." She grinned at my reflection. "I think it's perfect. Buy it."

The thing—I really didn't know the correct term for this garment—had an hour-glass-shaped panel of shiny fabric that began under my breasts, narrowed as it swept down my abdomen, then widened again at my hips. An oval mesh-filled cutout revealed my navel. More mesh stretched around my ribs and waist to the back, to join a band of black which followed my spine down to the crevice between my buttocks. The band then ran between my thighs to join a tiny satin triangle in front, which barely covered my trimmed pubic hair. I still had the paper protector between my pussy and the bizarre garment. Not that this did much good. The thin strip of material buried itself in my folds, forcing the paper up into my cleft to rasp against my twitching clit. How in the world could I ever wear this in public? I'd be on the edge of coming the whole time.

"You don't think this is too—oh, I don't know—too trashy?" The garment reminded me of some of the items I'd seen when Harry took me browsing on adult toy sites, except for the fact that the materials were clearly of the highest quality and the workmanship superb.

"Madame Mirasolle does not sell trash. Trust me. You're devastating—a walking orgasm."

Right. That was exactly the problem.

"He won't be able to resist you. I know it's not subtle, but believe me, this is what guys like. If you're embarrassed, just think of it as another weapon in your fight against Le Requin."

* * * *

When we'd finished at La Vie Douce and bid good evening to a beaming Madame Mirasolle, Toni took me to buy shoes — two pairs, both with heels high enough to make me feel dizzy — then to a back street bistro for a late night supper. We talked for a while about how I could attract Le Requin's attention, if in fact he was present at the race.

"Too bad you're not famous. His file makes it clear that he likes to hang out with celebrities."

I washed down my last *moule frite* with a sip of fruity Pinot noir. "Well, I *am* a public figure in the US. A TV star. After three months, I'm actually fairly well known, at least among the foodies."

"Pretty much everyone in France is a 'foodie'," Toni mused, scooping up the last vestiges of the tapenade with a crust of grilled bread. "But other than crime shows like *CSI: Miami* and *Law & Order*, they don't watch much American television. Still, I imagine there'd be a certain curiosity about a Chinese woman from American TV who cooks French food."

"I need to get on the public radar in just a day or two." I drained my wine glass then reached for the bottle to refill it. "Any ideas?"

"The Internet, obviously. How about Facebook?"

"Always viewed that as a waste of time."

"Do you have a blog?"

"Nah. I'm way too busy. Anyway, it takes ages to build up a reader base." The wine lingered on my tongue, mingling with the thyme from the barbecued lamb skewers we'd shared as an appetizer. For some reason, the sweet aftertaste from the wine reminded me of kisses, and that of course got me thinking about Harry and Etienne, languishing in the cruel hands of the Iron Hammer. I'd been so sure I'd be able to free them. Now the whole endeavor seemed impossible. It didn't matter how much I spent on sexy clothing. Among the thousands attending the Grand Prix, I'd be invisible.

All at once there were tears in my eyes. I blinked them away.

"Something wrong, hon?" Toni asked, observant as always.

"I— Oh, damn it all, the whole thing is just so hopeless. The clock's ticking, and every hour that goes by, the situation gets more desperate. Hooking up with Le Requin seemed like a fine idea, but now I don't have any idea how."

"Maybe we should go to Interpol after all. They're pretty together. Unlike my local colleagues!"

"I don't dare. That might be signing Harry's and Etienne's death warrant." Straightening up in my chair, I gulped down the remainder of my wine. "No, I've got to solve this problem on my own. I'm ranked four *dan* in *wei chi*. I should be able to outwit a conceited, self-obsessed French hoodlum."

"Don't underestimate Le Requin."

"I don't." Recalling his ice-cold eyes in the mug shots, I shivered. "He has weaknesses, though. I've got to find them and use them."

Deep in my purse, my mobile chirped for attention. By the time I'd managed to extract the phone, the caller had given up. I scanned the missed calls log. Oh, great demons of hell! It was Roger.

What was I going to tell him? That I'd learned his star and his top producer were in the clutches of the most brutal criminal organization in Asia? That I'd promised to rescue them by stealing a shipment of illegal drugs from an equally ruthless French gangster?

And what about the show? Would he want the crew to continue filming without Etienne? Or to return to the States? I wasn't about to leave France while my lovers were in danger, but perhaps Lisa, Marty and the rest should head back. It would get them out of any danger and save the network some money, too.

Roger could concoct some story about Etienne having fallen ill in France and the tour being canceled. With his years in the business, the network exec had great connections with both traditional and new media. That was one reason my partnership with Etienne had been so successful. Every week, Roger came up with some new angle on me, Etienne, or our relationship to feed to the press.

Ah, that was a good one! A cooking channel network head 'feeding' stories to the media...

I'm sure that thunder didn't really shake our table. But inspiration arrived so suddenly I felt that lightning had struck.

"I know!" I crowed. "I know what to do, Toni! I know what we need."

"Huh? What are you talking about?"

"We need a press release. A news story about the well-known French-Chinese chef Mei Lee Wong visiting France and attending the Grand Prix de Nice. A story that will attract The Shark's attention and send *him* looking for me."

"Sounds reasonable, but how are you going to manage that at such short notice?"

"You have any connections with newspapers here in Marseille?"

"Yeah, sure, a few."

"And the Internet news sites?"

"They're desperate for content."

"If I can get the story on the international news wires, can you push it into the local media?"

"I can try."

"Then leave the rest to me."

Chapter Seventeen

Bless Roger Elliot! Not only did he concoct a press release and get it on the wire services in record time, he actually managed to set up a press conference for me on the day of the race. Attired in my snazzy new suit, I posed on the steps of one of the Rococo buildings lining the Promenade des Anglais. Reporters, photographers and videographers surrounded me, all curious to meet a female Chinese chef who spoke fluent French and specialized in *canard aux champignons, homard au vin blanc* and *crochembouche.*

"Mademoiselle Wong!" A rangy young man with spectacles thrust his microphone in my face. "What is the most delicious dish you've tasted since you arrived in France?"

"Ah, can't you ask me something easier?" I favored him with what I hoped was a seductive smile and fluttered my mascara-heavy eyelashes. "Everything I've tasted here has been sublime. Don't make me choose!"

"You've been here now for"—a paunchy, balding reporter checked his tablet—"a week now. How have your fans back in America reacted to your French tour?"

"According to the network execs, ratings have climbed steadily since we began filming on location. At Tastes of France, we try to introduce viewers to the true flavor of French cuisine, but for many of them, the country itself remains an abstraction." I beamed at my questioner. An answering smile rewarded me. "The tour makes France real. It lets our audience actually see some of your magnificent sights, as well as to learn about regional specialties they might not ever encounter in the US."

"Why are you in Nice? Will you be filming a segment here?" a woman in a tricolor scarf inquired.

"No, this is just a side trip for me. When I heard about the race, I just had to attend. I've got a bit of weakness for fast cars—and the daring young men who drive them!"

"Speaking of men, where's your partner, Etienne Duvalier? Up until the last day or two, you've hardly been seen apart."

"Ah, poor Etienne!" I'd anticipated this question. My voice was steady as the foundations of Château d'If. "He's in the hospital back in Marseille, with a nasty case of the flu. The doctors are worried about the possibility of pneumonia. My bosses at the network won't let me near him—they're afraid I might catch it."

"There's a rumor that you and he are lovers." Another woman, her blonde hair swept into a classic twist, stabbed at me with her mic. "Is it true?"

"Please, Mademoiselle! You know it's not polite to kiss and tell." I favored the crowd with a conspiratorial grin, suggesting they could figure out the answer for themselves. "In any case, M Duvalier has a reputation as the most serious of chefs. I don't think he'd allow a mere woman to distract him from his vocation."

The assembled media chuckled.

A low-pitched roar reached my ears. "I believe the race is about to begin, ladies and gentlemen, and I'm sure that's of far more interest to you than an American television personality. Thanks for your time and attention."

"A few more photos please, Mademoiselle Wong!" Shutters clicked and television cameras zoomed in on my face.

I smiled until my cheeks hurt, nodding and waving as if I were on parade. The cars growled again, off in the distance. Gradually the media representatives drifted away, headed for the starting gates.

Crowds lined both sides of the boulevard, waiting for the first circuit to begin. Elevated by the stairs, I had an excellent view. Everyone's eyes turned to the west, where the race course started. Well, almost everyone. A lean, dark clad figure lounged against a lamp post across the street, just opposite the building where I stood. Even at a distance, I could tell his attention was focused on me.

A shock of recognition shattered my carefully cultivated composure. I knew those broad shoulders and narrow hips, those chestnut curls, that aura of self-confidence that bordered on arrogance. He looked exactly like Etienne. But of course it couldn't be — Etienne was a prisoner.

It had to be Le Requin.

My heartbeat revved like the engines at the gate. I couldn't breathe. My palms grew damp as I clutched by Louis Vuitton bag. This was it, the break I'd hoped for. And I was terrified.

I wanted to run, but I was pretty sure my rubbery legs wouldn't hold me. Not to mention the fact that I could barely walk in my absurd spike heels.

Anyway, if I fled, what would happen to Harry and Etienne? I had to follow through with my plan, as crazy and dangerous as it was. I drew in a lungful of petrol-laced air then released it slowly, willing myself to relax. *You can do this, Mei Lee. You can save your lovers.*

I didn't completely believe my internal pep talk. What choice did I have, though, but to act as if I did?

Across the promenade, over the heads of the spectators between us, I sought his eyes. Our gazes locked. Adrenaline zipped through me. He raised an eyebrow — how well I knew that gesture! — and I responded with what I hoped was an encouraging smile. With an answering smirk, ignoring the gestures of security personnel, he jumped the barrier blocking the street. He loped across the road, heedless of any danger from the racecars mustering a few hundred meters away. After elbowing his way through the ranks of spectators on my side of the track, he bounded up the steps to where I stood, transfixed by uncertainty.

From a distance, he was insanely attractive. Close up, he was even more devastating. He had all of Etienne's vitality and charm, amplified somehow by a complete disregard for convention. Attired all in black, with a leather jacket slung over his shoulder and boots polished to a mirror-like gloss, he was Belmondo, Brando and Dean rolled into one, the quintessential rebel. As he reached for me, I noticed a tattoo, an image of a bleeding rose, decorating his forearm below his casually rolled-up sleeve.

"Mademoiselle Wong, if I am not mistaken?"

Before I could react, he was touching me, his hand resting on my shoulder for a moment then sweeping down my arm. Warmth from his skin penetrated through my suit jacket and blouse. *Brazen bastard!* This was the guy ultimately responsible for Harry's and Etienne's kidnapping. If he'd just kept his nose out of Triad business... Anger swept through me. I struggled to maintain the mask of my eager, attentive smile.

He wore some kind of cologne, a spiky-sharp herbal scent quite different from the sophisticated Hermès fragrance that was Etienne's favorite. Underneath, though, I caught a hint of his natural man-musk, so familiar it made me ache. How bizarre that he not only looked like my lover, but smelled the same as well!

He *felt* different, though. Close up, I'd never have confused him with Etienne. Although he was physically attractive, something about Jean Le Requin made my skin crawl. Still, I had to act the part, had to appear charmed and susceptible.

"Monsieur? I don't think I've had the pleasure..." I raised my eyes to his, trying for an air of wanton innocence.

He licked his lips then slipped an arm around my waist, pulling my hip against his taut form. "Not yet, *ma belle*, but soon, perhaps." His lecherous grin made his meaning more than clear. "Jean Dunant, at your service."

"Monsieur Dunant..."

"Call me Jean. I don't think we'll be on formal terms for long. And I shall call you Mei Lee." Keeping me in a firm grip, he walked me down the steps to the street.

Despite his inappropriate familiarity with my person, I found myself grateful for his support as I struggled on my outrageous heels.

"I have seats in the grandstand." He steered me east along the boulevard, until we reached a spot where the racetrack veered sharply to the north. Tiers of chairs rose to our left, shaded by a blue and white striped awning. An aisle ran up the center. He released my waist, only to give my bottom a swat. "We're up in the top rank. Up you go!"

I bristled at Jean's domineering tone. He had no manners at all. It wasn't at all like when Harry gave me orders. I knew Harry, knew that despite his sometimes shocking ideas he'd never hurt me. I trusted him completely. Living without Harry was like losing one of my limbs. The ache of his absence was constant and unrelenting.

In contrast, this man commanding me was a stranger. A dangerous stranger, despite the sense of familiarity that derived from his uncanny similarity to Etienne.

The top tier of seats was empty.

"I bought the whole row," he commented, apparently reading my thoughts. "I like some space."

The Promenade des Anglais ran along the coast. From this height, I had a fine view of the Mediterranean stretching toward the horizon, a deep blue that mirrored the cloudless sky. I scanned the crowd. Toni was out there somewhere. She'd insisted on coming along to provide backup. She'd also convinced me to install a tracker program on my phone, so she'd be able to locate me if we lost touch. I saw no sign of her, but I was willing to bet she'd noted the gangster's approach. Toni was the consummate professional.

"Sit," he commanded, pointing to a chair in the middle of the row and taking the one adjacent.

I settled into the spot he'd indicated, deliberately crossing one leg over the other. My skirt rode up to reveal a sizeable length of bare thigh. Almost immediately, Le Requin took possession of that exposed flesh, resting his warm palm on the skin just above my knee. I expected him to take further liberties, but he seemed satisfied for the moment with this proprietary gesture. He waved his other hand at a white-uniformed young man maneuvering through the rows of spectators with a tray of filled glasses.

"*Garçon*! Champagne!"

The waiter clambered up to our level. Jean let go of my thigh long enough to grab two flutes. He handed one to me while berating poor kid. "Go get me a bottle. Veuve Cliquot if you have it."

"Uh…"

"Here." The gangster pulled a hundred euro note from the pocket of his black silk shirt and threw it down on the tray.

The waiter fumbled, struggling to catch the bill before the sea breeze blew it away.

"Hurry up! The race will start any minute."

The boy hastened away, ignoring the summons from other occupants in the grandstand.

Jean raised his glass and skewered me with his gaze. "To beautiful women. To you, Mei Lee."

I sipped at the chilled wine. The bubbles danced on my tongue. I drank more deeply, relishing the crisp semi-sweetness. "Thank you. But how do you know my name?"

"Your reputation precedes you, *cherie*. The feisty lady chef from Hong Kong who has taken America by storm. How did the article put it? '*Determined to show that gender and nationality do not constrain culinary excellence'."*

I had to laugh. Roger had outdone himself.

"When I read that you'd be here at the races, I was curious. When I saw the photo — well, I just couldn't resist." From the pocket of his tight Versace jeans, he extracted a newspaper clipping and held it up for me to see. The grainy image — me wearing the form-fitting *choengsan*, ornate wig and Oriental make-up Etienne had chosen for my first show — made me blush.

"Absoluement delicieuse!" He drained the remainder of his champagne then returned his hand to my leg.

I tried not to tense as he walked his fingers up to the edge of my skirt and grazed the skin just under the hem. All the while, his fierce blue-gray eyes kept me pinned in place, as if daring me to object.

"I'm flattered — Jean. But you have me at a disadvantage. I don't know anything at all about you."

"Me? I'm just a successful businessman, with a fondness for vintage wine, gourmet food, fast cars and lovely women."

At that moment, the waiter arrived. Jean grabbed the bottle, popped the cork and filled our glasses to the brim. "Today I expect to enjoy all four passions."

"Mesdames et Monsieurs!" The public address system saved me from the need to reply. "Welcome to the Grand Prix de Nice. The drivers are at the gate. The Mayor raises the gun. Ready…set…go!"

A single shot rang out from the speakers. Engines roared. The din, amplified by the sound system, echoed over the heads of the crowd. Jean downed the contents of his glass in two swallows then jumped to his feet, dragging me up with him.

The noise swelled. A sleek contraption streaked by — a bright blur of yellow and black. Two more vehicles hung on its tail, fluorescent green and fiery red, slung low between massive wheels, sweeping around the corner almost before I registered their presence. More roadsters sped past, hugging the track, a rainbow of hues smearing together, weaving in and out as they raced by the grandstand and out of sight.

Jean yelled and cheered. I could scarcely hear him above the deafening racket. As the growling of the cars faded, I realized I'd been shouting too. My throat felt raw and dry. I sank back into my seat, my heart slamming against my ribs, and guzzled my champagne like it was fruit juice. My companion refilled my flute with a laugh.

"Amazing, isn't it? The way it takes you over? The heat, the noise, the speed…It's so physical!"

I nodded and sipped my wine, adrenaline still buzzing through me.

"I find it's a bit like sex. Don't you agree?"

He accompanied his comment with a squeeze of my bare thigh, running his thumb along the skin. His other hand reached out, targeting my breast. I could see the future. In an instant he'd be twisting my nipple. What now? How could I keep him on the hook without actually giving in to him?

I jerked in my seat, pretending to be startled by the first brush of his fingertips against my jacket. My half-full glass tipped in his direction, soaking his lap with chilled champagne.

"*Merde!*" He leaped to his feet, dragging a handkerchief from his back pocket and scouring his designer jeans. "I'm drenched!"

"Oh, *Monsieur*! I'm dreadfully sorry…I'm so clumsy…" I noted with satisfaction that the substantial lump I'd seen earlier distorting his zipper had dwindled noticeably when doused with cold wine. "At least it's white, not red... Here, I have some tissues...I'll pay for the cleaning..."

At first, my placating tone did little to calm him. However, it appeared that he enjoyed having my attention focused on his crotch. He settled back into his chair as the cars swept past, the growling engines accompanied by the whoops and yells of the crowd below us.

"Never mind, Mei Lee." He leaned close, his tone conspiratorial. "You can make it up to me later."

Before I could react, he seized my shoulders and pulled me into a ferocious kiss. His lips sealed to mine. He forced his tongue into my mouth. Aggressive, with the same swagger that animated his walk, he took me over, his hands roaming over my body as if it belonged to him.

Etienne didn't kiss like this. He was gentle, sensuous, deferent, alert to my desires. Jean's mouth ravaged mine, taking more than giving, assuming control and forcing me to surrender. He had no subtlety at all. He'd be a selfish lover, I could tell, concerned only with his own satisfaction. Somehow, though, I had to make him believe that he'd snared me with his clumsy advances.

Disgust roiled in my belly. I tried to hide my reaction. I didn't fight him, much as I wanted to knee him in the balls. I had to give him something or I'd never succeed in my plans. So I feigned surrender, pretending that I wanted him as much as he obviously wanted me.

My ears hummed with a muted roar that grew louder by the instant. The world trembled, as though the earth were shaking. The noise was as penetrating, inexorable and unrelenting as his brazen tongue stabbing against my palate. The din built, overwhelming, deafening.

Le Requin chose that moment to slide his hand under my skirt. His fingers found the split in my panties. That was too much. With a moan of simulated pleasure, I twisted out of his grasp.

"Oh, no, please…not here! Not yet, Monsieur"

Trails of smoky exhaust hung over the track below. The sound of engines dwindled into silence.

"Why not?" His eyebrows knotted in a scowl, the Shark glared at me.

"Isn't this a—um—bit public?" I offered him the sweetest smile I could muster.

"Everyone's eyes are on the track. Except for mine, that is. Take off your jacket, Mei Lee."

I could hardly refuse. I had to keep him on the line. Shrugging the garment onto the chair back, I exposed my diaphanous blouse and the silky brassiere clearly visible beneath. Based on his expression, not to mention the swelling in his jeans, I'd say I'd got my money's worth from Toni's boutique.

"Your nipples are hard. You want me."

"Of course I want you," I purred, refilling his champagne flute. "But not this way. I don't want a furtive quickie out here in the hot, dusty street. I think you deserve a long period of my concentrated attention in luxurious privacy—don't you?"

I laid a hand on the Shark's hard-muscled forearm. "Let's watch the races, shall we? After all, as you said, they're absolutely thrilling. Maybe even better than sex."

"Nothing's better than sex," he replied. "Sex with me, at least. As you'll soon find out."

I batted my artificially-enhanced lashes and cooed. "Ah, Jean—I can hardly wait."

Chapter Eighteen

The race involved two dozen circuits around the four kilometer track. The total duration was perhaps a bit more than two hours. By the time it was over, I was emotionally exhausted as well as seriously intoxicated. It took every ounce of talent and will I could muster to keep up the pretense of attraction.

Every time he passed me more champagne, the Shark made a point of touching me—but never more than a momentary brush of his fingers against mine. I think he was trying to frustrate me. Maybe he thought that would make me horny. Fat chance! As for him, he certainly still showed signs of arousal. I was grateful he hadn't hauled me off and ravished me in some alley.

Meanwhile, I was focused on what came next. The first stage of my plan had succeeded brilliantly. Obviously I'd attracted his interest. Now I had to get him to take me back to his condo—not that I thought this would be difficult—and convince him that I should cook him dinner.

Depending on his level of impatience, that might be tougher to manage.

"Shall we go over to the winner's circle? We can get a closer look at Michel Juvernet's car."

"Ah, Jean! I think I'd better return to my hotel and rest. I'm not used to so much champagne."

"Oh, no you don't! I won't allow you to get away so easily, Mei Lee. I plan to take you to dinner tonight, at one of the best restaurants in Nice. But we'll have some hors d'oeuvres first."

His leer made his meaning obvious. My pussy was most likely at the top of his menu.

I gazed up at him in simulated adoration. "I'd love that, but please—give me a few hours. I really need to clean myself up. I'm feeling pretty sticky." I glanced down at my lap and raised my eyebrows.

He chuckled, believing he was the cause of my hot and bothered state.

"And I was thinking that perhaps rather than going out, I might cook for you. You told me you're passionate about gourmet food."

"But I don't want you to go to the trouble…"

"It's no trouble. I love to cook for friends." I let my voice linger on the last word. "And although I don't want to seem immodest—I'm very good."

"I don't doubt it." He sighed, suddenly wistful and charming. "You're sure?"

"I can't think of anything I'd rather do." I gave him one more eyeful of my transparent blouse and my lacy lingerie before donning my jacket. "Well, that's not strictly true…but I think you'll enjoy it, Jean."

"Okay, you've convinced me. But I'll take responsibility for the ingredients. Give me a list and I'll send Bruno out to get them."

"Who's Bruno?"

"My valet. Also my cook, driver and bodyguard—" He cut himself off, aware that he'd possibly said too much.

I pretended not to notice. "I have a pretty simple menu in mind. Do you like seafood?"

"I'm Provençal. What do you think?"

I glanced up at his handsome face. He sounded just like Etienne.

We strolled down the promenade, through the dwindling crowd. "How about *scallops gratinée, salade Niçoise*, almond pilaf and *crème brulée*?"

He swung his arm around my shoulder and gave me a hug. "Sounds luscious." Bending down to my level, he nuzzled my neck.

I forced myself to hold still.

"And don't forget the appetizers," he murmured.

"Don't worry," I laughed. "I won't."

"Where are you staying?"

"Hotel Alcatrice, near the Jardin Albert Premier."

The Shark nodded. "Right. I'll pick you up at seven." He trailed his fingers down my spine then squeezed my bottom. "Be ready."

"Don't worry. I will be."

* * * *

Back in my room, I stripped off my finery and stretched out naked on the bed. I stared at the gilded scrolls along the borders of the ornate plaster ceiling. Late afternoon sun slanted in through tall windows, patterning the flocked wallpaper. The alarm clock by the bed told me it was nearly five. I had two hours to prepare myself for what might be the battle of my life.

Where was Harry now? What was he doing? Was he thinking about me?

I was willing to bet my grandmother's jade earrings that he was.

* * * *

Jean arrived five minutes early, in a gleaming black Jaguar roadster with the top down. He swerved into the hotel driveway and squealed to a stop under the wrought iron and glass portico. I teetered out to meet him, swaying on the four inch heels Toni had chosen to go with my short, clinging black cocktail dress. The hunger in his eyes as he helped me into the passenger seat and the bulge distending his trousers made it clear that my costume had elicited the intended reactions.

Ignoring the speed limit, he blasted his way through the early evening traffic. My hair tangled and my eyes watered as the wind hit me in the face. Before long we were heading uphill, out of the city.

"I had the impression you lived here in Nice." I had to shout to be heard above the air whistling past us.

"On the outskirts. I have a condominium just off the Grande Corniche. You'll love the view."

I prayed it wasn't too far out of town. My tracker wouldn't help much if Toni couldn't reach me.

He reached across the center console to squeeze my thigh. My dress was short enough to reveal the satin garters gripping the scarlet borders of my stockings, but Le Requin focused mostly on his driving, much to my relief. The two lane road twisted along the edge of a cliff, high above the ocean. A flimsy metal rail was all that separated us from the precipice. Jean sped along the few straight sections and whipped around curves, far faster than I thought was safe. By the time he turned left into a steeply climbing side road, I was clutching the door handle, white-knuckled, and struggling to breathe.

The lane dead-ended in front of a modern building, all steel and glass, facing out to the sea. Surrounded by weathered boulders and green-gray scrub, it seemed totally out of place, some alien artifact plumped down in the wilds of ancient Provence.

"You live here?"

"A simple *pied à terre*, for when I'm in the neighborhood. My business involves quite a lot of travel."

"Not exactly what I'd call simple," I commented, as he led me through a soaring marble-tiled foyer to the lift. The building had eight stories, but there were only four buttons. Each unit, it appeared, comprised two entire floors.

The lift opened onto a carpeted hall that led to a massive oak door. It swung open without a sound when Jean and I approached.

"*Bonsoir, Monsieur – Mademoiselle.*"

The shaven-headed hulk who met us had to be Bruno. He had the build of a boxer, complete with a broken nose and a livid scar running down one cheek. I guessed that Jean was about six feet tall, the same as Etienne. Bruno loomed over him and probably outweighed him by forty or fifty pounds, too. Incongruously, the bodyguard wore a white chef's apron over his sweatpants and shirt. Elaborately tattooed muscles emerged from his short sleeves.

"'Evening, Bruno. Is everything ready for Mademoiselle Wong?"

Bruno nodded. "I went ahead and washed all the vegetables – to save you some time and everything." He flashed me a shy smile. "But I thought you'd probably want to put together the marinade for the tuna yourself." Despite his dodgy appearance, the guard seemed pleasant enough. However, my plans depended on being alone with Le Requin.

Fortunately, Jean's preferences in this area matched mine. "Thanks, Bruno. I don't think we'll need anything further from you this evening. You can head home."

"You sure, boss?" The bodyguard's bushy eyebrows drew together in an expression of concern. "I don't like leavin' you alone."

"I don't think I'm in any danger from Mei Lee, do you?" Jean shot a predatory grin in my direction. "Though the opposite might not be true."

"Okay. See you tomorrow then."

"Not before ten. Unless you have to be somewhere, Mei Lee?"

"No—I've cleared my calendar for the next twenty-four hours." Wiggling my hips in the most flagrant manner possible, I sauntered into the vast living room.

His breath hitched. I knew his eyes were glued to my bottom. Plumping myself down onto a white plush couch, I crossed one leg over the other again to show off my garters. "When it comes to pleasure, I don't like to be rushed."

I patted my wind-swept hair back into place, licked my scarlet-painted lips and fluttered my eyelashes. I felt like some overdone femme fatale in a forties movie.

Le Requin responded, though, exactly as I'd hoped. After hustling Bruno out of the apartment, he flipped the bolt to lock the door. Then he dragged me up from the sofa and into his arms.

"*Eh bien*. How about that appetizer?" He nibbled my ear lobe. "I'm starving."

His mouth locked to mine, demanding my surrender just as he had on the grandstand. I had to encourage him. For the moment, I gave him everything he wanted, wrapping my arms around his neck and sinking against his solid chest. He'd opened the top three buttons, enough to expose the red-brown hair scattered over his pectorals. He hadn't changed clothes since the races. Now the funky, masculine scent of his sweat overwhelmed the dwindling traces of his cologne — a scent that was dangerously familiar.

I struggled against my autonomic reactions, reminding myself that this man wasn't Etienne, no matter how similar he looked. Jean was a vicious criminal who wouldn't hesitate to kill me if he knew who I really was or why I was there.

One of his hands crept up my thigh to the bare skin above my stocking tops. The other fiddled with the zipper that ran up my spine. I felt a finger prodding at the satin of my undergarment.

I slid away from his lips and pushed myself back from his taut body. "Slow down, stud," I purred, letting my voice drip with lust. "I told you, I don't like to be rushed."

He grabbed at my arm, but I twirled away, laughing.

"Damn it, Mei Lee! I've been waiting all day!"

"And you can't wait a bit longer, *cher*? I do so want to impress you with my cooking. And I suspect that if I let you continue with what you've been doing, dinner will never happen. Wouldn't that be a waste?"

"If you *let* me continue?" Jean's face darkened.

I recognized the cold cruelty I'd seen in his mug shots. A chill skittered down my spine.

"I want you, woman. What's to stop me from simply taking you?"

"That would certainly ruin what's promising to be a lovely friendship…" I worked to keep my voice light, level, flirtatious. Reaching behind my back, I located the zipper tab. This wasn't the easiest maneuver but I'd practiced it in my hotel room. I eased the zipper down while I continued to soothe him. "Don't you know that building erotic tension can lead to far more pleasure, when it's finally released?"

Fists clenched by his sides, apparently torn between force and reason, Le Requin glared at me. "I don't give a shit about erotic tension. I just want to fuck you."

"Oh? You had me believing you a great lover. I guess I was mistaken." With an exaggerated sigh, I turned my back to him and slipped the dress off my shoulders. The crepe slithered down my body and pooled at my feet, revealing the satin and mesh costume I'd bought from Madame Mirasolle.

I didn't need to see him to gauge his reaction. His low moan was a dead giveaway. The jet black satin thong disappearing between the pale moons of my ass cheeks looked wicked as sin. I knew — I'd checked in the mirror when I'd put it on.

His mood shifted from anger to desperation. "*Merde*! Please, Mei Lee, have pity." Sidling up behind me, he rested his palms on my shoulders and pulled me back against his chest. "I'm so hard it hurts." He ground his massive erection into the crevice of my butt.

Given the evidence, I believed him.

I swiveled to face him — and to give him an eyeful of my plump nipples, distending the mesh panels that enclosed my breasts. I cupped his swollen cock. It jumped against my palm. "Be patient. I'll make it worth your while, I swear."

Standing on tiptoe, I brushed my lips over his, grazing my nipples against his shirt at the same time. I didn't want him. However, I was excited at being the object of his lust. Despite the danger, I was getting a charge out of teasing him. It was so easy to lead a man like Jean around by his cock.

"Let's play it this way. I'll make dinner—dressed like this. You can watch. You can undress if you want, even stroke your cock. Just don't come, okay? Save it for dessert, baby. Save it for me."

I gave his cock a quick squeeze. He groaned in answer. Without waiting for his explicit assent, I sashayed into the open kitchen and began my preparations.

I peeled garlic, slivered almonds, grated cheese, chopped vegetables, boiled potatoes, sliced the raw tuna and smothered it in marinade. After melting a generous tablespoon of unsalted butter, I sautéed the garlic and herbs, stirring in a splash of sauvignon blanc.

"Want some?" I held up the bottle.

The Shark shook his head. He'd stripped, as I'd suggested, and planted himself in a chair a few meters from the kitchen, on the opposite side of the breakfast bar. He fondled his swollen cock in a desultory fashion, while he watched my every move.

Jean's cock bore an uncanny resemblance to Etienne's. The rosy head gleamed with moisture. The pale skin sheathing the shaft looked smooth and soft as velvet. Saliva filled my mouth as I recalled sucking Etienne.

I poured myself some wine and drank deep to wash away the tempting memory. Normally I preferred reds, but this vintage was excellent, crisp and fruity with a hint of lemon.

"Mmm. Lovely." I stepped around the bar and pranced up to him. Standing between his splayed legs, I pulled him into a brief, juicy kiss. "Don't you agree?"

His cockhead rubbed over my satin-cased torso, streaking me with pre-cum. Before he could grab me, I scampered away, back behind the counter.

"You're playing a dangerous game, girly!"

His growl sent my pulse into overdrive. He had no idea how truly he'd spoken. I remembered where I was — and why. This was not about my playing the vamp. This was about finding the dope and ransoming my lovers. One slip might mean Harry's life.

I sipped at the sauvignon to disguise my nervousness. "But it's so much fun," I simpered, when I'd regained my self-possession. "Isn't it?"

"You have a strange notion of fun. This is torture."

"Delicious torture. Just hold on for a while longer, Jean darling. Dinner's almost ready. That will distract you."

"I doubt it," he grumbled, but he settled back into his chair anyway.

I was rather astonished by his compliance. Maybe he really liked me and wanted to make me happy. Maybe under that bossy surface he had a streak of submissiveness, like his double.

I'd tossed the greens and scattered them with the black olives, potato cubes and seared tuna. The pilaf was steaming. The scallops lay in neat rows in the Pyrex baking dish, drenched in the buttery herb sauce, sprinkled with Parmesan and bits of *chèvre*. Ten minutes under the broiler and they'd be ready.

Now came the riskiest moment. I emerged from the kitchen and, giving the naked owner of the condo a wide berth, headed for the table where I'd dropped my purse. I brought it into the kitchen and extracted my phone.

"Got to check the recipe," I told Jean. "Meanwhile you could make yourself useful by setting the table."

"Make myself useful? Just wait till I get my hands on you, Mei Lee Wong...!"

"I'm looking forward to it." I gave him my most lascivious smile. "And I really appreciate your restraint, baby."

"I'll show you restraint..." he muttered. Still, miraculously, he followed my instructions, pulling placemats, silverware and wine glasses out of various cabinets and drawers and setting them on the table to the right of the kitchen.

As soon as I was sure he was looking the other way, I slipped my hand back into my bag and located the little bottle of white powder Toni had given me. A harmless, fast acting barbiturate, she'd told me, tasteless and without side effects. A quarter teaspoon should be enough to knock a man out for four to six hours.

I prayed that would be enough time for me to find the opium.

Chapter Nineteen

"God, that was delicious!" Jean leaned back in his chair and drained the last of his wine.

"Didn't I tell you I was a great cook?"

"You're a culinary genius, Mei Lee. Best meal I've had in— Well, I can't remember when I've had better. True ambrosia." He picked up my hand from the table and nuzzled my palm. "Thank you."

"My pleasure." I searched his face, seeking signs of sleepiness. Were his eyelids drooping, just a bit? "How do you feel?"

"Full. Completely sated. At least as far as food is concerned." He rose from his chair and stretched, letting me admire his trim, muscular body. "I have other hungers, though, that need to be satisfied. And you've made me wait long enough."

His cock reared up from the reddish tangle in his crotch, urgent as ever. His steel-blue eyes glittered in the flickering candles, hard as diamonds. He appeared to be totally alert, and definitely horny.

Oh dear. Had I misunderstood the dosage? Had some ingredient in the scallops neutralized the drug's effect? My mind flew back to the disastrous consequences the last time I'd tried to spike someone's food with a psychoactive agent. Well, maybe disastrous was too strong, but certainly not what I'd planned. I couldn't afford a mistake tonight. I sent a little petition winging toward the Wise Ones, for better fortune this time.

"Into the bedroom, girl. I can't wait to peel that slutty get-up off you and see what's underneath."

"Mmm. Sounds like fun..." I began to gather the plates. "Just let me do the dishes first."

"No!"

I jumped at his shout. The china crashed to the floor, scattering greasy shards in a semi-circle around me. "Now look what you made me do, Jean."

"I don't give a fuck. Get your ass into the bedroom, you wretched little cock-tease..."

"No, please, let me..."

"No way, baby! Your ass is mine. I've earned it."

He lunged at me, arms outstretched. I dodged away, into the kitchen, putting the bar between us. With grace and strength that stunned me, he vaulted the bar.

Just at that moment, my phone rang. I tried to grab it, but Le Requin snatched it from the counter and flung it against the wall. The case flew apart, the battery flying in one direction, the rest of the device in another.

"Jean! That cost me a small fortune!"

"Tough titties. It's your own fault."

"No! Get away from me!"

He backed me into a corner. "You're going to be very sorry you teased me."

I shrank against the refrigerator. "No...please..."

He spread his legs and planted his arms on either side of my head, trapping me. "I'm going to fuck you till you scream for mercy, baby. And then I'm going to fuck you some more."

He leaned in, pressing his hard body against me. I could scarcely breathe. The stainless steel surface of the fridge was cold against my bare back. His massive cock rooted blindly between my thighs. I shrank away from him. I'd teased the tiger. Now I was paying for my foolish audacity.

His mouth sought mine. Without thinking, I turned my head, trying to avoid those fierce lips of his. Seizing my chin, digging his fingers into my flesh, he jerked me back to face him.

"Take it, slut!" He drove his tongue into my mouth. One hand reached between us to tear away the satin triangle that guarded my pussy. His cockhead slid across my lower lips.

Fight him. I heard the voice in my head. Harry's voice? My gran's? My hands were still free. I groped for his eyes, raked my short fingernails down one of his cheeks.

With an animal bellow, he snatched my hand from his face and slammed my wrist against the refrigerator. Grabbing the other wrist, he held it in a grip of iron while he continued his attempts to impale me.

I flailed and squirmed. I wouldn't give in. A Dragon would never surrender. He'd have to knock me out if he wanted to fuck me.

I tried to bring my knee up. Before I could connect with his balls, he whipped me around and pushed me against the unyielding steel surface. The impact left me dazed.

"You want to play rough, girly? I'll show you rough!" He tugged at the thin strip of fabric in the back of my costume. It gave way like paper.

Pinned by his weight, my hands immobilized, I was helpless. The Shark was too strong. Despair washed over me. I held my breath, waiting for him to take what I'd so rashly promised. Knowing that all was lost — my life, Harry's, Etienne's...

Instead, his body went limp. Suddenly, without warning, he slumped to the kitchen floor in a heap. I sucked in a lungful of air and coughed until tears ran down my cheeks. He didn't stir.

Finally, my fit passed. Blinking the moisture from my eyes, I stared down at Jean Le Requin, lying loose and relaxed next to my fuck-me shoes. His eyes were closed. His lips were parted. His features had taken on a boyish cast, almost innocent. His sculpted chest rose and fell in a gentle, even rhythm. Even his cock had subsided. It lay against his thigh, a fleshy cylinder leaking residual pre-cum into the auburn fur that dusted his limbs.

He looked harmless.

I knew better.

* * * *

Four hours. That was how long I had to find the drugs and get away — if the shipment was here at all. Uncertainty seized me. How did I know he'd keep the opium in the condo? Toni had said he owned property all over France. Indeed, would a thief keep stolen property at his residence, where it could incriminate him? Maybe he had some secret hideout where he stashed his loot.

I hadn't worked out any plan beyond this point. Well, I'd just have to improvise. I was usually good at that.

We had reason to believe the Iron Hammer people were in Marseille. That's where the tip from Toni's informant, months ago, had indicated the drugs would be delivered. There was a strong probability that Le Requin had ripped them off in that city. After all, that's where the Triad had grabbed Etienne. They'd been expecting The Shark to be in Marseille. Starting from Marseille, Nice was Jean's closest base, a natural place for him to bolt to.

Assuming the drugs *were* here, though, where would he hide them? How much space would twenty kilos of raw opium require? Too big for a normal safe, I guessed. So I should be looking for a cabinet, or a closet, or maybe some clever hideaway built into the wall or under the floor...

Stepping carefully over Jean's inert form, I returned to the enormous living-dining room and glanced around. The furniture was minimalist modern. No bookshelves or other storage lined the plain, cream-colored walls. To my left, a vast expanse of glass, three meters high, looked out toward the Mediterranean, offering, as he'd promised, a breathtaking view.

I didn't have time to admire that now. This room occupied the entire lower floor of the condo, aside from the kitchen, a pantry and a bathroom. I didn't dare search the kitchen cabinets—the chance of bumping into The Shark and waking him was too great. However, I thought it was unlikely he'd cache the drugs in such an accessible location.

I surveyed the food storage room. It was all open shelves and wire baskets. Methodically, working from left to right, I checked the contents of each. I found thousand dollar bottles of wine, at least ten kilos of imported Italian espresso and an entire shelf full of caviar, but unless he'd emptied a dozen tins of Scottish shortbread cookies, filled them with dope, and resealed them, the opium wasn't in the pantry.

With just a freestanding black porcelain sink and sleek matching toilet, the bathroom took no more than a couple of minutes. Before I headed up the spiral staircase in the corner to search the second floor, I checked on Jean.

Sleeping like a baby. As I gazed on his physical perfection, his somnolent cock twitched and swelled a bit. Maybe he was dreaming about me.

Upstairs, the condo held two huge bedrooms, each with an en-suite bath, and what looked like an office. Every room offered a magnificent ocean view. However, there were no paintings or other wall hangings that might conceal a safe. Wall-to-wall shag carpet covered the floors. It seemed to me that would make under floor storage too obvious to be useful.

Fortunately, Le Requin's spartan taste in furnishings held up here as well. A gigantic bed, easily the size of two normal kings, occupied the larger bedroom. I searched the drawers in the tables flanking it. In the left one, I discovered gold-plated nipple clamps—really, talk about conspicuous consumption!—mink-lined leather cuffs, a neat little flogger, a top-of-the-line bullet vibe, and four boxes of condoms.

Definitely not a submissive.

In the table on the other side, I found a revolver.

The air in the condo was comfortably warm. My shiver was not due to my state of undress. I've never been comfortable with guns, unlike some members of my family.

Take the gun. You might need it.

Where had that idea come from? I didn't want to touch the thing. I was a terrible shot. In any case, attired as I was in the remnants of Madame Mirasolle's kinky satin costume, I had no way to carry it.

I shut the drawer and moved to search the walk-in closet, finding only more confirmation that Jean had expensive tastes. The bathroom and the other bedroom also yielded nothing of interest.

My spirits sank lower with each failure. If the drugs weren't here, what then?

A Dali-esque clock on the office wall told me it was almost eleven. Barely an hour had elapsed since Le Requin passed out. I still had time to do a careful search.

The L-shaped teakwood desk that was the room's main feature had half a dozen drawers, but none were locked, and none contained anything unusual. Could there be a secret compartment? Using a ruler I found among the stationery supplies, I measured the outside and inside dimensions. There might be a small discrepancy, but certainly not enough room to store what I was seeking.

The top drawer of the half-height filing cabinet, also unlocked, yielded folders packed with contracts, invoices and receipts. Carefully sorted and labeled clippings from wine and restaurant reviews occupied the bottom drawer.

I sank into the fancy ergonomic chair behind the desk and gazed down at the glittering ribbon of the Grande Corniche, defeated and despairing. The Shark must have stashed the goods elsewhere. Now what?

Get out. But how? I'd need my clothes, still on the floor downstairs. And given our remote location, I'd either have to find the keys to Jean's Jaguar, or call a taxi.

Oh, merde! I recalled my shattered phone, victim of Le Requin's violence. If I reassembled it, would it still work? That meant going back to the kitchen. Did I dare risk waking the slumbering gangster?

I had no choice. Toni would be frantic, too, seeing the signal from me had gone dead. I had to get in touch, as soon as possible.

Making a decision to leave helped improve my mood. New energy surged through me. I'd get back to Marseille and come up with some other plan. Perhaps I could make the Iron Hammer believe I had the goods, even if I didn't. I thrust the chair back from the desk, ready to descend, dress, grab my mobile and get the hell out.

The leather-and-stainless-steel chair hitched a bit underneath me, as though the wheels had caught on some minor discontinuity. Focused on my next steps, I almost didn't notice. Everything else in the luxury condo seemed so smooth and well-crafted, though, that an irregularity in the carpet struck me as strange.

I rolled back toward the desk. There it was again, just the smallest bump transmitting itself to my naked rear.

I dropped to my knees on the furry carpet, pushing the chair out of the way. Where was it? I couldn't see anything, but as I ran my palm back and forth across the stretch where the chair would normally reside, I felt the cold touch of metal. A bit of groping and I discovered a steel ring about an inch in diameter, flush with the floor but hinged so that it could be pulled upright.

Yes! A sense of triumph swept through me. Hooking my forefinger through the metal loop, I tugged. As I'd expected, a section of the floor swung up, also hinged, with the carpeting still attached. It was too dark under the desk for me to see much, but obviously the panel concealed a fairly large space under the floor.

I'd been right all along! Harry and Etienne would be free soon. A tiny shimmer of lust illumined me as I imagined our reunion. All I had to do was grab the dope and hand it over to the Triad.

I reached down into the cubbyhole—it was at least half a meter deep, easily large enough to hold a package of the size I imagined. I was surprised to find myself touching the bottom surface. Where were the drugs? I felt around, skimming my fingers along the walls of the compartment and across the bottom. Nothing.

I couldn't believe it. The opium had to be there. It must simply be smaller than I'd envisioned. I needed some light. I remembered I'd seen an LCD flashlight in one of the desk drawers. Just the thing...

As I started to rise, pain exploded at the back of my skull. Multi-colored stars streaked around me. My first thought was that I'd clumsily bumped my head on the desk. The world went black before I had time for a second.

Chapter Twenty

Fog blurred everything around me. In the distance, I heard a deep moan — a foghorn? Was I on a boat somewhere? I didn't sense any rocking of waves but my stomach definitely felt queasy. The back of my head throbbed, but that seemed far away too. The pain barely made an impression.

How had I gotten here? I had no recollection. My eyes felt glued shut. I didn't want to open them anyway. That would have taken far too much effort. The fog seeped underneath the lids, coloring my world a comfortable gray.

A lock of hair tickled my nose. I tried to ignore the annoying sensation, but at last I had to take action. I raised my hand to brush the errant strands back into position.

Nothing happened.

The sudden understanding that I was bound snapped me into full consciousness. At the same instant, pain exploded in the back of my skull. A hundred suns clicked into being and the fog turned a fiery red. Agony blazed behind my eyes

"Ow! Turn that damn light off!" In my urgency, I slipped into Cantonese.

"What?"

"*La lumière — éteignezla lumière, s'il vous plait.*" I blinked against the glare. Le Requin had the goose-necked desk lamp aimed directly at my face.

"Just trying to wake you up, baby. You've been out for almost half an hour." He leaned in, close enough that I could smell the wine on his breath and see the ice in his gaze. A long, vicious-looking blade flashed by, a few centimeters from my face. "I was starting to think I'd have to do something — extreme — to get a rise out of you."

The gangster spoke with casual cruelty, but he did divert the light enough to let me fully open my eyes. A spike of adrenaline scattered the last shreds of my mental confusion. I kept my mouth shut, not wanting to provoke him, while trying to assess my condition.

I was in the rolling chair, which had been turned so that my back faced the angle of the desk. My wrists were fastened to the chair arms with leather cuffs I recognized from my search of Jean's bedroom. Plain, old rope looped around my ankles, affixing them to opposite spokes on the base, so that my thighs were parted. The fur lining of the cuffs reduced the chafing but there was nothing even remotely arousing about this bondage. I was helpless, at the mercy of a desperate criminal who wouldn't hesitate to hurt me in order to get what he wanted.

But what did he want? Although he was still nude, he was only partially erect. At the moment, his mind was not on sex.

"I should have figured it out a lot sooner." He pricked my cheek, just a tiny sting.

When I shrank away, he released an ominous chuckle. "But I was thinking with my dick. Pretty little China pussy, dancing around, leading me on. Flashing those sweet tits of yours and promising me heaven."

He held the knife poised at my throat. I stopped breathing. He ran the tip down along my breastbone, into the valley between my breasts. I couldn't stop myself from shuddering.

"Better hold still, girly." One flick of his wrist and he'd severed the satin panel between the mesh cups. "Wouldn't want my hand to slip." Easing the knife under the left cup, he hooked into the stretchy material and peeled it down to reveal my naked breast. "It would be a shame if I were to cut off one of those juicy nipples." He laid the flat of the blade against the areola. Despite my terror, the flesh tightened from chill.

"Anyway, I can fuck you later—at my leisure." To my vast relief, he straightened up, moving the knife somewhat farther from my skin. "Right now, you're going to tell me why you're here."

"You invited me," I replied, trying to buy some time. How much should I tell him? Given my current situation, was there any benefit in lying?

"Don't bullshit me. You're working for the chinks, right? Those fucking Triad morons? They looking for revenge or something?"

"No, no." I swallowed the lump that was threatening to strangle me. "Nothing like that."

"I heard you speaking Chinese."

"I'm from Hong Kong—you know that. Chinese is my native language."

"So the Iron Hammer didn't send you? You expect me to believe that?" He waved his knife in front of my face. "Try again, girly."

I took a deep breath then released it slowly. I couldn't see any reason not to tell the truth.

"They didn't exactly send me. But I *am* here to recover the opium you stole from them."

The Shark barked out a laugh. "Hah! That's long gone. I had an eager customer lined up even before I nicked the drugs from under their noses. Turned the goods around the very same day."

"Oh, no!" A sob crept into my voice, much to my chagrin, and my eyes brimmed with tears.

Le Requin peered at me with a mix of surprise and suspicion. "What's wrong? Why'd a sweet piece like you want the dope anyway?"

"To use as ransom. They're holding my lovers hostage."

"Lovers? Plural? You're even more of a slut than you look." He gave me a slow once over that would have had me blushing beet red under other circumstances.

I ignored his leer to continue my tale. "If I don't get the drugs back, the Triad will kill them both."

"Hmm. You're in quite a pickle, aren't you, *cherie*? But I'm confused. How did your lovers end up in the hands of the Iron Hammer in the first place? Are they members of a rival gang or something?"

"Nothing like that. One's a chef. The other's a TV producer."

"Huh? Then why should the Iron Hammer care about them?"

"The Hammer thought that one of them was you."

"What? This is getting more and more interesting." He placed the knife on the desk and folded his arms across his muscled chest. "Tell me more."

"We were having dinner at some North African place in Marseille, two nights ago. When we left the restaurant, four thugs drove up in a van and snatched the two men. I had no idea what was going on until I saw your picture. You look almost exactly like Etienne — the chef."

"Really? I don't believe it. Got a photo?"

"On my phone," I responded through gritted teeth. "The one you smashed."

"Ah, it's probably okay. I've got to see this. Another guy, as good-looking as me? *Incroyable!*"

He loped off, leaving me to squirm against my bonds and wonder if I could turn his curiosity into sympathy.

In less than a minute he was back, holding up my phone, which indeed appeared to have survived. "What's the touch pattern to unlock the screen?"

"Untie me and I'll show you."

"Hmm. I don't think I should trust you, after you fed me those knock out drops."

"Hey, I could have poisoned you, right? I just wanted time to search for the opium." I adopted an expression of utmost sincerity. "Look, Jean. I'm right handed. Undo just the left. What can I do to you, strapped to the chair like I am?"

"Okay, okay." He hiked himself up onto the desk and reached behind me, then brandished a gun — probably the same one I'd seen in his bedroom, and very likely the one responsible for my splitting headache. "Try anything funny and I swear, I won't hesitate to shoot you."

He leaned down to fiddle with the left cuff. It sprang open. I clenched and released my fist, trying to get the blood flowing.

"Unlock it." He held up the device so that I could punch in the code. "Let's see this imposter."

With some degree of awkwardness, I flicked through my gallery until I found a shot of Etienne that

I'd taken that day on Montmatre. He looked more relaxed than usual, his hair a bit mussed and a big grin on his kissable mouth. "Here. Quite a resemblance, don't you think?"

The Shark stared at the screen as though he was hypnotized. He let out his breath in a long hiss. "*Sacre bleu!* It's Jet! It has to be."

"Jet?"

"My cousin, Jet. Haven't seen or heard from him in decades. What did you say this guy's name was?"

"Etienne. Etienne Duvalier."

My captor let out a bleak chuckle. "He used to be Etienne Dunant. I guess he didn't want to be associated with his old mates. Wanted to turn over a new leaf and all that."

"So you and Etienne—you're related?" That could certainly explain their uncanny similarity, right down to the level of the way they smelled.

Jean paced back and forth in front of me, waving the gun as he spoke. "Our fathers were brothers. Jet's dad died when he was just a kid. Mine ran off with his secretary. Jet and me…we were tight. We got into a lot of trouble together. Ran with a gang of Algerians from Marseille. Nothing serious, petty theft mostly, lots of drinking and drugs. Jet was the leader—he's a year older than me. I really looked up to him. Then one night we robbed a liquor store, and I got caught. The rest of the gang managed to escape."

I recalled Etienne's comments about his teen years, the night he'd been snatched. He hadn't mentioned a cousin.

"By the time I got out of jail, Jet was gone. His mother had sold their house in St Rémy. Nobody knew where she'd moved her wayward son. 'Away from bad influences', they'd whisper. They meant me."

I heard pain in Jean's voice, and regret. Could I use that?

"I'll bet he'd love to see you now," I began, cautious, feeling my way through his emotions.

"Oh, you think so? I doubt it." He sounded so bitter. Despite the fact that he'd almost raped me then knocked me unconscious, I almost felt sorry for him.

He halted his restless progress to stare at my bound, skimpily clad form. "So you're fucking my cousin Jet?"

"Etienne and I have been in a – um – relationship for a couple of months."

"No wonder you seemed so turned on by me."

He'd really bought my act. Amazing.

"I'll bet I remind you of him, don't I?"

"Um – yes – to some extent."

"But he's not as much of an animal as I am, right?"

Something compelled my honesty. "Right," I murmured, dropping my eyes.

He wanted me. I heard it in his voice, felt it in the air. The hard shaft poking up from his groin only confirmed what I already knew.

"And I never had a chance with you, did I?"

He bent to me, his lips gentle and questing against mine. I didn't have the heart to turn away – or to answer.

"Freeze, scum! Don't move or I'll blow a hole in your head as big as the Channel Tunnel!"

Holding a gun twice the size of Jean's in both hands, Toni strode into the room. "Drop the piece. That's right. Now back away from her, slowly. Good boy. Give me those wrists now. You know the drill."

Still keeping the gun trained on Le Requin, she unhooked a pair of handcuffs from her belt and fastened the man's wrists together. "Now lie down on the floor, on your stomach."

"Just a fucking minute, lady..."

Toni whipped out her badge and waved it in front of his eyes. "I'm no lady. I'm an officer of the law, and you, sir, are in major trouble. Lie down if you want to keep that nice fat sausage of yours intact."

I didn't believe Toni would really shoot him, but he clearly didn't want to take the risk. He lowered himself to his knees then stretched his rangy body out on the fluffy carpet.

"Are you alright, Emily?" She crouched to pick up Jean's weapon then tucked it into her waistband with her own. With one eye on The Shark, she busied herself with my bonds. In mere seconds I was free. "Did this bastard hurt you?"

I palpated the swelling at the back of my head. "He gave me quite a wallop, but I'll survive." I tried to stand and discovered I was a bit woozy. "I could probably use some aspirin or something."

"I'll get you some in a minute. What happened?"

"Well, everything went like clockwork—more or less—except that he woke up two hours early."

"It's all the drugs I did as a teenager." Le Requin's voice came from below, a bit muffled by the rug. "Raised my resistance."

"Nobody asked you," Toni returned her attention to me. "So did you find the opium?"

"It's gone. He said he sold it right away."

"Oh, *merde*! All of this was for nothing?" She sighed. "When the tracker went offline, I knew something must be wrong. I jumped in my car and headed for the last position I'd recorded. This isn't the address we have in our records, though."

"Just bought the place a year ago," The Shark commented. "Got to keep you cops on your toes."

"I told you to shut your trap, Dunant."

"Anyway, I'm really fine, Toni. Actually, Monsieur Dunant and I were just having a fascinating conversation. It seems that he and Etienne are related — first cousins, in fact."

"Well, that explains a lot." She seated herself on the edge of desk, where Le Requin had perched only a few minutes before. "But without the drugs, how are we going to spring them?"

"I can help." Jean wasn't very good at following orders, was he? So unlike his cousin. "I can take you to the chinks' hideout. That's where they're probably holding your men."

"Oh, really?" Sliding off the desk, Toni went over and nudged the recumbent man with the tip of her boot. "Turn over so we can hear you better."

Jean rolled onto his back, his cuffed hands crossed over his flat belly. "Can I sit up, so we can talk face to face?"

"I guess so. Don't try anything funny, though."

The handsome gangster drew his knees to his chest and managed to prop himself against the wall. "Let's make a deal. I'll lead you to the Triad people. Arrest them, kill them — I don't really care. I just want them out of my territory. I'll help you free my poor cousin and Mei Lee's other squeeze. In return, you let me walk free."

"Are you kidding? Police officers don't make deals with criminals."

"I don't think you're here in your official capacity — Toni, isn't it?" He flashed her a smile drenched with charm. "I suspect your superiors would take a dim view of your encouraging Mei Lee here to drug a man and ransack his house."

"Not just any man—one of the most wanted men in France."

"You don't have anything on me. I'm clean."

"How about Battery? Kidnapping? Attempted Rape?" Toni had obviously noticed the damage to my costume.

"Only if the alleged victim presses charges. And she's not going to do that. Are you, Mei Lee?"

I searched his face. "Can we really trust you?"

"At the moment, our interests are aligned. I want to drive the Iron Hammer out of France. You want your fuck-buddies back. I propose that we join forces to achieve both those goals."

I turned back to my formidable friend. "It might be our only hope, Toni."

She frowned. "I don't know. We could pretend you have the drugs, to lure them out…"

"That's what we'll do anyway," Le Requin interrupted. "You'll set up a rendezvous, to deliver the goods. I can put together a fake package that will fool them for a while."

"Will they fall for that?"

"I have some ideas that will give you some leverage. Buy you some time. You'll insist they either bring the hostages to you—which they won't do, I guarantee—or take you to their place. I'll be waiting at the hideout, ready to pounce."

"But there's only three of us—" I began.

"Four. Bruno will come too."

"Okay, four, whatever. It's not enough, Jean. I saw four guys at the kidnapping and I have a feeling from talking to Harry when they let him phone, that there are at least a few more. We're badly outnumbered, especially when you consider that I've never attacked anything more threatening than a leg of lamb."

Jean Le Requin's face lit up in a nasty grin. "Ah, Mei Lee. But you speak Chinese. You *think* Chinese. You're our secret weapon."

Chapter Twenty-One

Toni decided that the three of us should spend the night at The Shark's condo. She shackled Jean to his bed with one of his own bondage devices—just to be sure he didn't have 'a change of heart', as she'd put it. From the quick work she'd made of the process, I had the feeling she knew her way around a dungeon. My attempts at restraining Etienne had never been so competent.

"What if I need to take a piss?" he complained.

She handed him the empty wine bottle from dinner.

"Oh come on! My dick won't fit in through that little opening!"

Toni gave him a sweet smile. "Oh? You think you're that big? Guess you'll have to hold it till morning then."

"Bitch."

"Sleep tight, Jean." She shut the door and locked it from the outside.

We retired to the other bedroom.

"Don't you think you were a bit hard on him?" I asked, wriggling out of the remnants of my costume and donning a Yves St. Laurent dress shirt I found hanging in the closet. After swallowing a couple of aspirin, I collapsed onto the bed. I was too tired to stand up any longer. A shower would have to wait until morning.

"That's the kind of treatment guys like him understand." She'd stripped to her bra and panties, both sensible cotton that provided full coverage, though they hugged her curves. "He wouldn't respect me if I showed any sort of sympathy."

She flopped down next to me and enjoyed a long, luxurious stretch. "Have to admit, I'm pretty destroyed. Talk about stress! When your phone went dead — well, I pictured the worst."

"He's not so bad," I replied, recalling his wistful tone as he'd recounted the tales of his youth. "He actually treated me pretty well."

"Up until the point he tried to rape you, you mean?"

"Well, he was frustrated... I'd pretty much promised to screw him then backed out."

"Emily, get real. He may look like your friend Etienne, but he's a different sort of person all together. I don't trust him, not one bit."

"But you agreed to cooperate with him."

"Out of necessity, girl. For your sake."

I glanced over at Toni. She lay on her side, her jaw propped up in her palm, watching me. Her predatory expression didn't differ all that much from what I'd seen in Jean's eyes earlier.

Toni noticed my faint shudder.

"Don't worry, Emily. I won't touch you. You've made your inclinations — or lack thereof — quite clear."

Now I blushed. "I'm so sorry. I like you a lot, I really do. Just not...like that. Women don't do anything for me, sexually."

"You never know until you've tried, hon..." She chuckled at my obvious alarm. "Just kidding. You're as safe with me as you'd be with Mother Theresa. Get some sleep. You look like you need it."

She was right. I could barely keep my eyes open. I pulled the sheet up over my aching body and snuggled into the fluffy down pillow.

"Thanks, Toni," I mumbled. "Thanks for everything."

Sleep descended so quickly I didn't even hear her response.

* * * *

Jean's mood the next morning was surprisingly cheerful. While I foraged in the kitchen for breakfast—poached eggs with leftover tuna, apple slices sprinkled with crushed almonds, toasted baguette with a bit of caviar, and a big pot of French roast coffee—our new ally was rummaging in a storage closet just inside the condo entrance, that I'd somehow missed during my search the night before.

He emerged with a coil of electrical wire and some other bits of electronics, plus a silvery Samsonite suitcase on wheels, a bit bigger than a typical carry on.

"What's that for?" Toni inquired. She sat at the dining table, intent on cleaning her gun. Her handcuffs lay next to the gun parts, conspicuously available.

"You'll see." The Shark flashed her a grin. "Do you have to do that before breakfast, by the way? Kind of turns my stomach."

"My apologies." Toni sounded less than sincere. "In my business, I've got to be ready for anything." She clicked the magazine back into the handle, twirled the revolver around her finger then stuck it into her shoulder holster. "But I'm done for now." She did not remove the cuffs from view.

"My business, too." He seated himself in the same spot he'd occupied the previous night. "Look, Toni, you don't have to worry about me. I'm on your side in this thing."

"I'm not worried. Just well prepared."

"Stop bickering and eat." I set full plates in front of each of them.

"Mmm. Smells wonderful," Toni gushed.

Jean dove in without any commentary but with obvious appreciation. I might not be able to tell one end of a gun from the other, but when it comes to cooking, I know what I'm doing. Occasionally that comes in handy.

After cleaning up—Toni made Jean do most of the work—I dialed the number the Triad boss had given me and left a brief message in Mandarin. In less than ten minutes, he returned my call.

"*Huay.*"

"*Huay.* Do I understand correctly that you have recovered our property from the French thief?"

"Yes, esteemed uncle. I will deliver it to you as soon as you free the barbarians."

A cynical chuckle came from the other end of the line. "Please, young lady! Do you think we are fools? We will release the hostages, but only after the goods are in our hands."

"Once you have your property, you will have no incentive to let my friends go. It would be far easier for you to dispose of them in some other way."

"We could do that in any case."

"And I could keep the goods myself. I have made some inquiries, uncle. This package of yours is extremely valuable. It might even be worth sacrificing the lives of my associates."

A moment of silence. I held my breath, waiting for his response. I knew that when you're bargaining, you've got to make your opponent believe you're ready to walk away.

"I was under the impression that these individuals were important to you."

"Everyone is expendable, under certain circumstances."

God, I could imagine Le Requin saying something like that. He was eyeing me with a combination of curiosity and lust. Was there any chance he understood Mandarin?

"You told me you were a 'private citizen'. Without the necessary contacts, you'd have difficulty turning our property into cash."

"I have connections, esteemed uncle, both here in France and in Asia. In fact, I already have a potential buyer."

Another pause. Would he call my bet?

"If you pass our property onto a third party, the situation could get very messy."

"I would venture the opinion that it is already messy. I am sure that the resources you are using to guard my associates could be better employed in more productive activities. Release the foreigners, take back your property and everyone will be satisfied."

"Why should we trust you?"

"Have you been bothered by the police since you seized my friends? I have kept my part of the agreement, uncle. Now you need to keep yours. Let us meet at some neutral location. I will bring your goods. You bring my friends. We will make the exchange and go our separate ways."

More silence. I had the feeling he was conferring with his henchmen.

"Do you know the Wang See Restaurant, on rue du Rimbau? North of the port?"

"I can find it."

"I will meet you there at five this evening. Come alone."

"With my bodyguard. I am sure you will understand my position."

"Very well, but no weapons."

"As you wish. And you will bring Mr Duvalier and Mr Sanborne with you."

"After I have confirmed you have our package, we will take you to them."

Should I push harder? On the other hand, if they brought us to the gang's headquarters, Jean and Bruno would get the chance to get in on the action.

"Until five this evening, uncle. I look forward to meeting you in person."

"The sentiment is mutual. I'm extremely curious about you, young miss. There are not many women who could take on The Shark."

I glanced over at Jean, who was fiddling away with wires and switches, under Toni's watchful eye.

"Quite true, uncle. Quite true."

* * * *

Overriding Jean's loud objections, we drove Toni's Peugeot back to Marseille. The policewoman was formidable, granted, but I still found it astonishing that the gangster followed her orders. What kind of hold did she have over him?

They dropped me at my hotel while they went to make some sort of mysterious preparations. I settled down in the coffee shop, with a *croque monsieur*, a cup of Earl Grey and the local newspapers. I found nothing about the abduction, much to my relief, but *Marseilles Matin* had a two page spread on the previous day's race. Mixed with photos of drivers and their flashy girlfriends, footballers, politicians, movie stars and the like, I discovered a picture of me posed in front of an ornate nineteenth century door, smiling and waving. I looked stylish and feminine, almost delicate. Fragile. Not at all someone one would expect to have dealings with the mob.

Of course, that wasn't exactly what I'd expected when I'd come to France.

It was barely two. Toni had promised to come fetch me at four-thirty. After the feverish activity of the last thirty-six hours, I wasn't sure what to do in the interim.

I glanced around. At this hour, I was the café's sole customer. One waiter hung out behind the bar, peering at his mobile and ignoring me.

All at once, I felt utterly alone.

Roger had called the Tastes of France team back to the States. No one knew how long it would be before Etienne and Harry were freed, and meanwhile, we didn't want one of the crew to let the secret slip. If the police decided to take another look at the case, the Triad might respond by cutting their losses — and their prisoners' throats.

We broadcast the official story that Etienne was in isolation due to complications from influenza. Apparently, the studio had been deluged with get well cards and messages of sympathy.

I'd stayed in France 'out of concern for my colleague', a tale that only confirmed the popular assumption that Etienne and I were a couple.

Meanwhile, Harry was such a low key presence—at least outside the bedroom—that nobody even seemed to realize he'd disappeared.

Nobody but me, that is. I hadn't had time think much about my Master since we'd spoken two days ago. Now it hit me, like a speeding train with failed brakes—sharp fear and terrible need. My beloved, rumpled, horny, bossy Harry! There was some possibility I'd never see him again. That he, or I, might not get out of this alive.

My stomach lurched and a sour taste filtered up into my throat. This wasn't a game of Go. One false step and his life could be forfeit. I liked to imagine I was clever, some sort of woman of international intrigue, bargaining with the Iron Hammer as if I had the upper hand. But what did I have, really? Nothing. No drugs. No weapons. Nothing to offer in trade for Harry's life. Nothing I could use to protect him.

Hysteria built in my chest. Tears blurred my vision. I had to get out of here. I tossed a twenty onto the table and ran for the elevator before the storm burst.

Back in my room, the floodgates opened. I sobbed and wailed, face down on the bed, until the pillow was soaked with tears. A fit of hiccups seized me. My moan became a silly yelp with each rhythmic clench of my diaphragm.

'Get hold of yourself, girl.' I could almost hear my grandmother, scolding me. 'Crying won't help.'

Closing my swollen eyes, I breathed deeply, trying to will the spasms away, along with my despair. I needed a clear mind for what was to come. Fear would only muddle my thoughts and corrupt my judgment. Gradually my panic ebbed. I released it, grateful for my Dragon training.

I focused my thoughts back on my lover. Harry wouldn't want me to be upset. He'd tell me to relax, to let go, to trust myself and him. He'd take me in his arms and I'd know that all was well. New ease flowed through me as I remembered the magic he could work on my body and my spirit.

The hotel room held no trace of my lover's scent. He'd been snatched before we could consummate our nocturnal plans.

I tried to recall Harry's distinctive musk, without much success. The sense of smell is the one most intimately entwined with emotion, but also the most difficult to conceptualize or describe. I couldn't summon the sense of well-being I always found in breathing him in, burying my nose in his clothing or his body.

Touch, then. When it came to touching me, Harry was a virtuoso. His repertoire ranged from the most delicate brush of fingertip over flesh to fiery caresses as painful as they were thrilling. Whether by instinct or by observation, he knew exactly how much I wanted, and how much I could take.

Rolling onto my back, I let my fingers graze my jaw then sweep down my neck to the hollow of my throat. This was one of his favorite gestures — and mine — one that never failed to send delicious shivers straight to my sex. Sure enough, my clit started to tingle. With just my forefinger, I continued into the valley between my breasts. I circled to the right, caressing the sensitive underside through the T-shirt Jean had provided.

The soft fabric transmitted the delicious, barely-there sensation. Moisture leaked from my cleft, dampening the seam of my borrowed jeans.

My eyes still shut tight, I summoned memories of Harry's caresses. He'd go from gentle to intense in a breath, and so did I, seizing both nipples and pinching as hard as I could manage. Like turning the knob on a stove, this raised the heat level. My gluts tensed and my hips bucked. Meanwhile, my erect nipples throbbed, aching but craving more. I clamped down on them with even greater force, digging my fingernails into the swollen flesh. The first quivers of an orgasm stirred in my depths.

'You love it when it hurts.' I could hear Harry's warm, teasing voice in my mind. *'You're a natural sub. The more I torture you, the more you want.'*

But of course, Harry's ministrations weren't torture, they were bliss. Every slap or spank he inflicted upon me, every kiss of the whip, every brutal thrust of his cock, was edged with delight.

In my mind, he knelt between my spread legs, gloriously naked, stroking his substantial erection and grinning down at me with a heady mixture of lust and love. My pussy clenched around emptiness at the image, so vivid I could see the black hair that furred his powerful thighs and the pre-cum beading on the head of his cock. I needed him — needed him with me, on top of me, inside me.

I interrupted my fantasy just long enough to strip off the shirt and jeans. I was nude underneath. Pulling open the drawer of the bedside table, I retrieved a black velvet drawstring bag and extracted its contents. Harry had hidden it somewhere in his luggage and handed it to me with a triumphant grin the first night in Paris.

Though I was alone, I couldn't help blushing at the sight of the massive dildo. Fashioned of jet black silicon, it was nine inches long and a full two inches in diameter. Harry had insisted I buy it. He'd stood laughing in the background at the adult store while I'd stuttered and fumbled with my credit card, unable to meet the clerk's eyes.

"It will never fit," I'd protested, after I'd obeyed his order.

We'd strolled arm in arm down Market Street, my cheeks still hot with embarrassment. I'd felt as though every passerby knew what I carried in the plain brown paper bag.

"Oh, you're wrong, love. It will fit perfectly—not just in your pussy, but in your ass too."

He was right of course. If I was sufficiently aroused—and I was always that way, around Harry—it slid right in. The first time he'd commanded me to fuck myself with the obscene object, I'd had one of the most intense orgasms in my life. He hadn't inserted it into my anus yet—nor forced me to bugger myself—but I knew he would eventually.

How would that feel? My rear hole tightened at the mere thought of such an invasion.

Stretched out on the bed again, I feathered my hands over my bare breasts, across my belly and down to my cunt. The lips were slick and swollen under my fingertips. Spreading them with my left hand, I rubbed the toy over my inner folds, gathering wetness. My clit screamed for attention, but I held off, as I knew Harry would, building the tension. Instead, I eased the first inch or so of the artificial cock into my channel, pretending it was Harry's cock.

As always, going farther felt impossible. The silicone rod was too big, too hard. My poor, tight pussy could never accommodate such a bulk. Pain flickered through the haze of my arousal as my flesh protested. "I can't," I moaned out load.

'Of course you can. You will. For me.'

For Harry, I'd do anything. I released my labia, grabbed the dildo in both hands and pushed. A few more inches disappeared into my cleft. My thumb grazed my clit, triggering a bolt of pleasure that spiraled deep into my core. The pain faded, replaced by extreme sensations of fullness, sensations that pumped energy into my gathering climax.

'Fuck yourself. Ram it in.'

I drew my knees up that I could tilt my pelvis to a better angle. With all the force I possessed, I drove the phallus into my cunt. The tip hit my cervix. I gasped in sudden agony. Then pleasure welled up, drenching me and spilling over, washing away even the memory of discomfort.

I pulled the toy part way out then slammed it back in, using the same sort of rough, fast strokes Harry favored. *Incredible!* Of course, the lifeless hunk of silicone couldn't begin to match my lover's hot supple flesh, melding with my own.

But the sense of transgression was thrilling—the knowledge that I was fucking myself with a huge toy at the orders of my Master.

'Good girl.'

Eyes closed, I summoned my lover. I wanted the dildo to be Harry's cock, but stubbornly, I could only picture him watching, a delighted grin lighting his face.

'That's right, love. You keep working on your pussy. Meanwhile, I'm going to bury my cock in your ass.'

Oh, by the Wise Ones! He'd been threatening to take my rear hole for months. So far he'd done no more than talk, knowing how the notion both scared and thrilled me.

I thrust the dildo in and out with my left hand, my right toying with my clit. Just a week before we'd left for France, he'd drizzled massage oil down my crack and worked three fingers into my anus, fighting my resistant muscles. I'd thought I'd faint from the perverse pleasure of that intrusion. At the same time, I'd almost been ready to use my safe word. It was just too private, too embarrassing. I felt unbearably filthy—all the more so because I liked the feeling so very much.

But his cock—impossible—unbearable—unbelievably hot... I tried to imagine those sensations magnified several times. When I wrapped my hand around the dildo, my fingers barely met my thumb. Something that big, forced into my ass...?

I came suddenly and catastrophically, gushing around the dildo, thrashing on the bed, my pussy and rear hole both contracting in delicious spasms. As the knot of tight-wound tension unraveled, I had a clear image of Harry, snatching his cock from my ass with an obscene pop and spraying me with his cum. That sent me over the edge again.

As my heart rate returned to normal and my limbs relaxed, a sense of peace stole over me. Whatever the Fates decreed, I was ready—ready to give everything to save my love. Even, if necessary, my life.

Chapter Twenty-Two

By quarter past four I was in the hotel lobby, waiting for Toni. I wore a tailored silver-gray suit with a knee-length skirt and a black silk blouse, both far more conservative than my racing day outfit. I'd opted for flats. I might need to run.

I felt much calmer than before my fantasy interlude—a chilly calm with more than a hint of fatalism. 'You can't bargain with the gods', as Gran would say. I planted myself in an armchair with a view of both the door and the clock over the registration counter. The minutes crawled by so slowly that I wondered if that timepiece was defective.

When Toni finally appeared, I almost didn't recognize her. She'd slicked her hair back with some sort of gel. It clung to her skull in a masculine style that exposed her ears—one of which sported a diamond stud—and made her look even more formidable than usual. Dramatic makeup exaggerated the slight tilt to her eyes and gave her a Eurasian look. She'd exchanged the loose jeans and button-up shirt she'd worn earlier for form-fitting leggings and a long-sleeved turtle-necked top, both black. The sheen of the fabric suggested it was partly Spandex. Over the shirt, she'd donned a stiff black vest with several pockets. On her feet she wore thick-soled lace-up boots of black leather, polished to such a sheen that someone kneeling at her feet could have seen his reflection in the toes.

"Toni?" I rose to meet her. "What in the world...?"

"Hey, I'm supposed to be your body guard. I have to look the part."

Certainly, I wouldn't have wanted to tangle with her. The outfit showed off not only her curves but also her muscles. She looked like some manga character, a cross between Emma Peel and the Terminator.

"Let's go, Emily. I'm double parked."

Rue de Rimbeau was only two or three kilometers from the hotel, but with rush hour traffic, we made slow progress. We pulled up in front of the Wang See Restaurant with just a few minutes to spare. Toni managed to locate a parking space just down the block. Stepping out of the Peugeot, I started toward the building which, aside from a sign in Chinese characters, had the same stucco moldings and wrought iron balconies as its neighbors.

"Wait a sec." Unlocking the hatch back, she pulled out Le Requin's suitcase. She unwound a coil of wire from the handle. It terminated in a sort of metal cuff that she locked around her left wrist. Also attached was a cup-like device of rubber, which she placed on her middle finger. The other end of the wire disappeared through a hole drilled in the bag.

"What in the name of Kuan Yin is that?"

"Booby trap." She explained the system The Shark had rigged up to prevent the Iron Hammer from opening the case prematurely.

I shook my head. "They'll never buy it. We're supposed to be private citizens, not James Bond."

"They won't risk anything that might destroy the opium. That's their primary interest."

"I hope you're right."

A cricket-like chirping accompanied the opening of the restaurant door. From the outside, the Wang See Restaurant looked like any other Marseille building. Stepping into the entry way, though, was like being whisked away to China.

Heavy red brocade curtains draped an arch framed by gilded carvings of a dragon and phoenix, and hid the interior. A gigantic blue and white porcelain vase occupied one corner. The other corner held a miniature fountain fashioned of river stones. The scents of star anise and dried herbs tickled my nostrils.

A young, well-built Chinese man stepped through the curtains. He wore a Western business suit that fit as though custom made. Most likely it had been. The excellent tailoring made the bulge of the firearm at his waist all the more obvious.

He gave me a cursory, rather dismissive glance then turned to inspect Toni. His eyebrows arched and his thin lips pressed together.

"This is your bodyguard?" he asked in Mandarin.

"Yes. As we agreed."

"She must surrender her weapons."

"She is unarmed, as I promised. However you may search her if you wish." I turned to my companion. "He wants to check you for weapons, okay?"

Toni shrugged. She was playing the strong, silent type.

He gave Toni another worried look. I had the feeling he was reluctant to do anything that might antagonize her. I didn't blame him. "I suppose your word is sufficient guarantee. I am sure you are aware that your companions' lives depend on your behavior."

I gave a small bow of assent.

He responded in kind. "This way, then, young miss." He swept the drapes aside and gestured for us to precede him.

We entered a vast room with a ceiling two stories high, hung with decorative red lanterns. Round marble tables surrounded by rosewood chairs occupied the center of the room. There were no customers in evidence. Wooden booths with red-cushioned benches lined the left and right walls. Our guide led us to one of the booths on the right, which was occupied by a balding, middle-aged man with wire-frame glasses.

"Please sit down, Miss Wong." He addressed me in Cantonese and appeared amused by my astonishment. "Of course we know who you are. Your friends were happy to cooperate."

"I am glad to hear that."

"You may call me Mr Zhou."

I nodded, feigning calm agreement. Meanwhile I tried to work out the implications of his knowing my identity. Was he aware of my secret? Was now the time to play that card?

"In any case, you are a bit of celebrity." He gestured at the table, where a folded newspaper displayed the photo of me at the Grand Prix. "You went to Nice to try and lure The Shark from his lair, did you not?"

I seated myself opposite the Triad boss. "Yes, exactly."

"A clever ploy. I am impressed."

"Thank you. Highly effective, as well." I gestured at Toni and the case affixed to her wrist. In her role as my bodyguard, she had remained standing, flanking me.

"And where is the French upstart now?"

"In the hospital, in Nice. It's likely he will survive. However, he will never be the man he was." I assumed a serene smile, allowing my opponent to draw his own conclusions.

"You continue to surprise me, Miss Wong." He pointed to an exquisite porcelain teapot in the center of the table. "Some tea?" Without waiting for my assent, he filled two cups and handed one to me. "Let us drink to the success of your mission."

I waited for him to take a sip before tasting mine. I, of all people, knew the dangers of foreign substances introduced into food or drink. "I believe I have already succeeded, Mr Zhou."

"I must check our property first. Open the case, please."

"Not until we are in the presence of Mr Duvalier and Mr Sanborne and you have freed them from all restraints."

"Miss Wong, do not try my patience." He waved a hand at the young man who'd admitted us, who waited off to the side, then at the suitcase. "Xifeng. Force the lock."

"I do not recommend that, uncle. In addition to your opium, the suitcase contains a modest quantity of Semtex, which will be triggered if the bag is opened by force."

"Then you will tell me the combination."

I shook my head. "The lock is keyed to Reki's — my bodyguard's — thumbprint. Furthermore, there's a circuit that will detonate the explosives if it stops receiving a feed from her pulse."

I lay my hands palm up on the marble inlaid table top in a placating gesture. "Please understand, we have no desire to cause you difficulty. We are only trying to protect ourselves and the ransom until you have delivered your prisoners into our hands."

Zhou's eyes narrowed. "I feel confident we could persuade your guard to open the case. Everyone has limits to what he or she can endure. Or perhaps it is you that we should torture, Miss Wong?"

I took another swallow from the delicate china cup, hoping he wouldn't notice my shaking hands. "All she has to do is snatch the heartbeat monitor off her finger and we'll all be nothing more than piles of bloody body parts. Is that what you want?"

The mob boss drank his tea in silence. His henchman hovered uncertainly a few feet from Toni, who stood at my shoulder, stony-faced and forbidding. It was unfortunate that she could not understand the conversation. However, she probably got the gist.

I gave Zhou the sweetest smile I could manage. "Uncle, why should we fight one another? Take us to your headquarters. Make the exchange as you've promised. We'll give you the drugs, take our people, and never trouble you again."

Mr Zhou sighed in obvious frustration. "Very well. We will blindfold you, of course."

"Of course. I understand completely."

"And bind your hands."

"Agreed. I understand that you need to protect yourself and your business." The steady confidence I heard in my voice astonished me. "However, if you make any attempt to take the drugs, Reki will detonate the explosives." I rose to my feet. "Shall we go?"

Chapter Twenty-Three

I recognized the vehicle parked at the curb as the SUV used to snatch my lovers. My stomach churned with anxiety as Xifeng slipped a black mask over my eyes, helped me into the back seat, and buckled the safety belt across my chest. He then used plastic handcuffs to fasten my wrists to the belt. A flurry of movement followed by a surge of warmth, told me that Toni had been deposited in the seat beside me.

"They are taking us to their headquarters," I told her, in English.

"I figured that was what was going on, boss." We stayed in character, given that there was no way to know whether Zhou and his minion understood the language.

"Do you have the suitcase?"

"Of course. Between my legs."

"Good. We'll open it as soon as Duvalier and Sanborne are free."

"Sure thing, boss."

No one said anything else throughout the rest of the hour long drive. I sensed the difference in speed when we turned off the city streets onto some sort of highway. Before long, we turned again, onto a much rougher road that wound up and down over what must have been fairly hilly terrain.

Why hadn't I studied a map of the area before our appointment? Then I might have been able to recognize something about our trajectory. As a native, perhaps Toni had some idea where we were. I prayed that Jean had been telling the truth when he'd told us he knew the location of the Triad's hideout—and that in fact, that was where Zhou was taking us. Otherwise, we were in serious trouble.

Finally the vehicle crunched to a halt on what felt like a gravel surface. My door opened. The plastic biting into my wrists was cut. I blinked as the blindfold was removed.

Xifeng had parked the SUV next to a simple, one story stucco building with a terracotta roof, perched on a slope and surrounded by weeds a meter tall. Tumbled heaps of gray limestone rose behind the hut. In front, the land swept down to a precipice that overlooked a V-shaped bay. The sea glowed indigo under the darkening sky. Off to the right—the west, obviously—bars of purple and gold streaked the horizon, where the sun had recently disappeared.

Salt and the dusty scent of dry vegetation spiked the crisp breeze. We were too far away to hear waves crashing against the cliff, but every now and then the lonely call of a gull reached my ears.

It was one of the loveliest, and most desolate, spots I'd ever seen.

With some assistance from Xifeng, Toni extricated herself and the suitcase from the other side of the vehicle. Dragging the case over the uneven surface, she joined me.

"Calanque de Sormiou," she murmured in English, leaning close to avoid being overheard. "Twenty, maybe thirty kilometers from the city. You'd never know we were so close to civilization, would you?"

"This way." Zhou broke into our tête-a-tête.

I didn't have the chance to ask Toni whether this was the hideout Jean had mentioned.

"Your friends are inside," the Triad boss added.

Harry! Etienne! My pulse quickened at the thought of seeing them at last.

Xifeng unlocked the door and motioned for us to enter.

I stepped into a room with whitewashed walls and a concrete floor, lit by fluorescent fixtures in the low ceiling. A wooden bench strewn with calico cushions extended almost the length of the room on the left, under a line of windows. A counter ran along the back, holding a propane stove. Behind it I saw a small refrigerator and a microwave oven—clearly a makeshift kitchen. The blank right wall held a closed door.

Four men clustered around a table in the center, playing mahjong.

Neither Harry nor Etienne was among them.

My spirits plunged to a new low. Four Triad members here, plus Zhou and Xifeng—unless Jean and Bruno showed up soon, we were hopelessly outnumbered. And where were my lovers?

"Bring out the prisoners," Zhou ordered one of the men in Cantonese.

The player on the right, a lanky man in his thirties whose hair grazed the collar of his white business shirt, sprang up from his chair. He dug in his pocket, coming up with a heavy ring of keys. As he turned toward the door on the right, the gun strapped under his arm was more than obvious. He entered the other room then closed the door behind him.

"Sit down, Miss Wong," the boss invited, as cordially as if I were a welcome guest. I suspected he felt much more confident now that we—and the drugs—were on his turf. "Your associates will be out in a moment."

I perched on the edge of the bench, ready to bolt if I had the need or the opportunity. Once again, Toni remained standing, her wrist cabled to the 'booby-trapped' loot.

What were we going to do? My mind whirled, seeking some plan. In a few minutes we'd have to open the suitcase and our ruse would be revealed. I needed to stall for time somehow, to delay that moment as long as possible. But how?

The click of a lock interrupted my frantic musings. The door opposite me swung wide. A disheveled but smiling Etienne stepped through the opening.

I sprang up and hurried to meet him. "Etienne!"

For a guy who'd spent nearly a week in captivity, he'd held up well. He wore a blue-striped matelot jersey and tight navy blue pants that clung to his muscular thighs. His hair was a bit ragged, and he hadn't shaved, but as usual, Etienne Duvalier looked good enough to eat.

As I was about to embrace him, I remembered my comment to Zhou. Everyone was expendable. If the Triad boss realized the depth of my feeling for his captives, he'd use that against me. Instead of hugging Etienne and planting a kiss on those ripe lips of his, I squared my shoulders and gave him a critical once over.

"Monsieur Duvalier, you've caused me a great deal of trouble," I told him in French.

He fell into his role immediately. "I'm very sorry, Mademoiselle Wong. I hope to be able to make it up to you."

Zhou watched this interchange with obvious surprise.

"You will be punished for your carelessness. As usual. Go stand near Reki. I will deal with you later."

I pointed at Toni, standing tall in her ninja gear on the other side of the room. Etienne's eyes grew wide as he took in her formidable appearance. He flushed and licked his lips. It appeared he was having some difficulty breathing. Rocking a bit on the balls of his feet, clearly hesitant, he did not immediately follow my instructions.

"Didn't you hear me?"

"Uh, yes, yes, Mademoiselle Wong." His voice betrayed both fear and excitement. I glanced down at his crotch and found what I'd expected—a massive bulge, shamefully obvious in the tight sailor pants.

Toni had skewered him with a fierce gaze. He shivered and took a reluctant step in her direction. I gave him a push between the shoulder blades. "Well then, get over there."

Toni drew herself up to her full height, a few centimeters taller than Etienne. Peering down her proud nose, she gave him a withering look, as though he was some sort of vermin. The chef wilted, folding his hands in front of his body, trying with minimal success to hide his prominent erection. At the same time, I recognized the smile he struggled to suppress.

"Perhaps I should let Reki punish you," I added. "She'd teach you how to behave."

Etienne choked back a moan.

"Ms Wong."

That warm, rich, nuanced voice! My attention snapped back to the doorway, which framed my other lover.

Harry was as rumpled as ever. Though he wore the same sort of striped shirt as Etienne, Harry's was too loose to show off his broad shoulders and sculpted chest. On the bottom, baggy jeans hid his lovely muscular thighs and solid butt. A few days' beard gave Etienne a dashing appearance. Harry's stubble, in contrast, just made him look scruffy.

None of that mattered.

Joy swelled in my chest. I forgot, for a moment, our desperate straits. My nipples pebbled under my blouse. My pussy moistened. I yearned to sink to my knees before him and beg to serve him.

There was more, though, beyond the immediate and importunate desire his presence kindled. A dizzying rush of gratitude swept through me. Harry was safe. He was well. He was here, standing before me, a hint of his characteristic mischief sparkling behind his glasses despite our current danger.

The pain of days without his presence melted away. That hurt had become so habitual I'd almost stopped noticing it. Now, with the burden lifted, I realized how terrible it had been to be separated from him. My spirit danced, lighter than air. I wanted to laugh, to cry, to sing praises to the Wise Ones who had brought him back to me. I wanted to share the truth I finally understood, that I loved him and wanted him beside me. That I was his — body, heart and soul.

All this emotion and knowledge flooded me in an instant. In the next moment, I understood that I must hide it.

"Mr Sanborne." I kept my voice level, neutral, matter of fact. Even if the gang didn't speak English, they'd pick up on my tone. "I'm happy to see you are in one piece. You are of no use to me with a smashed skull."

"My skull is fine, thank you."

"You should have taken better care of Mr Duvalier. Letting him be kidnapped—you haven't exactly earned your salary."

"You're right, of course. I'll make it up to you, I promise. Just give me the chance to show you what I can do."

Harry wasn't quite playing the game. I heard the innuendo in his smooth apology, and it was enough to set my pulse racing. I made my voice stern.

"I haven't decided yet whether to keep you on my staff. If I can't rely on you, Mr Sanborne, I will have to find someone else."

"Trust me. I won't fail you again..." Did he believe me? His plea sounded remarkably sincere.

"Go sit with Mr Duvalier—Etienne—over there. Mr Zhou and I have business to conclude."

Zhou recognized his name, at least. "Are you satisfied? As you see, your associates are unharmed and unrestrained. Now you must unlock the suitcase and give me the opium."

"I greatly appreciate the care you took with my associates, esteemed uncle. It's a pleasure to work with someone so professional."

"Never mind the flattery. Open the case."

"Of course, whatever you say. I was wondering, though, whether I could have some tea." I cast a longing glance in the direction of the kitchen nook, where a kettle sat on one of the propane burners. "The Mediterranean air here is so dry and dusty. I'm quite parched, especially after scolding your two former prisoners."

"The suitcase, Miss Wong. No more stalling."

"Very well, uncle." I switched to French. "Reki, bring the suitcase." Sweeping the mahjong tiles to the side, I gestured at the surface of the table. "Put it up here. Press your thumb to the touchpad. That's right."

As Toni fiddled with the gadget Le Requin had constructed, I tried to distract Zhou. "Couldn't you ask one of your men to make me some tea, while we are checking the goods?"

"All right, all right, if you insist." He turned to the five men who huddled behind him, eager for a glimpse at the contents of the suitcase. "Tea for Miss Wong. Get me a cup, too."

Two of the guards hastened to obey, one filling the kettle, the other retrieving a pot and two cups from a cupboard under the counter.

Zhou focused his attention back on Toni, who was pressing her thumb repeatedly against the liquid crystal panel and looking puzzled.

"Well?" he growled.

"It won't open," Toni said in French.

"What do you mean?" The concern in my voice sounded quite convincing.

"The lock won't operate. The LED flashes but other than that nothing happens. The lock won't release."

"Try the other thumb."

"I did, Mademoiselle Wong. No reaction."

"*Merde!* Let me try." I shifted into Cantonese and bowed to the boss. "I deeply apologize for this, esteemed uncle. This technology is supposed to be highly reliable. Perhaps the dust has something to with the problem. Or maybe jolting when Reki dragged the case over the stones outside."

"I don't care about the cause. Just open the damn thing."

"We're trying, honestly. Give us a few minutes." I seated myself at the table and peered at the mechanism. "There's a manual combination that can be used as a backup, if the biometric sensor fails. I memorized it when we had the security system installed, but I never expected to use it..."

"Your tea, Miss." Xifeng placed a steaming cup at my elbow and one next to Zhou, who had seated himself opposite me.

"Thank you. Let me see..." I punched a random quintet of numbers into the miniature keypad above the fingerprint reader. "No, that's not right. 77094? No? Was it 70794? I'm so sorry, uncle. Please be patient. I'm sure I'll remember..."

"I've had enough. Break it open!" He handed Reki a metal spatula that had apparently come from the kitchen. "Now!"

"But the explosives..."

"The locking circuits appear to be out of order. Let's just hope, for your sake and your friends', that the detonation electronics are as well." He nodded to his subordinates.

Four of them pulled out their guns and repositioned themselves, one on each side of Harry and Etienne. Xifeng and Zhou backed away from the table, far enough from to avoid the brunt of a possible blast, their weapons still trained on Toni and me.

"But if the bomb does go off...? If the drugs are destroyed...?"

"In that case, it will be too late for you and your bodyguard, won't it? We'll finish off your associates without delay. Then we'll hunt down that bastard, The Shark."

He took another step backward, increasing the distance between him and the suitcase. "Open the case, Mei Lee Wong, or I'll shoot you now."

My mind whirled. If they saw the case was empty, they'd kill me. If I didn't open the case, they'd kill me. Jean might be here at any moment, but until he arrived, I had to stall.

Only one option occurred to me.

"Esteemed uncle, you might want to think carefully before you murder the great granddaughter of Gao Xi Wong. You could bring great trouble down upon your organization."

"What? What is this nonsense? Master Gao Xi has been dead for thirty years."

"But he is still revered by members of the Black Dragon, uncle. And I am his direct descendant." I turned my back to him and raised the hair off my neck. "My proof."

Zhou leaned closer. When he saw the tattoo, he sucked in his breath.

"What's happening?" Toni asked in French.

My straight locks fell back into place as I turned to answer.

"I've given Mr Zhou a persuasive reason not to kill us."

Zhou offered me a bleak smile. "I find myself less surprised by your cleverness, knowing who you are. Of course a woman of the Black Dragon Triad would be more than a match for The Shark."

I bowed. "I can only hope I have inherited at least some of my ancestor's sagacity."

"However, your illustrious pedigree has no bearing on my problem. I need those drugs, Miss Wong. Open the case or I will be forced to end your life."

"And risk a Triad war? Do you recall the cost of the last one? Hundreds of dead, uncle, and both organizations reduced to mere specters of their previous power."

"That was in the 1920s. The world has changed."

"Only by becoming more lethal."

Zhou sighed. "I'm losing patience, girl. I don't give a damn about the possibility of a Triad war. All I want is my opium. If I don't deliver it to my customer within forty-eight hours, I'm the one who will die."

"We may all die if the bomb detonates, sir."

"That is for the fates to decide. You have until the count of three. One."

I took the spatula from Toni and tried to insert it at the seam where the top and bottom halves of the case met.

"Two."

"I'm doing it. I'm *doing* it. Don't rush me, please!" The blade slipped into the gap. I twisted it a bit. At the same time, I thumbed the secret latch Toni had shown me.

"Three."

The suitcase sprung open. Glass shattered. Thunder crashed around me. The lights went out. For a moment I almost believed that the imaginary bomb had, in fact, exploded. Then more gunshots split the darkness and I understood. Jean had arrived.

Instinctively, I dropped to the floor and crawled under the table. Bullets whistled above me, flying in all directions. My ears rang with the noise.

"Emily! Here." Toni crouched next to me and put a hunk of cold metal into my hand.

"But I don't... Ow!" A hot poker pierced my calf. My leg was suddenly wet. I gritted my teeth. I'd endured worse pain. I could bear this.

Harry. Where's Harry?

Another projectile whizzed by my ear. I couldn't see a thing. At this rate, my friends might well kill each other.

A racket erupted above me, rapid fire that drowned out the individual reports of the mob's revolvers. One of the ceiling lamps flickered back on. I peered out from under the table to see Toni, feet apart, head high, gripping an automatic rifle and spraying the kitchen area with bullets. Two bodies clad in business suits lay sprawled in front of the counter. Obviously Toni believed there were still other people behind it.

Over by the bench, Jean grappled with Xifeng. He hacked at the Chinese man's wrist with a glittering knife, forcing the Triad member to release his gun. Just when I thought Le Requin had the upper hand, though, Xifeng executed some sort of maneuver that flipped the Frenchman onto his back. The next thing I knew, Xifeng had straddled Jean's body and pried the blade from his grasp. Le Requin freed one arm and rammed his index finger into Xifeng's eye. Xifeng howled, but didn't let go. He swiped blindly at Jean's chest. Jean gripped him by the throat and held him at arm's length.

Bruno and the skinny, long-haired thug rolled on the floor in the opposite corner, twisting each other's arms, pummeling each other's faces, each struggling to reach a discarded gun a half meter away. Meanwhile Toni lowered her weapon, strode over to the closed door leading to the next room, and kicked it down. Shouts came from within. She entered the dark space. For another thirty seconds her gun spat death.

Aside from gurgles, groans, gasped curses and the thud of fists against flesh, the place fell quiet.

Where was Harry? And Etienne?

I ventured another look toward the smashed windows. Jean and Xifeng had disappeared.

Maybe Harry and Etienne had escaped. They weren't armed. That would have been the sensible move, if they could manage it.

I twisted to check out the door to the shanty. Was it open a crack? I should try to get out, too. Despite my heritage, I was no warrior. This fight belonged to Jean and Toni, not to me.

Awkward because of the gun in my hand, I started to crawl toward the door. It wasn't far, no more than two meters, but every movement sent a spike of fiery pain sizzling up my leg. I was still mostly under the table when the lights died once more. All the better. No one would see my progress across the open floor.

"You little bitch!" The Cantonese curse almost stopped my heart.

A fist gripped me by the hair and hauled me to my feet. My gun fell to the floor with a clatter. Zhou spun me around and rammed my kidneys against the table edge. Between that and the bullet lodged in my leg, I almost fainted from the pain.

Zhou gave my face a jaw-rattling slap. "You set me up. Betrayed me. But you'll pay. Oh, yes, you'll pay, Black Dragon or not!"

His hands encircled my throat. I coughed and sputtered. He tightened his grip, pressing his thumbs against my windpipe. "I'll teach you not to mess with the Iron Hammer, slut. I'll hang you from the ceiling, slice you open and pull out your guts. I'll brand you with the mark of the Iron Hammer, until your flesh smokes and burns. But I won't let you die, oh no, not for a long, long time. Not until you've paid for making a fool of me."

Despite his threats, he seemed likely to choke me to death within the next few minutes. His vise-like fingers made it impossible to breathe. Blood pounded in my head. Sparkles danced in front of my eyes. The ache in my wounded calf faded in contrast to the agony of my tortured lungs.

Harry. Etienne. Toni. My Gran. I'd never see any of them again. How stupid of me to believe I could cheat the Triad! How arrogant! Hovering on the edge of consciousness, I wallowed in self-disgust.

I didn't even hear Zhou's imprecations any more. The ringing in my ears drowned out his venom. This was too hard. I wanted to just let go, to stop fighting. Relax. Let go. That's what Harry would tell me...

My hands clenched involuntarily, banging against the table. Something hot burned my right knuckle. Hot?

My tea, or maybe Zhou's. It seemed as though hours had passed since Jean and Bruno had burst into the shack, but most likely it had only been a few minutes. The tea had barely cooled.

I grasped the china cup, ignoring the effects on my skin. With one final burst of strength, I raised it and flung the near-boiling contents in Zhou's face.

"Aiyee! Ah!" Like magic, he released his hold on my throat.

I wheezed, sucking air into my lungs, letting the precious oxygen cleanse and revive me. Blinded and burned, Zhou screamed and cursed, flailing his arms in a wild attempt to catch hold of me once more.

I slipped to the floor and resumed my slow crawl toward the door and freedom. I didn't think I'd make it, but I had to try...

Pain was my only reality. Throbbing pain in my leg. Searing pain in my burned palm. Aching pain in my bruised throat.

Move your leg, Emily. Now your hand. Now the other leg.

A single shot rang out above me. I collapsed, belly to the concrete. Zhou released a strange, gurgling yell. Then silence reigned.

My world went black.

Chapter Twenty-Four

I opened my eyes to find Harry staring at me, his mouth pursed and his forehead furrowed. His expression of worry melted into a brilliant smile when he realized I was conscious.

"Em, love! You're awake."

I stirred, gradually becoming aware of the myriad types of pain inhabiting various parts of my body. "Evidently." My voice sounded hoarse. My throat felt like I'd swallowed steel wool. "Where am I?"

"A hospital in Marseille." My lover seized my hand and brought it to his lips. "You've been out for nearly twelve hours. I was so scared. I mean, the doctor warned me that the sedative he'd prescribed was pretty strong, but watching you lying there, not moving, hour after hour—it was tough."

The buttery light of the Mediterranean poured through the open window. I scanned his familiar features, noting the circles under his eyes, like smudges of ash. "You've been here all night?"

"Of course, love. After everything that's happened, I wasn't going to let you out of my sight!"

He leaned over the bed to give me a gentle kiss. I tried to raise my head, to meet him halfway, but the ache in my neck forced me back onto the pillow.

"Ow! That Zhou really did a job on me!"

My lover just nodded, more serious than usual. "We're all lucky to be alive."

"Everybody made it out? Etienne? Toni?"

"Jean's man took a bullet in the shoulder, but other than that, you're the only casualty."

I remembered searing pain blazing through my leg. I made a feeble attempt to move the limb. "Ay! Is it broken?"

"The bullet nicked the bone, but didn't shatter it. You lost a lot of blood. The doctor says you should be able to walk normally in a week to ten days."

"Thank the gods! And the Iron Hammer?"

"Dead."

"All of them?" Despite my recollections of the gun battle, that seemed impossible, unreal. "Zhou? Xifeng? All gone?"

"Yup. Between Toni and The Shark, they got more than they bargained for."

I shuddered. Six deaths laid to my account. That was a heavy burden to bear into the future.

"It's not your fault, Em." As usual, Harry seemed to read my thoughts. "They started it, by kidnapping Etienne and me. Plus they would have been perfectly happy to slaughter us all, given the chance. The world is better off without them."

"I don't know if that's ever true, Harry."

He settled on the edge of the bed, cradling my hand in both of his own. I caught a whiff of his distinctive scent. All my pains eased a bit.

"Look at it this way. We're free now. If any of the Triad guys had survived long enough to report to their superiors, we'd have a new set of thugs coming after us. Jean says it's very unlikely Zhou told his own boss about the stolen dope. He'd want to save face and his own skin, try to get it back without anyone knowing he'd screwed up."

"Hmm. You're probably right."

"So now, all the big guys in Hong Kong know is that someone wiped out half a dozen of their operatives and that the opium's gone. There's nothing to pin it on us — or The Shark, either. We can get on with our lives, without worrying about their payback."

What he'd said made sense. Still, I couldn't quite shake the feeling that I was responsible. I was the one who'd agreed to do the French tour, despite my qualms regarding our ménage. If we hadn't come to France, six men would still be alive. I wouldn't be lying in a hospital bed racked with so many pains I couldn't label them all. Harry and Etienne would never have been subjected to the horror of being abducted and held captive.

But I had allowed desire to overrule reason, and this was the result.

I couldn't change the past, though. 'You can't force spilled wine back into the bottle', as Gran would say. I'd have to live with the consequences of my actions.

One consequence, of course, was realizing I loved Harry. I couldn't possibly regret that.

"By the way, what did you tell Zhou that made him look so worried? Right before all hell broke loose? And why did you show him your tattoo?"

"Ah — well..." Sudden panic seized me. Would Harry still want me, if he knew about my criminal roots? I couldn't risk it. "Nothing, really. Nothing that would mean anything to you, at least."

"Come on, Em. Can't you trust me enough to be honest? You know I'll keep your secret, if you want me to."

He raised my hand to his lips and pressed them to my palm. "Please, love. Don't shut me out. I don't care what it is, if only you'll share it with me. There isn't anything that could make me love you less."

His voice was so earnest. How could I not believe him?

"Well — ah — I told him something about my family."

"Yes? What?"

"That my great-grandfather was one of the biggest Triad bosses in the history of the gangs. From 1917 until 1932, he led the Black Dragon Triad."

Harry's breath whistled out. "Wow! No wonder you knew how to deal with Zhou and his crew. Did you have a bodyguard, growing up? Weapons training? Was it like in *The Godfather*, where the children are expected to carry on the work of the family?"

"No, no! Not at all! Great-grandfather Gao retired long before I was born. The bloody Triad wars sickened him. He passed the mantle of power to a distant relative and moved to Lantau Island to grow flowers. I remember him as a diminutive, white-haired man who loved to tell stories. He died when I was six."

"So his son didn't take over?"

"He had no sons, just a single daughter, my Gran. She married a poet instead of the Black Dragon he'd chosen for her. The family went on to pursue legitimate businesses. Our Triad connections faded."

"But they still gave you the tattoo."

"As protection. I told you. Anyone with Dragon blood has one."

"Protection against bad luck? Against other Triads?"

I shrugged. "Whatever. These days it's mostly superstition."

"It might have saved your life. You managed to keep Zhou busy until The Shark showed up."

"I suppose. Anyway, I'm sure my grandmother will insist that my children be tattooed—if I ever have any, that is..."

Harry didn't seem the least bit perturbed by my revelations. He leaned in to kiss me, cupping my cheek in his palm. "I'm sure we will have kids, one of these days. But not until you're ready, Em."

Something melted inside me. He grinned in delight, as if he knew what was going on in my heart.

"That's some secret, though."

"Don't tell anyone else about this, okay?"

"My lips are sealed, darling. No one else will ever know, unless you want to reveal it."

"Thank you. It's not really something to be proud of."

"I don't know about that. But speaking of other people, there's someone who's very eager to see you. If you feel up to it, that is." The distinctive glint behind Harry's lenses told me who he meant.

"Etienne? I guess I have to face him sooner or later. But Harry..."

"Yes, love?"

"No more games, okay?"

"What do you mean?"

"From now on, I want just the two of us in our bed. I care about Etienne, but you're the only lover I want."

Harry's eyebrows shot up. "Really? You don't want to be worshiped? By someone other than me, I mean?"

I stroked his arm. "You're more than enough for me—Sir."

"What if I decide to share you with someone else? Would you obey?"

Would he actually do that? Knowing his kinky mind, anything was possible. I didn't know how to answer.

Fortunately, he acted as if the question was rhetorical. He flipped his hair out of his eyes and pressed his lips to my forehead. "Whatever you say, Em. You're the boss."

"Yeah, right," I muttered as Harry went to the door to call the chef in. My decision felt right to me. But how was I going to tell Etienne that our dalliance was over? That I had no further interest in playing the role of his Mistress?

I didn't get much chance to worry about this issue. Etienne swept into the room, resplendent in a suit of charcoal gray, paired with a goldenrod shirt and a silver tie. He seized my hand and gave it a firm squeeze. "Mei Lee! How are you?"

"Don't be so rough!" Toni scolded. "She's in a fragile condition right now."

Toni came up beside Etienne and elbowed him in the ribs. He dropped my hand as though he'd been scalded.

"It's okay, Toni. I'm not in that bad shape. Can you hand me the bed control?" I managed to raise myself to a half-sit without too much discomfort. "Wow! You look fantastic!"

Like Etienne, Police Detective Antoinette Leblanc was dressed to the nines, in an off-white skirt and jacket that looked like raw silk, a peach blouse, and — I could hardly believe it — shiny silver high heels.

"Thanks, Emily. Etienne and I have an appointment this afternoon."

"Huh?"

"At *le mairie*—the city hall." Toni sounded smug. "Monsieur Duvalier has asked me to be his wife."

My mouth fell open. Maybe I was hallucinating from the medication.

"My wife—and my Mistress," Etienne added with a bit of a blush. "I hope... I hope you don't mind, Miss Wong."

If the dragons on the eaves of Wong Tai Sin temple had taken flight, I could not have been more astonished. "Um—isn't that a bit sudden? You've known each other less than twenty-four hours!"

"I've never believed in love at first sight, but Toni has proven me wrong." He turned his adoring gaze to his partner. "Forgive me for saying this to you, of all people, but she's the Mistress I've always dreamed of."

Momentary jealousy fluttered in my chest, before I remembered that I'd *wanted* to disentangle myself sexually from Etienne.

"You do know she's been married before? Three times?"

Toni frowned down at me. "Emily, are you trying to spoil our happiness?"

"No, no, not at all." I recalled Etienne's very physical reaction when he'd first encountered Toni. "I just don't want to see either of you hurt by rushing into something so official. I'd recommend waiting for a while...but if you're sure..."

"I'm completely certain Etienne will succeed where my other husbands failed. And if he falls short in any way—well, I don't doubt that I can induce him to improve. Don't you agree, darling?"

"Yes, ma'am." The silly grin on Etienne's handsome face made it clear that he, at least, was delighted by the hand fortune had dealt him.

"Well, I guess congratulations are in order, then…" I began.

"Hey, I heard there was a party going on in here." Jean Le Requin poked his head into the room. "Can I join in the fun?"

"Jean!" Etienne sought Toni's eyes.

When she nodded her permission, he hurried over to give his cousin a bear hug. The gangster's face showed a mix of joy and embarrassment.

"Hey, Jet! You're looking snazzy."

"It's my wedding day. You're invited to the ceremony, if you'd like to come."

"You want *me* there? Your crooked cousin?"

"You saved my life, Jean. You'd be welcome even if you weren't family."

The gangster grinned. "Well, my plane doesn't leave until midnight, so I guess I can make it."

"Where are you off to, Dunant?" Toni's professional manner reasserted itself. "Got some new caper lined up?"

"You promised you'd let me walk, Toni. Don't disappoint me by breaking your word."

"Don't tempt me. But I won't be a cop for much longer."

"You're retiring from the force?" I interjected. "That's a shame. You're so good at what you do."

"I'm going into — um — private practice, hon. Something that makes better use of my skills. I can't stand the bureaucracy anymore. Not to mention the sexism."

"I'm sure the fact that you killed a bunch of people last night has nothing to do with it," The Shark taunted.

"Your hands aren't exactly clean either."

"True. And I don't mind admitting I'm bit concerned that the Triad might send someone after me. I'm a bit of a celebrity in the criminal world."

Toni released a snort of derision.

Le Requin continued as if he hadn't heard, "So I've decided to retire. Get out of France, at least for now. I'm headed for Bangkok tonight, though I might ultimately end up in Laos or Myanmar. Somewhere with great food and beautiful women."

"What about the vintage wine and fast cars?" I teased.

"I can usually get what I want." His gaze met mine. "Though not always."

We chatted for a few minutes longer — or more accurately, my visitors talked, and I listened. I was thrilled they'd all survived, delighted at Jean and Etienne's reconciliation, amazed by but grateful for Toni and Etienne's connection. My head ached, though. My throat was lined with sandpaper and my wounded leg throbbed as though it would explode.

An aching weariness stole over me. My eyelids drooped. Harry was first to notice.

"Emily needs some rest, people. I think you'd better go."

"Sure thing. See you soon, girl. Come on, Etienne. You can take me to lunch before we tie the knot."

"Mind if I tag along, Jet? I know a wonderful little brasserie just a few blocks away."

"Why not? One might consider this our wedding dinner. And you're practically the best man."

Harry herded the trio out of the door. I stopped fighting the urge to close my eyes.

"Go to sleep, baby." He pressed his warm lips to my forehead. "Your body needs to heal."

"Thanks so much, Harry." I peered at his smiling face through fluttering eyelids. "I love you, you know."

"I know, baby. You just lie back and snooze now. Don't worry about anything."

"And you'll be here when I wake up?"

"Always."

Chapter Twenty-Five

"You could spank me some more, you know. I won't break."

We'd just gotten to the point where my butt started to glow, all tingling and warm, when Harry had stopped. Since I'd gotten out of the hospital, he'd treated me as though I were made of glass. No bondage to speak of—oh, maybe a few symbolic ribbons tying my wrists together above my head, but nothing more. No clamps on my nipples or my labia, though I'd reminded him several times that I'd suffered no injury to those parts. He had taken his belt to my ass once, much to my delight, but after a few thwacks, he'd tossed it aside, buried his face in my pussy and eaten me until he'd summoned three thundering orgasms.

Not that I meant to complain. Everything he did to my body, I found arousing. What he did to my mind, too. But I didn't like the notion that he was holding back, denying himself satisfaction out of misplaced concern for me.

"Topping from below, are you?" He swept one finger down through my slick cleft, from back to front, ending with a flick to my clit that made me squirm. "Who's the Dom here?"

"You are, Sir." The honorific still gave me a thrill, after all these months.

He stroked the flat of his hands over my tenderized buttocks, waking little sparks here and there, where his previous slaps had landed. Each one shimmered down to my sex, moistening me further, but I craved more.

"I'll spank you as much or as little as I please, girl. I'll give you more when I think you're ready."

"But I'm fully recovered, Harry! Haven't I done three shows in the past five days?"

"Yes, and taken a two hour nap after each one. It still hurts to stand, doesn't it?"

"After a while it does start to ache a bit," I confessed. "Lying here on the bed, though, doesn't put any stress on my leg at all..."

He had laid me out on my stomach, my pelvis propped on a mound of pillows to elevate my rear, my face turned sideways and resting comfortably on my crossed arms.

"Hush, girl!" Whack! His palm made contact at the tender junction of cheek and thigh, with more force than he'd used in all his earlier blows put together.

Lightning arced down to ignite a fire in my pussy. That was more like it!

I arched up, grinding my pubis against the cushiony support and presenting my ass to tempt him further.

Instead he stretched his body out on top of mine, his cockhead nudging the base of my spine, his furry chest tickling my bare back. He nuzzled my neck, just below my ear, in that special spot that always turned me to complete mush.

I sighed and relaxed against him, grateful for whatever he was willing to offer.

"I love you, Em. I don't want to hurt you." After licking his way along my cheek, he planted an awkward half-kiss on my somewhat inaccessible lips.

I strained my neck, trying to capture his mouth full on, but he scrunched down to nibble at my shoulders.

"Don't get me wrong. I adore the way you writhe and scream when I whip or spank you. I know it's as much a turn on for you as it is for me."

I whimpered as he bit down hard. I swear I felt the marks of his teeth on my clit.

"I'll beat you when I think you're ready."

"But, Harry..."

"When *I* think you're ready, woman! Don't you trust me?"

"You know I do."

"Then give me control. Be patient." He ground his swollen cock against my ass crack. "You won't be sorry, baby."

Bestowing one last kiss between my shoulder blades, he heaved back, onto his knees. I moaned a bit at the loss of his warmth against my skin.

"Tonight I have something other than spanking in mind for you, Em."

There was the tiniest edge of menace in his voice. My already-taut nipples throbbed and new moisture flooded my pussy.

Weight shifted as he got off the bed and puttered around our hotel room. "Toni invited us to join her and Etienne tonight."

"What?" Shame and arousal streaked through me, so mingled I couldn't tell one from the other. I was eager to see how Toni managed my former slave. I wasn't sure, though, that I was ready to reveal the depth of my own submissive urges to the ex-police detective by letting her see me with Harry.

"I declined, though," Harry continued. "For now, I want to keep you all to myself."

I released the air from my lungs. Was I relieved or disappointed?

Before I had time to decide, I felt a slick finger prodding my rear hole. Without thinking, I clenched down, resisting the incursion, even though the very idea made me tremble with lust.

"I thought, though, that you and I might try something new."

"Oh…" Something cool and wet dribbled down the crevice between my butt cheeks, flowing over my anus and down into my pubic hair. The fingertip circled my pucker, smearing the lube over that forbidden spot, urging it inside. "Oh, ah—oh, Harry…"

"I've wanted to butt fuck you since that first night you surrendered to me, up on Mount Sutro. I still remember the pale gleam of your rear cheeks when I stripped off your panties, and the shadowy promise between them. Your sweet, juicy cunt is a delight, but I've dreamed for months about driving my cock into your hot, tight ass."

"Oh—ah…"

He'd slid one well-lubricated digit into my channel and was working it back and forth, trying to loosen the rubbery ring of muscle that guarded my back passage. The sensations were strange, scary, but not unpleasant—no, quite the contrary. But those sensations—I wasn't supposed to like this, was I?

Being poked and opened and entered *there*, in that filthy spot?

"That's right, love. Relax. Let me in."

He pushed deeper. I jumped at the suddenly increased intensity.

"Does that hurt?"

"No, not at all... But oh, Harry..."

"What is it? Should I stop?"

"No, not unless you want to... But I don't know if I can..."

"Your first time, right?"

A second digit slid in, then a third, stretching me farther. I gasped for breath. "Ah — yes — oh, by the gods, Harry, that's unbelievable..."

So full... Compared to his fingers, his cock was enormous. Could I really take more?

"Open up, baby. Trust me." More lube slithered down my crack. "I'm so honored to be your first, Em."

I heard love, respect, even awe in his voice. It melted me into a puddle of pure need.

"Come on, Harry. Do it. Before I chicken out."

He eased his fingers out. I moaned in frustration and in fear. I was gaping, lubed, stretched and ready for his cock, or as ready as I'd ever be. He pressed his cockhead against the swirl of muscle and for the first time, I felt a twinge of pain. He was so big. Could I really bear it?

"Here goes."

The pressure increased. My first instinct was to clamp down, but I fought that inclination, determined to give my Master what he craved. "That's right. Relax your muscles. Let go. I'm going to thrust a bit now, to get the head inside. If it's too much, just tell me."

A brief sensation tore at me, bright and sharp, as he stretched me to new limits. Then he was inside, his cock embedded in that narrow passage, filling my most secret recess and triggering the most awful, delicious pleasure I'd ever experienced.

"Okay, love?"

I sucked in my breath, fighting the urge to expel him. "More," I groaned. "Give me more."

"Oh, Emily!"

He jerked his hips. His cock settled deeper inside me. The pleasure built as I let myself experience every shameful and miraculous sensation.

One more thrust and he was in to the root. His crinkly pubic hair ticked my rear cheeks. His musk washed over me, mingled with my own scent, plus a hint of something darker. Pausing once more, he let me adjust to his impossible bulk.

My clit pulsed and shuddered. The luscious feel of his cock embedded in my ass spread through my whole pelvis. I ached for friction and force.

"Oh, Harry—please! Fuck me! Fuck me before I die!"

I'd thought I'd reached the pinnacle of pleasure when he sheathed his full length in my channel. As he started to move, I discovered I'd been wrong.

He slid his shaft out of my hole then drove back in, smooth and slow, stimulating nerves I'd never known existed. At first he kept his strokes gentle and measured, but he couldn't keep that level of control for long. Soon he was slamming into me with the same ferocity he used in fucking my cunt. In, out, hard and fast, he plundered my ass, taking me over, making me his. In gratitude and ecstasy, I surrendered. Each thrust forced my clit against the pillows, pushing me closer to climax.

With each breath, I expected to tumble over the edge. Instead, the tension just coiled tighter on each stroke, trembling, explosive, looming like thunderheads swollen with rain. I'd never felt such an overwhelming need, and yet it seemed he'd take me higher still.

I focused on his cock, the astonishing sense of connection when his flesh mingled with mine. *This is my love.* Only that thought remained, as he pounded into me. His nails scoring my rear cheeks, he held me open so he could thrust deeper, into the very heart of me.

His rod twitched and shuddered. "Emily!" he bellowed, driving into me one last time. There was an instant when the fullness increased, as he swelled. Then he burst inside me, bathing me in hot fluid.

Lightning flashed. The storm broke. I came like wind and rain, with gasps and tears, showering my pleasure down on my lover.

"God, I'm sorry, Em." Harry traced the raw crescents his fingernails had left in my flesh. "I'll get some disinfectant."

"No!" I rolled onto my back—wincing a bit as the wounds grazed the sheets—and pulled him down on top of my prone body. "You're not going anywhere right now." I wrapped my arms around his neck and my legs around his waist to enforce my statement. "Kiss me."

"You're pretty uppity for a sub, aren't you?" he laughed. However, he obeyed my command, sealing his lips to mine.

He let me control the kiss at first, and I took advantage, probing his sweet, hot mouth and nibbling at the corners. Before long, though, he reasserted himself. He bore down, till my lips were bruised and sore, drinking me in like he couldn't get enough.

Finally he allowed me to catch my breath. His nutmeg-brown eyes were hazy with exhaustion and desire. "I love you so very much. I'm not sure you can understand…"

"I have some idea, Harry. I feel the same. Well, I don't know if it's exactly the same, since you're Dominant and I'm…well, not. At least not usually."

"You can kick ass when you want to, Ms Wong."

"Yeah, well, whatever." I knew he was thinking about Etienne and about Jean. I was annoyed to find I was blushing. I blundered on. "Harry, when I saw you out there at the Hammer's hideout—well, I knew…that I didn't want to live without you."

"Whooee! Is that a proposal, Ms Wong?" He hiked himself up onto his forearms and grinned down at me.

"Well, uh—I'm not sure. Maybe. Something like that." I hadn't thought in terms of marriage but if we loved one another, wasn't that the next natural step? It seemed to have worked out well for Toni and Etienne, though maybe it was too early to tell.

"I accept. When should we have the wedding?"

"Um, wait a minute—let's not jump into things."

"Are you or are you not asking me to marry you, Emily Wong?"

"Uh—I think—um—yes. Yes, I am."

Quick as a cobra strike, Harry grabbed my wrists and forced them down onto the bed. He bent to my chest and took my nipple in his teeth. I gasped as new pleasure streaked to my extremities.

"Definitely too bossy for a submissive. But I know what to do about that."

Epilogue

Ten p.m. in San Francisco. Two in the afternoon, tomorrow, in Hong Kong. I typed my username and password into the Skype dialog then clicked on the icon for my grandmother.

In less than sixty seconds, her wise, lined face came up in the video window.

"Hello, Grandmother."

"First Granddaughter. I'm so pleased. I missed hearing from you. Have you returned from *fàguó*?"

"I got back last night."

She peered at me—at my image, presumably—and pursed her red-painted lips. "You look tired."

"It was—um—a complicated trip."

"I warned you. Two men is one too many."

"You were right, Grandmother."

"Of course I was right. You youngsters! You should have listened to me—"

I cut her short to forestall her impending lecture.

"I have some good news to share with you, Grandmother. I hope you'll tell the rest of the family for me. The network has offered me my own cooking show. 'Asian Accents with Mei Lee Wong'."

"There in Gold Mountain?" She tried to smile. I'll give her credit for that. "You sound excited."

"You know I am. This is what I've been working toward. This show will be a springboard to a whole new career. Cooking videos. Cookbooks. Maybe even my own chain of restaurants. I have tons of ideas."

"But in America, Mei Lee! What about the family?"

"I'll come visit. And you can visit me here."

"And the great-grandchildren you promised me, First Granddaughter?"

"Well — um — "

Now she interrupted me, "Anyway, how is the rich, handsome chef?"

"He's married, Gran."

Her eyebrows shot up. "Really? That was fast." Her jade eardrops swayed as she shook her head in obvious disapproval. Then a look of shock crossed her face. "I assume you mean he married someone other than you."

"Of course. Don't you think I would tell you if I was getting married?"

"Before you get engaged, we expect you to bring the man here for our approval."

Should I tell her about Harry? Skype seemed like such an informal way to announce an engagement. "That might not be possible, Grandmother."

"Please, First Granddaughter. Make an old woman happy. Follow the old ways for once." She released a dramatic sigh. "Too bad about the chef, though. Will you still be working with him?"

"No, he stayed behind in *fàguó* with his bride. They're planning to start a restaurant in his old home town. That's one reason I got the new show. In some sense, I'm his replacement."

"Ah, I see. And the other one, the one who wasn't rich?"

"He's still around." I shot a glance at the bed, where Harry lounged, deliciously naked. Of course he couldn't understand our Cantonese conversation.

"Maybe you should go after him, if he's the only one left. Let me remind you, you are no spring flower."

"Perhaps you're right, Grandmother."

"We elders are always right. When will you young people learn?"

"You know what Confucius said. 'We only learn through our mistakes.'"

My quote managed to elicit a smile. "Probably I should not worry about you so much. You've always been clever."

"Not as clever as you, Grandmother."

Now she grinned. "Thank you."

"I have to go. It's late, and I'm still quite tired from the trip."

"Sleep well, First Granddaughter. Good luck with the not-rich man who wears glasses."

I glanced again at my love. He was fondling his swollen cock, using long, lazy strokes that made my mouth water.

"Thanks, Gran. I'll talk to you soon."

I thought she was about to close the connection, but she paused as something occurred to her. "Are you sure you don't want me to send you more *dōngchóngxiàcǎo*? It might help you get his interest."

I suppressed a laugh. "Thanks for the offer, Grandmother. But I don't think that will be necessary."

I stashed the tablet, shucked my clothes, and climbed onto Harry's inviting erection.

"Hey, lover. Looks like we might need to make a trip to Hong Kong."

About the Author

I became addicted to words at an early age. I began reading when I was four. I wrote my first story at five years old and my first poem at seven. Since then, I've written plays, tutorials, scholarly articles, marketing brochures, software specifications, self-help books, press releases, a five-hundred page dissertation, and of course, lots of erotica and erotic romance.

My lifelong interests in sex and the written word became serenditipitously entwined more than a decade ago when I read my first Black Lace book by Portia da Costa. Her work inspired me to take my fantasies out of the closet (and the private email files) and expose them to the world. The rest, as they say, is history (although granted, no more than a minor footnote!)

I've always loved traveling; my husband seduced me in a Burmese restaurant by telling me tales of his foreign adventures. Since then I have visited every continent except Australia, although I still have a long travel wish list. Currently I live with him and our two exceptional felines in Southeast Asia, where I pursue an alternative career that is completely unrelated to my creative writing.

Lisabet Sarai loves to hear from readers. You can find her contact information, website details and author profile page at http://www.totallybound.com.

Totally Bound Publishing